HARD NOX

WILD SCOTS, #1

JOLIE VINES

WWW.JOLIEVINES.COM/NEWSLETTER

PRAISE FOR JOLIE VINES AND THE MARRY THE SCOT SERIES

A selection of five-star reviews:

- I loved this book! It had all that I would expect with hot Scots and rambling castles - Paula

- Jolie Vines has fast become a one-click author for me! - J. Saman, Bestselling author

- I'm impatiently waiting for the next book - I just know it'll be another sizzling story from Jolie Vines - Zoe Ashwood, author of the Shift series

- (Hero) is an amazing work of art, highly recommended for anyone looking for a modern-day Highlander to swoon over - Viper Spaulding

- I swear, every time I pick up a Jolie Vines book I think: this is him, my favorite hero, no one will be able to top him. And then I read the next book and the process begins again - Chikap09

- If you haven't read the other books in the series Marry the Scot, you should really start with Storm the Castle, then move on to Love Most, Say Least before diving into Hero. I cannot wait to see what Ally and Wasp get up to in their stories! I've enjoyed the first three books immensely! - Pam Graber

• Jolie Vines is an amazingly talented writer. I am so completely obsessed with this series and so madly in love with the characters. Each book gets better than the last and when you start off with a 5 star? There just aren't enough stars - Carmen Davis

Editing by Emmy at Studio ENP

Proofreading by Zoe Ashwood

Cover design by Elle Thorpe at Images For Authors

❀ Created with Vellum

To those who raise us and those who follow in our footsteps

BLURB

Hard Nox (Wild Scots, #1)

He's a brawler, she's a speed racer. Together, they're explosive.

Isobel
Heir to the McRae estate, Lennox is the huge Highlander everyone respects. But deep down, he's a dirty fighter. He crashed my car, stole my first kiss, then walked away with another woman.

There's no reason why, years later, when I see him in a fight, I should be lusting after his body. They call him Hard Nox, but I know him, and damned if he's getting an easy ride back into my life.

Nox
Isobel is a menace. She races cars and has tattoos in places I can't even imagine. I shouldn't want her. But I can't

forget the one kiss we shared as teenagers. Fresh out of the military, I have one thing in my sights – her.

Isobel Fitzroy is my best friend's sister, and I'm going to tame her wild heart.

From the author of the *Marry the Scot* series comes a brand-new generation. *Wild Scots* brings you everything you love about Scottish heroes and contemporary romance but sexier, faster, and supercharged.

READER NOTE

Dear reader,

Thanks for picking up my new series! You're in for one heck of a ride.

The Wild Scots are a new generation, with their parents' romances already told in the *Marry the Scot* series. (All can be read as standalones.)

You can find the origin series here, starting with Storm the Castle. Get swept away with the alpha laird and the lass he can't have: mybook.to/StormtheCastle

Hold on tight and enjoy the fun.

Jolie x

THE LASS WAS A MENACE

*L*ennox

There was a sixth sense that came from being the oldest of my group of cousins. At eighteen, and heir to the vast Highlands estate that was our playground, I'd grown up with sharp instincts for spotting trouble.

I slowed the Land Rover at a bend in the road, easing around the snowy track, then spared a glance at the kids in my back seat. With rosy cheeks from our afternoon snowboarding on the mountain, they chattered away, no mischief in their looks.

Still, something was wrong.

Ahead, Castle McRae stood proud, the centuries-old building guarded by an enormous illuminated Christmas tree to the right of the entrance. Tonight was Christmas Eve, and my father, the chief of Clan McRae, was hosting a party. Kin and friends alike were invited, and Da was as excited as a lad. He had a choir, special logs to burn on the fire in some ancestral ceremony, and had been going on about it for weeks.

I wanted it to be perfect for him.

In the car park, I rolled to a stop. The kids yelled thanks then ran inside the castle, and I followed, trudging over the gravel, my boots leaving deep prints in the newly fallen snow.

Da appeared in the doorway to the great hall.

I raised a hand. "I know I'm late. Any problems?"

He rested a shoulder on the carved stone and furrowed his heavy brow. "Nae problems. The hall is decorated, most of the family is already here. Guests should arrive in an hour, then we'll have carols, food, and a walk to the church for midnight mass for those staying. Why do ye have a face like a wet weekend?"

I debated for split second telling him about my spike of intuition but shook my head. "No reason. It's going to be a grand evening."

"Aye, the best Christmas ever. All the more important now you oldest three are heading out into the world."

In a few weeks, I was joining the army. Sebastian, my best friend and sort-of cousin, was signing up, too. Then my twin sister was leaving for university. We'd aged up and were shipping out. Rarely a day went by where Da didn't stare at us with a wistful gaze.

Not that it helped me any. I'd had an alternate plan, but my father had shot me down in flames. Fuck it. The military would do me good. Use up the energy I never seemed to be able to control.

Behind me, a car rumbled into the yard.

Da's gaze sought it, and a grin lit his face. "James and Beth!" He stuck his head in the doorway and bellowed the same into the depths of the great hall.

I stared at the car. Aunt Beth had a garage full of expensive vehicles, and today she drove a glossy red Bentley Continental. They were the only two people inside. Sebastian, their son, was driving himself, but where was Isobel?

My premonition grew stronger. If anyone was going to be causing mischief, it was their sixteen-year-old. The lass was a menace.

Side by side, Da and I approached the car. The couple climbed out. They were my parents' closest friends, but we kids called them uncle and aunt.

"How was your trip?" Da hugged them both, his big voice booming.

I held back while they made their greeting. "Where's Isobel?" I finally asked when they turned to me.

Beth smiled. "Good to see you, too, Lennox. Isobel is travelling with Sebastian. They should be here soon."

Fuck. Now I knew we had a problem.

Da ushered them into the castle, and I made my excuses and headed the other way. Once out of sight, I jogged, rounding the building until I reached the tower's exterior door. In a minute, I was inside and up the stairs to my apartment, frustration driving me on.

I placed a call, shucking my snowboarding jacket and pants to my couch.

Sebastian answered on the first ring. "Nox, how's it going?"

"Where's your sister?" I demanded, no time for pleasantries. Seb was my best friend in the world, and he'd forgive the rudeness.

There was a pause. "Isobel was to travel to Scotland with our parents." Then he groaned, no doubt working out the reason for my urgency. "Fuck."

"Aye, fuck. They just got here, and she wasn't in the car. They think she's with you."

He swore viciously. "Hold on. Let me pull over and call

her."

While I waited for him to come back on the line, I strode through the hall into my bedroom and grabbed my jeans and a jumper.

Isobel Fitzroy was a problem child and then some. I hadn't seen her in over a year, but I'd heard about her exploits from her far-too-patient brother. She'd changed schools after outrageous behaviour had her expelled. She smoked, drank, had apparently and inexplicably gotten a tattoo, and seemed to be doing everything to draw attention to herself.

There was no way in hell she was ruining Christmas.

Sebastian returned. "She's not answering. I'll ring the garage at home. She usually hangs out there."

Another twenty-second wait brought worse news. "The Tesla is missing," Seb said, his deep voice flat.

I slapped my hand to my forehead. Our runaway had taken a car from her ma's collection as if she were entitled to it. "Where the fuck would she go?"

He grumbled. "No idea. Isobel has some issues right now. Is Skye there? I'd bet any money that she'd answer the phone to her."

Sebastian was right. My sister would know. "I'll call ye back," I muttered then stepped into my boots and hotfooted it out of my apartment, descending the spiral stairs to the interior of the castle.

Skirting the great hall and the large number of relatives already present, I found my twin in the dining room.

I glared at her, unable to help my mood. "Skye, a word."

She pushed her blonde hair behind her ear then blinked at my expression. Rising gracefully, Skye set aside the pastel paper Christmas chain decorations she was making with two of our younger—and comparatively well behaved—

cousins. The girls exchanged an uh-oh glance but didn't complain about my interruption.

I dragged her through the busy main kitchen where our uncles prepared the evening's feast and outside into the night. Chill air fought the furious heat blazing in me.

"Are you going to tell me what's going on?" Skye asked.

"Isobel has taken a car from Belvedere. She lied to her parents about coming here with Seb. She's missing."

"Oh heck." Skye shivered, wrapping her bare arms around her torso.

Twins we might be, but she was slender to my brawn. Instantly, I shed my jumper and stuck it over her head.

"Thank you. Have you tried calling her?"

"No. Her brother did, and she won't answer. You try," I ordered.

Skye grimaced but took her phone from her dress pocket. "Just don't bark at her in the background. She's going through a hard time right now."

A hard time? I planted my balled fists on my hips. Isobel had a charmed life. She lived in a mansion with two doting parents and she wanted for nothing. She wasn't the one who'd have to take on a title and ownership of an estate one day, like her brother and me, or lead a clan, like I would.

What the ever-loving fuck did she have to worry about?

The dial tone sounded on Skye's phone. A voice answered.

My sister pressed her finger to her ear and half turned away from me. "Is? Where are you?"

A clear laugh came down the line, and my back stiffened.

Skye listened intently. "Right," she said. "But the party starts soon. Will you be here in time? That's at least an hour's drive away. I'm worried about you."

Skye knew where she was! I seized the phone from her hand.

"Isobel Fitzroy, what the bloody hell do ye think you're playing at? Are you out of your mind? What the hell is wrong with ye?"

A shocked intake of breath came, then silence met my ears. I checked the screen.

She'd hung up?

Fuck!

"Lennox! That was really rude!" Skye grabbed her phone back. She poked me in the chest. "We'll be lucky if she shows up at all now, and you know how excited Da is about this party. He's got most of the clan coming. It has to go well."

"How is any of this my fault? Tell me where she is," I demanded.

With a resigned sigh, she gave me the name of a tiny town south of us.

"What's there?" I asked.

"I've no clue. She said she needed to drive." Skye poked at her phone again. "I'll search for it."

I dialled Sebastian. "Seb. We think she's in Balliedun. It's about an hour south."

"There's an airfield there," Skye reported.

"God's above." Seb growled, clearly overhearing. "Then she's racing."

"Racing? As in cars?"

"Yeah, she's just taken it up. Legally, I mean. But she keeps going on about these drag racing meet-ups and she's taken the fastest nought-to-sixty car in the garage. What else can she be doing?"

With my nerves fraying to the very edge, I relayed this wee nugget of joy to Skye.

She paled further. "We need to help her."

"I'm the wrong side of the Cairngorms," Seb said in my ear. "I won't be able to reach her in time."

"I'll go." I jammed my fingers into my hair. "Just get here safe, aye, Seb? We can't have two Fitzroys missing on one evening."

"Shit. Fine. Thank you. Keep me posted."

I hung up and eyed my sister. "Don't tell anyone what's happening. If asked where I am, say I had to see a friend and I'll be back soon."

"Agreed. Da will have a head fit if he knows what's going on."

He would, but better that he had it after the fact with Isobel in front of him. Maybe then she would finally get the discipline she needed.

Skye blew out a frosty breath. "I don't know how you're going to get there in time."

"Leave that to me." I had an idea in mind but I'd have to be quick. "I'll see ye before the fun starts, aye?"

"Be careful, and don't be too hard on her." My sister held up a hand, pausing me in my steps. "I still need to talk to you," she said.

I'd forgotten all about that. Earlier, Skye had told me she had something important to ask me. A favour she needed. I'd assumed it was to do with her and Sebastian. Ever since we'd been tiny, everyone—me included—had assumed they'd one day be a couple. I couldn't imagine how she'd need my help with that, though.

"It'll have to wait, but whatever it is, consider it done." I took off at a jog, leaving my twin behind.

I had to see my uncle about a helicopter ride. There was only one way I could stop Isobel before she did something stupid, and it meant getting there fast.

ADRENALINE RUSH

*I*sobel
  Engines rumbled, the vibrations combining to shake the disused airfield under my wheels. I'd pulled up at the end of the line of cars, ready to race, but now, I couldn't bring myself to step out of the Tesla.

Impulsiveness and a need to burn off my anger had primed my muscles, but I hesitated, gazing at the accumulated racers.

The vehicle next to mine, a Lamborghini Huracan, belonged to someone I knew. Casey Warwick. His younger sister, Erika, was in my year at school.

Erika was my own personal bully.

After what that bitch had done to me, I wanted to ram her brother and his fancy fucking car off the fucking road.

Not that I'd ever be so violent, but the thoughts danced around my head, entwined with images of her mocking message.

At least in the Tesla Model S, I'd kick her brother's ass.

Casey stepped out of his vehicle. "Engines off," he yelled to the petrolheads assembled.

I slid my window down a quarter to hear him better but kept to my seat.

Eyes soaked in Mum's newest ride.

She'd kill me if she knew I'd taken it, but I wouldn't hide the fact. I could hardly avoid the truth as I'd arrive at the castle in the Tesla later this evening. But the details of the illegal drag race could wait until after Christmas.

"Rules are simple. See the headlights down the airfield?" Casey reached into his car and flashed his lights. Two answering flashes came from a car farther along the dark, wide concrete expanse. "To the Subaru and back again. Winner takes all. If you crash, it's your problem, but deliberate ramming means disqualification. Got it?"

A series of replies came back, all male, all gruff, and tinged with testosterone-fuelled excitement.

In the background, a chopping noise came. Distant but distinct. I'd know the sound of a helicopter anywhere—Dad's friends often came to Belvedere by air. One of the McRae uncles ran a helicopter training school. But the airstrip we were on was in the middle of nowhere. It must be a passing military chopper. Nothing to worry about. We'd be long gone before any reports of the race could be acted upon.

A knock on my bonnet startled me.

Casey peered in the tinted windscreen. "Hey, Tesla, are you nuts? If you wreck this ride, that's a fucking waste."

I squirmed in my seat.

Earlier today, I'd been a howling, raging little beast. Casey's sister had somehow come across a Christmas card I'd written for a friend. She'd taken a photo of my writing and posted it everywhere, her mocking jeers intended to hurt.

She'd got her wish.

I never wrote anything by hand. I had agreement from my teachers that all schoolwork could be done on my laptop and printed if necessary, and I'd carefully avoided the kids at school knowing about my problems. But then, on the last day of Christmas term, I'd broken my rule and handwritten a card for a boy I liked.

Sort of asking him out.

Erika somehow got hold of my note and played her trick. School was hard enough, particularly ours where every kid came from a privileged background and bullying was almost mandatory. I mean, I didn't even like the guy that much. That wasn't the source of my embarrassment. Memories of my spidery scrawl and mixed-up letters had me cringing. Next term was going to be rough. I was already being watched for my hot temper.

The leather steering wheel dented under my nails.

I hated that school, with the constant pressure on whose parents earned the most or what celebrity they'd had dinner with that weekend. My parents had picked it because Skye, my sort-of cousin, had gone there and thrived. She was even friends with Erika and Casey's elder sister, Amber.

If it made me miserable, why should I go back?

"Shit." Casey reached my window, clocking me through the gap. "It's a girl. Wait, I know you."

Summoning my will, I popped the door and climbed out. "What if you do? Got a problem racing a girl?"

His lip curled, and his gaze took on a predatory glint. He adjusted his sunglasses, perched in his over-styled brown hair. "Can you drive that thing, babe?"

I narrowed my eyes. "Better than you can your Lambo, *babe*."

Casey's smile dropped. "Seriously, this isn't a game. There's money on this race."

I already knew that. I'd read about it in the motor forum where the race had been planned. His sister boasted about her brother's illegal activities like it was some clever achievement rather than a rich kid taking risks because he could.

Though wasn't that me, too?

Maybe. But if I didn't offload this anger, I was going to ruin Christmas for my family. Driving aggressively would get the angst out of my system. The adrenaline rush, one I'd been used to since Mum taught me to drive the moment I was old enough to help her in the garage, would tire me out and shut my damn brain down.

"Scared to lose to a girl?" I taunted Casey.

His mouth twisted. "If you can pay, I don't give a fuck who you are."

From the pocket of my leather jacket, I extracted the race fee. Then I pressed it to Casey's chest. "Good. Then let's go."

"Isobel!" a voice boomed across the field.

I hesitated, my ears burning.

There was *no way* that could be Lennox McRae.

I swung around and spotted him, his long legs eating the black night between us. At his back, the helicopter I'd heard but blotted out sped off into the distance, lights flashing.

Oh God.

I'd had no problem telling his sister Skye where I was because I'd be at the castle before any of them could think twice about it. No one could reach me in time to ruin my race.

Lennox was not fucking this up for me.

"Got company?" Casey quipped at my back.

"Whatever. Let's race." I jumped into the Tesla and buckled myself in.

Lennox's voice thundered again, but I ignored him, watching Casey for his mark. I started the almost silent engine, getting comfortable in my seat. A couple of cars along, a guy was still hanging out of his door, chatting, and I growled, impatient to go. Time was running out.

"On your marks," Casey finally yelled over the snarl of engines.

I breathed through my nose and set the car in gear. My pulse thrummed, and my stomach contracted into a tight ball. I needed to get away before Lennox tried to stop me.

The passenger-side door of the Tesla opened.

My sort-of cousin jammed into the seat and shut himself in. "Stop what you're doing. Right now."

I didn't take my eyes off the next car. "No."

"Isobel, stop the fucking engine."

"Go!" Casey hollered.

I floored the accelerator.

We shot forwards, instantly ahead of the pack. The deep-blue metallic Tesla was second to none on take-off— nought to sixty in under two-and-a-half seconds—the exact reason I'd been unable to resist choosing it as my ride.

Still, I had never driven this fast.

G-force pinned me to my seat and stole my breath. Fear, panic, and speed-lust held me tight in their grip.

Fighting the shock of what I was doing, I spluttered a laugh, glancing in my rearview. The Lamborghini was the only real contender, and it was closing.

Then I spared a glance for Lennox.

His hulking presence at my side couldn't be overlooked. With muscles straining at his neck and a rabid expression on his face, he bit out, "You're insane."

"I'm not. Put your seat belt on."

"No. Stop the car!"

We were halfway to the Subaru—the marker point for making the turn.

"Len! Put your fucking seat belt on!" I only had seconds.

"Pull out of the race, Isobel."

Anger flooded me. "I'm about to take the corner," I snarled.

I passed the Subaru. With the Lamborghini on my tail, I pulled right.

Lennox grabbed the wheel and yanked it left. Brakes squealed, and our path straightened.

"What the fuck do you think you're doing?" I wrenched against his hold, but he didn't budge.

We swung wide, off the makeshift track and out onto the dark airstrip. Now I was out of the way, Casey's Lamborghini took the lead.

"I'm going to lose!" I yelled.

"You lost the second you stole this car."

"I didn't steal it!"

"You don't even have a driving licence!"

Ha, I had him there. Though I was still only sixteen, our home was rural enough for me to apply for special dispensation, and I'd taken my test earlier in the year, passing with flying colours.

"Wrong. I've had one for months. Get your hands off my wheel."

"Brat! Do as I tell ye."

"Asshole! You have no rights over me!"

We tussled, struggling for control. With no knowledge of what lay ahead and visibility only as far as the headlights reached, I eased up on the accelerator. I might be a speed freak but I didn't have a death wish.

"You want to drive fast? Put your fucking foot down. Let's break your record." Lennox switched his grip on the wheel then leaned across me, grabbing my knee in his meaty hand. By force, he had me flooring it again.

The car punched into the black.

"Len!" I fought him, beating his arms and shoulders, trying to dislodge my foot from the gas pedal. "Get the fuck off. You're going to kill us!"

If we crashed, he'd die. The Tesla topped out at over two hundred miles per hour. Not strapped in? He stood no chance.

Outside, the empty night zipped by. The flat airfield could end in a wall at any second. A broken section of the old security fencing could flip the car.

"No fucking way. You wanted a thrill? This is it. You wanted to drive fast like the fucking idiots back there? Soak it up."

"That was a controlled race! I knew what I was doing."

"Knew what you were doing? You don't have the sense you were born with. What the hell is wrong with your head? Are ye stupid or something?"

My mouth dropped open, and my words died.

Silence buzzed.

Lennox seemed to notice the difference in me, in how my muscles slackened following his slur. He eased up the pressure on my leg, and I yanked my foot from the pedal. We slowed.

But, too quickly, a solid wall appeared in the headlights.

"Fuck!" I screamed.

Together, we hauled the wheel, spinning the car. I stamped hard on the brake.

The edges of my vision blackened, but the car performed. We made the turn.

It wasn't quite soon enough.

With a sickening squeal, my side of the car scraped along the brick. Metal tore and crunched. We came to a halt in a cloud of smoke.

I stared in shock at the wall, inches from my face outside the window.

In a flash, Lennox opened his door, unfastened my seat belt, and dragged me across the car. Outside, the enormous man dropped me and took two steps back, his eyes wide and his hands flying to link behind his dark-blond head.

God, he was pissed off.

My emotions railed.

Then the strangest thing happened.

In the midst of disaster, and with my mother's prized car battered and dented, my brain fixated on the swell of Lennox's biceps either side of his head.

Oh shit.

He was my brother's best friend. On our visits when we'd been growing up, the two of them had usually been together. At best, I'd seen him as an irritating, bossy relation. Self-appointed king of the cousins. Except we weren't related. Not by blood.

My teenage hormones decided at that very second to wake up and take notice. At his size. His brawn. The way his t-shirt stretched over his chest, no jumper or jacket to hide his tight, muscular body.

When the fuck had he gotten so attractive?

Then I realised he was looking at me in exactly the same dazed way.

And it snapped me back into reality.

"This is your fault," I said, only half believing my own words.

Lennox blinked. "Ye have to be kidding me?"

Another argument was brewing. An explosion. Yet my energy drained, and my head drooped. "No, I'm not kidding. Whatever you have to say, save it. I need to drive this to the castle and show my mum what I did."

"What we did," he muttered, giving up a tiny concession. Then he shook his head. "Fuck are ye driving me. I'll get behind the wheel. If it will even go anymore."

"You think you're driving me? Go home in your own car." I suddenly realised the big picture—the helicopter had dropped him off. He had no other way of getting home. Ugh.

"Sorry. You're stuck with me." Lennox shouldered past and clambered through the car to the driver's seat.

Looked like I had no choice but to follow.

3

RED-BLOODED MALE

*L*ennox

Empty roads took us home to the castle. Lucky for us, the damage to the Tesla hadn't affected the engine, though I did have to suffer the indignity of needing Isobel to show me how to drive the thing. No gear stick. What the fuck was up with that?

We drove in absolute silence, and I alternated grinding my teeth in frustration and worrying that I'd overreacted. Had I caused the crash? Aye, perhaps. Wait, no. I wasn't the one who'd stolen a car and gone to an illegal race.

I had lost my temper, though. This was why I needed the military—to help control my energy so I didn't end up doing idiotic things.

Like forcing a lass to drive until we smashed into a wall.

I grimaced at the road and huffed, then glanced at Isobel. In the dark passenger seat, she'd curled away from me and was gazing out of the window, her hand to her mouth. Her tight leather jacket and jeans skimmed curves I hadn't known her to have.

She dragged her knuckles over her lip, and my breath caught.

Fuck. There was no reason why I should find her attractive. None at all. It was the adrenaline. The fuss.

That was the only reason my blood had heated when I'd been yelling at her.

Isobel was a terror, and her actions—and the car she'd trashed—were going to send our families into havoc. Right on Christmas.

Yeah, that was better—thinking about Da's face worked wonders to kill my erection.

"You know, if you mutter any more to yourself, I'm going to think you've lost it," Isobel said, her tone dry.

I ignored her, peering ahead for non-existent traffic.

After a minute, she hadn't said another word, and I stole another glance.

"That outfit is ridiculous. I hope ye have a change of clothes for the party," I grumped.

Isobel raised an eyebrow then stretched between us to grab a bag from the back seat. She opened it, extracted a dress, then tossed the rucksack behind her once more. Then the damn minx sat forward, winked at me, and unzipped her jacket.

A lacy black bra sprang into view, with Isobel's high, firm breasts gleaming in the low light. The pattern of a black tattoo ghosted over her ribs, but that was barely worth my notice.

Her fucking lingerie, on the other hand... My kryptonite.

I was an eighteen-year-old red-blooded male. Dragging my stare off her took a Herculean effort.

"Fuck," I whispered, gripping the steering wheel.

A snort of laughter met my bewilderment. Isobel's jeans went the same way as the bag, then she stuck her arms into a dress, pulling it over her head. She wriggled it down her body then smoothed the frock over her hips and legs.

No way could I clap eyes on her damn legs.

"It's safe to look now," the lass deadpanned.

No, it wasn't. Not even for a second. I gritted my jaw and sped on.

$\mathcal{W}$e rolled into the castle's car park barely an hour after I'd left. The journey had been at pace—maybe I'd broken a speed limit or two in the sweet ride, earning me a dark laugh from Isobel—and we'd returned in time to witness a swathe of guests entering the great hall.

The party was starting.

Da greeted his friends at the door. He took in the damaged car, and his shoulders rose. Isobel shrank in her seat. Good. Maybe he'd make a dent in her cast-iron attitude.

I trundled the wreck around the corner and out of sight then parked up and leapt out. Isobel dragged her feet, and I clapped a hand to her biceps, marching her ahead of me.

At the castle steps, Da regarded us with a firm look. "My office," he barked.

We trailed him inside. Isobel slipped in ahead of me. I ignored the hollers of friends and family, but Da caught the eye of Uncle James, Isobel's father, and the man moved to join us. Isobel waited for her da then drew his arm over her shoulders. Against, him, or anyone, really, she was tiny. Five feet of absolute trouble. He tucked her in and dropped a kiss to her wild black curls.

Huh. He wouldn't be so kind if he knew what she'd done.

"One second," Da said to us, pausing our steps at the top of the hall. He turned to his guests. "Friends, family, clan, and kin, I am glad and honoured to host this McRae Yule gathering. There is nothing more important to me than the knowing ye are all safe and well under my roof. Christmas is a time for family, and we'll celebrate together." He gave a meaningful glance to Isobel who inched closer to her father. Then he cleared his throat. "Mathilda, my beautiful wife, where are ye, lass?"

Ma raised her crystal wine flute, and Da raised his chin, earning a nod in response. My parents had an uncanny way of knowing what the other was thinking.

My mother tinged her glass, drawing the attention to her. "Thank you, Callum. As my husband says, we are so happy you all came. Please, everybody, refresh your drinks and fill your plates. The carol singers are ready to wow us, and there is food enough to see us all well-fed."

She continued on, but Da ushered us away, guiding our unhappy little group down a corridor. Singing started at our backs, and the chatter of the crowd recommenced.

At his office, Isobel and Uncle James went inside. Da halted at the door, and I stood before him, ready with my report.

"Are ye hurt?" He ran his gaze over me.

"Naw."

"Is she?"

I shrugged. I'd assumed not, but I hadn't thought to ask.

Da heaved a sigh. "Go on and find your mother. Help her host while I deal with this."

I drew my head back. "Don't ye want to hear what happened?"

"I know this was nothing to do with ye, my lad. It isn't anything to do with me, either, but I'll see if her da needs my help. For the rest of it, Isobel can speak for herself, aye?" He turned on his heel and disappeared into the room, closing the door behind him.

I stared at the pitted wood for a second then did as he asked, inordinately annoyed that I hadn't got to rant about the drama. Weaving through groups in their suits and sparkly dresses, I stomped across the great hall in search of Ma. She was easy to spot. Like the rest of my family, she stood a head taller than most, but it suited my regal mother.

The lady of Clan McRae gave me a soft smile, adjusting the drape of her long silver dress. "Is all well? I take it from your father's forced smile that something is going on."

"There is," I admitted. "Trouble with Isobel. She stole a car."

"The bigger the child, the bigger the problems," Ma said with a sigh. She drained her wine and placed the glass on a table garlanded with pine boughs. "Is her father handling it?"

"Aye."

"Then it'll be fine. Well, until her mother gets back from her jaunt to Braithar to collect your Aunt Ella's forgotten dress. Beth wanted her children to be confident drivers, but I'm not sure this was her goal." She shook her head, her elegant jewellery sparkling. "Come with me and greet the newcomers. This will be your role one day."

I dawdled after her, still not feeling right. Across the hall, Uncle Ally headed down the corridor to Da's office. Why would they call him in?

For a quarter of an hour, I made polite conversation as best I could, but I was itching to find out what was happening behind the closed doors. Eventually, Da emerged. He joined us and kissed Ma on the cheek. She asked him a quiet question, too low for me to hear over the choir, and he intoned something in response.

Ma pressed his fingers then left us.

I stood tall under Da's attention. "Is Isobel in trouble?"

He tilted his head then took me aside, under the row of arches that made up one side of the great hall. "I think the shock she'll get when she shows Beth the damage to the car will be enough, don't ye?"

No, I really didn't. "What about taking away her licence? What about curbing her freedom?" A good couple of months stuck in her room should do it. Better still, they could send her to the military, like her brother and me.

I opened my mouth to continue, but Da cut over me.

"Just imagine her state of mind and don't jump to judgement. The learning disability diagnosis hit her hard, the bullying has been far worse. How would ye feel in her shoes?"

I stared at my father. Isobel had never showed any signs of having a learning disability. Nor had I heard of her being bullied. "I didn't know," I managed.

"Well, now ye do. When you're managing a team of soldiers, you'll need to bear this in mind. Bad behaviour is a symptom, aye? You can't fix it with punishment, you have to work out the underlying issue. Now stop worrying about Isobel Fitzroy. She isn't your problem." He palmed my shoulder, shook me once, then left, following my mother into the crowd.

Skye arrived at my side. "You're back!" my sister said. "Is everything okay? I need to talk to you."

Another person loomed behind her. One of her friends. The lass whose name I couldn't recall wiped a tear from her eye and gazed at me with a hopeful expression.

I stifled my sigh and raised my chin. Whatever this favour was, I didn't think I was going to enjoy it.

Maybe I deserved that.

I left the great hall by the side door, bursting out into the bitter air. Fuck! What could I do, go and yell at the loch? I'd agreed to my sister's request. With her tearful friend pleading with me and making doe eyes, I could hardly say no, but I despised lying above all things.

Turned out this Christmas I'd be a bully *and* a liar.

Good fucking thing I was shipping off in a few weeks.

I stalked along the castle's defences until I came to the car park exit. A lone figure came into view up ahead. They blew a plume of frosty breath into the black night as if they were smoking, one foot kicked back to rest on the wrong side of the stone wall. The model of nonchalance.

Isobel.

Though my blood spiked, I swallowed down my ire and joined her. This time, I kept my damn mouth shut and took a position at her side, facing out into the dark landscape. Ahead, the loch glistened in the faint starlight. Warm lights marked the village, owned by my family. Upstream was Braithar, another McRae castle, owned by my Uncle Gordain and his wife, Ella. Ella was Isobel's dad's sister. Their marriage connected our two families beyond our parents' friendship.

Isobel and I were kin. I'd behaved like she was something other and I regretted every action I'd taken.

She broke the silence first. "Mum's on her way to inspect the damage. She's been at Braithar so hasn't seen it yet. She's going to go spare."

I grunted acknowledgement. "I'll stay to see her, too. It's half my fault."

The lass's stare bored into me. She tried twice to start a sentence before settling on, "I'm sorry. You shouldn't have been put in that position."

I gaped now and turned to her. Shite. I hadn't counted on her being reasonable. "I didn't know you'd had problems. I'm sorry, too."

"No. You were looking out for my family. I appreciate that."

"I do daft things when I'm fired up. I cannae help myself."

"Same."

We watched one another.

Isobel had the prettiest eyes. In fact, her pert features made her almost beautiful. How long had it been since I'd last seen her? At some point, she'd stopped being a child, and though I called her brother my cousin, a fact not strictly true, I had no idea what to do with this new version of Isobel.

On impulse, I reached out and brought her into a hug. My family were huggers, always ready with open arms. But her warm body on mine was something else.

In a second, my frustration, anger, and guilt switched to a newer, more powerful emotion. Hotter. Wilder.

Isobel pulled back an inch and gazed up at me.

My words had escaped. I could only hold still and hope the thoughts running through my head weren't apparent in my expression.

"Jeez, Len," Isobel breathed, then she uttered a laugh, pushed up on her toes, and crammed her lips on mine.

4

WHAT A DOUCHE

*I*sobel

I was full of bad ideas. Made of them, maybe. This had to be my stupidest yet. Lennox froze under my kiss, his soft lips unmoving.

Oh God, what a mistake.

Then the huge Scot gave a hungry growl, clamped me to him, and stole my breath. He attacked my mouth with a vengeance, delivering a powerful kiss that had my knees weakening. His tongue slid over the seam of my lips, and I parted them on instinct, allowing him entrance.

My whole body went into a kind of horny shock from the taste of him.

His hot tongue tangled with mine.

His hand grasped my head, the other found my backside.

Rough stubble scratched my skin and woke my senses. It was all I could do to hold on but, God, this was the best idea ever.

I really liked this kiss.

I was seventeen in a couple of months. It was about time

I had some face time with a boy. Or a man. Lennox was almost nineteen and built. There was nothing boyish about him.

A moan erupted from me, and Lennox answered with a groan that shook me to my boots. Then, without warning, he tore his lips from mine.

He took two steps back and jammed his fingers into his hair, his brown eyes wide in alarm.

I might not be the quickest person, but even I could see his instant regret.

"What's wrong?" I asked, though I knew the answer. Me. I was wrong.

"I shouldn't have…" he started.

Shit. My eyes teared up. Call it delayed shock, but fresh humiliation slammed into me with the force of a battering ram. It was ridiculous, but Lennox's rejection *hurt*. I clutched my arms around the ache in my middle.

I should've said something, but my mouth wouldn't give up the words.

Instead, I dropped my chin, turned, and fled.

---

*M*um found me in the Tesla where I'd hidden myself from the world. She rapped on the window with a knuckle then let herself in.

"Hmm," she said, closing the door, and she reached for my hand and interlaced our fingers.

Mum's warmth had my bottom lip trembling all over again.

In Callum's office, Dad had listened to my story then hugged me hard and told me, in no uncertain terms, how it would break him to hear that I'd been injured. My father was the very best person I knew. He was good and kind and he rarely yelled. Mum yelled, but she also loved fiercely.

Poor them for having me.

Dad had summoned Ally, Callum's brother, to talk to me. The other men left the room, and Ally explained to me how all his life he'd coped with extreme dyslexia. He hadn't tackled it at school and had dropped out early. He offered no opinion on what I should do but told me to specialise in the things I was good at and find coping mechanisms for the things I couldn't change.

It was kind of him to take the time, but why the fuck couldn't I just be normal?

"I killed your car," I said to Mum.

"Yup." Her thumb swept over my knuckles. "You'll work in the garage with Mr Hinchcliffe until the repair debt is paid."

A laugh burst out of me. "That'll take forever."

Mum's lips twitched. "Good. It'll keep you out of trouble. Are you going to tell me how all this started?"

I did. My hatred of school, Erika's bullying throughout term, the final straw with the handwriting jeers, it all fell from my lips.

"And I kissed Lennox," I added fast with no real idea why.

"You didn't?" Mum gaped. "No, I'm sorry. You can't kiss boys because you're still my baby. Even if you raid my garage. Even when you're thirty."

"I prang your car, drop out of school, and you're more worried about my first kiss?"

Mum leaned over and hugged me. "Cars can be fixed. Hearts take longer."

"My heart wasn't involved." No worries on that score.

Mum *hmmed* again and then ordered me out of the

Tesla. We inspected the damage, and I fudged a retelling of the events that led up to the crash, leaving Lennox's part out of it. No reason to drag him into my mess.

Then Mum and I returned to the castle to join the festivities. Now the fuss was over, I just wanted to unravel.

Even though I wasn't a child anymore, I loved Christmas. I adored the smell of pine in the air, the shiny, Edwardian decorations Dad unearthed from some remote storeroom in Belvedere. I loved carol singers and the million and one traditions we had as an old family. How the catering staff in Belvedere's visitors' centre served mulled wine and mince pies.

We always came here, to Castle McRae, for a few days during the season. The echoing yet cosy open space of the great hall had set the scene for many snug days spent playing with my cousins. Sebastian would disappear with Lennox out on the estate somewhere. Skye and I led the younger kids in games. We'd go out on toboggans, or even ice skating if the loch froze.

It was with a strange sense of an ending that, now, I gazed into the great hall. The boys were moving on, Skye was leaving, too. Our childhoods were over.

Mum led me to join our family group. At some point, Sebastian had arrived, and I got a serious stare from my brother with a promise to talk more later.

A short distance away, Lennox stood, his spine stiff and a tic to his jaw as if he was annoyed. I caught his eye and tilted my head. I didn't want to be angry at him. Not at Christmas. The kiss was yet another mistake, and I had to get over it.

But then my gaze skirted down his body and stopped at his hand. A hand that was very firmly clenched in someone else's.

A sick sensation hit my stomach.

I followed the female arm up to its owner. A slender blonde woman with shiny hair and boobs brimming over her satin dress.

Oh fuck, no.

Amber Warwick. Elder sister to my bully, Erika, and to Casey who I'd raced earlier.

Amber was Skye's friend. Was that why Lennox was holding her hand?

Then she snaked her arm around his waist in a possessive, claiming move and laid her pretty head on his broad shoulder. Next to her, an older couple tipped their heads at Amber and Lennox.

The woman smiled and said, "Young love, eh?"

Love?

Around me, conversation buzzed. Mum chatted, Dad laughed, none the wiser to my turmoil.

The whole time, Lennox didn't take his eyes off me. That regret I'd seen? It was guilt. Because he'd kissed me knowing he had a girlfriend.

Schooling my features with untypical self-control, I held his gaze for a beat, letting my disdain show through.

What a douche. What a shitty way to behave.

The king of the cousins had tarnished his crown.

5

GOLDEN BOY

Isobel – Belvedere, 4 years on

"Excuse me? Young man?" a voice called into the depths of the garage.

I tightened the last bodywork bolt on the Jaguar Mark II restore I'd been working on and rolled from under the car. I was alone in the garage, aside from whoever it was interrupting me, but I'd just about finished and I cast an appreciative eye over the repair job. This car had been a wreck, but it had been a breeze to cut out the rusted parts and patch it up. All it needed now was a respray, and an engine tune-up, and it would be as good as new.

I wiped my fingers on my overalls and turned around. A middle-aged lady peered at me.

"Can I help you?" I asked.

"A girl! I do beg your pardon. I saw legs under a car and I assumed you were male. My mistake." She waved a hand at the park behind her. "I'm visiting on a coach trip but I don't think I should be back here."

She was right. The garage and gardens between us and

Belvedere were private and not open to the public like the rest of our estate.

I gave the woman a smile. "You're lost. I'll take you to the gate."

She thanked me, and I stowed my tools and hit the button to close the overhead garage door, the only one open on the long row. We set off across the frozen grass, and the chilly February wind had me wrapping my arms around myself. In a few weeks, Mum was hosting a car rally here on the estate, and I had to hope that spring would make its presence known by then.

"You have oil on your face, by the way," the woman at my side said.

"I usually do." I grinned and made a half-assed effort to swipe at my cheek.

She leaned in as we walked. "What are the family like who live here? They're royalty, I heard."

I stifled my grin, stopping it from growing bigger. No one who saw me like this would ever guess I was Lady Isobel Durant Fitzroy. And I liked it that way.

With practiced ease, I summoned a shocked grimace. "I hear the parents are lovely but the children are quite wild."

The lady tutted. "That doesn't surprise me one bit. Imagine growing up in a place like this. Never having to worry about money or work. Not like the rest of us." She nodded at my grease-stained get-up.

"I know! Rich kids have it so lucky."

We reached the footpath gate that led back into the public park, and I tapped in the code and let her through.

"Thank you, young lady. I apologise for taking you away from your job, I hope you won't get into trouble!" the woman said, then disappeared out of sight behind the thick hedge, into the main part of our grounds.

Actually, her interruption had been timely. I checked my phone and goggled at the hour. I had to be in and showered in twenty minutes—Mum's request. Sebastian was coming home today, his four years in the military done, and we were celebrating with a dinner in his honour.

I jogged across the expanse of lawn that stretched to the east wing of Belvedere, our family home.

I'd missed my brother terribly. Not that things had been quiet around here. The stately home and estate always had something going on. Case in point: the upcoming rally with its hundreds of cars and thousands of visitors.

Which left me with no further excuse to keep from doing the job I'd avoided all day. Ugh. My procrastination time was up.

There was nothing quite so awkward as calling an ex-hookup to ask for a favour.

One of the big suppliers for the rally was unconfirmed. Warwick Supercars, owners of a fleet of gorgeous, powerful motors, had agreed to attend, but we'd heard nothing since. They would bring Ferraris, a sweet Aston Martin Valhalla, then the cherry on the top, a Bugatti Chiron. A three-million-dollar gorgeous beast I'd always wanted to drive. We had a decent garage, but nothing matched the Chiron.

The supercars were a huge public draw. We'd scheduled time trials, and nothing got people more whipped up than fast cars flying by.

The Warwick family—Casey Warwick in particular—knew fast cars.

In the past four years, my relationship with the Warwicks had gotten even more complicated. After I'd dropped out of school, my parents had insisted on two things: that I work with private tutors so my general education was sound, and to choose a career I loved and find a way to specialise.

I'd chosen cars, unsurprisingly, and raced as a hobby, meaning I'd often be at the same meets as Casey Warwick. Not long after my eighteenth birthday, away from home, I'd drunkenly kissed him. Luckily, I'd come to my senses before it could go any further but, in the years since, he'd alternated between flirting outrageously and taunting me like his sister used to.

What a massive error. My skin crawled whenever I remembered it.

Strangely, the other kiss I'd made in error, with Lennox McRae, I didn't regret in the same way. I thought about that damn kiss far too often, even if I'd avoided the jackass himself since that Christmas.

I crunched across the frozen grass, fighting memories.

Shame I couldn't avoid Casey. I needed him to persuade his stepdad to confirm the club's attendance. The rally was in a matter of weeks, and it would be too late notice to find an alternative. I dragged in a breath, sucked in my ego, and hit *Call* on my phone.

It rang, and I stopped and clamped my finger to the opposing ear.

To my right, a car slowly circled the drive. I squinted. A metallic grey BMW 8 series coupé. It was Seb!

A voice answered the phone. "You've reached the voicemail of—"

I hung up and carefully sent Casey a text—because what kind of monster left voicemails?—and then picked up my feet. Family parking was on the north side, and I rounded the corner, a big grin ready on my face.

Sebastian stood tall from the driver's seat, his smart

uniform a familiar sight from ceremonies and previous visits home.

His gaze found mine, and he laughed and slammed his door. "Is!"

I pelted to him, and he picked me up in a swinging hold.

"Ah! Call a parade! The golden boy hath returned," I cried and messed his black hair before strangling him in a hug.

My big brother grinned and kissed my cheek in return. In his regiment, he'd parachuted out of planes and had been deployed more than once. He'd always been a thrill-seeker, but at least in the army it had been controlled. I had to wonder what he'd be like now as a civilian.

"Mum and Dad around?" He placed me on my feet.

"Probably hanging up bunting."

Seb rolled his eyes. "I ordered my own naked dancers. Have they arrived?"

The passenger door to Seb's BMW swung open, and I stopped my retort. His windows were tinted, so I hadn't noticed that someone else was there.

Lennox McRae stood tall.

Oh fuck. Heat shot through me. He'd visited a handful of times over the years, and I'd been to Castle McRae once or twice, but I'd purposely steered clear of the man. I didn't understand what had happened between us, not the kiss, the rejection, or the girlfriend.

Nor did I care.

There was no place in my life for someone who made me feel the way he had.

Resisting my instinct to walk away, I stood my ground. "Lennox," I said, cool as you like. I didn't even taunt him with a 'Len'.

"Isobel," he replied quietly.

I hated the way he said my name. Gruff but almost musical in his soft Scottish brogue.

His gaze wandered down my oil-splattered clothes. I narrowed my eyes.

"Sebastian! Lennox!" Dad called from the mansion steps, breaking the moment.

Both of our parents whooped and flew to rain hugs and questions on the two men. Then we were ushered into the house where travel stories were swapped for updates on home.

As soon as I politely could, I slipped away up the wide staircase to my apartment, my boots almost silent on the plush runner. I took care not to touch the gilded balustrade for fear of marking it with my oily fingers.

When Dad married Mum, they altered Belvedere's public areas to create a family house within the enormous mansion. The house was considered a national treasure and had rooms filled with antiques, grand master paintings, and even wallpaper that was listed and protected. Not so good for small children to be around. Now, those rooms were entirely public and our wing entirely private. I had my own suite, decorated as I pleased. Dad had hated growing up in a museum, as he'd put it, and wanted us to have a normal life.

Normal had its limits, though.

My father was one of England's wealthiest men—the tenth Earl Fitzroy, and descended from a long and noble line that included kings and queens. Sebastian held the honorary title of viscount and would one day own the lot. Just like Dad, he looked the part: tall and commanding. Under the surface, my brother had the same wild heart I did, but, at a glance, you wouldn't guess at how bad he could be.

At the hall to my rooms, I slowed my steps.

Then there was me. I'd never felt like I fitted in. I had a mean temper and I wasn't going to win any prizes for brains or beauty. At best, I was cute, at worst, a pain in the ass. After the humiliation that led to me leaving school, I'd knuckled down. I should be proud of my achievements.

But I was nothing compared to Sebastian.

"Isobel?" Lennox's voice came from behind.

I whirled around, embarrassed at how gloomy my thoughts had become. Today was for celebrating. Instantly, I stuck my armour back in place.

"Hi, Len. How's the girlfriend?"

Fuck it. I hadn't meant to say any of that.

He cocked his head at me. I refused to absorb even a tiny detail of his increased bulk under his dress uniform. But his expression, I couldn't miss. Growing up, Lennox had always carried a stern glare. Now, he seemed tense or worried.

"Sebastian and I are going out after dinner. He thought you might want to come."

Despite myself, my interest piqued. Seb frequented the strangest places. Ones I'd never go to alone. "I might."

"Good," he replied.

Then he just stood and waited, like I owed him a further answer.

Closing him on the wrong side of my door had never felt sweeter.

---

*A*fter a long scrub in the shower, I tamed my black hair into a manageable wedge of curls and searched through my wardrobe, selecting a black camisole and floaty trousers in black and white. Mum would like it if I dressed nice.

From a drawer, I chose a new lingerie set.

The fact I was into cars left fewer chances for me to be feminine, so I never, ever skimped on my skimpies. Whenever we could, Skye and I hit the lingerie stores, bonding over our shared love of silky clothes. There was something about having a gloriously sexy set of underwear beneath my work attire or racewear. It gave me a secret buzz of power.

I drew the cherry-embroidered nude lace knickers over my smooth legs, then donned the bra, getting my ladies into place before finishing dressing. Ready, I stared at myself in the mirror in my dressing room.

Couldn't change my five-two height. Couldn't fix my upturned nose or my punky attitude.

At least clothes-wise, I'd do. For my family, I was good enough.

Downstairs, rich cooking scents filled the hall. My stomach growled. I'd worked solidly all day and only stopped for a quick bite at lunchtime. My appetite had noticed.

In the dining room, Dad waved from the bar, and Mum joined me, two tall glasses in her hands.

"Isobel! Look at you! Here, I thought you might need this." She handed me what looked like a Kir Royale.

"Thanks." I raised the glass in a *cheers* then drained the cocktail. Yum, blackcurrant. "Did you know Lennox was going to be here?"

"Nope, though I had a suspicion. He and Sebastian signed up and signed out of the army at the same time. I figured we'd see them together while they worked on what to do next."

I raised a sardonic eyebrow. I looked just like my mother, though my bigger backside and blue-green eyes must've come from Dad's branch of the family. "You could've warned me."

She knew that, in the past, I'd avoided him. I was terrible at keeping secrets so I rarely tried.

"I've barely seen you for days, so it didn't cross my mind. Hey, while we have a second, can I persuade you to rethink and let us throw you a birthday party after all?"

My twenty-first was fast approaching, the day before the rally. With it came responsibilities I didn't want to face.

"No, thanks," I replied. "But I appreciate the thought."

Mum sighed. "Fine. Oh, which reminds me, did you get hold of anyone at Warwicks?"

She meant the car club. I tapped my phone in my pocket, concealed in the folds of my loose trousers. "Waiting on a callback from Casey."

Mum wrinkled her nose. "Awkward."

Argh. "Need food." I changed the subject. "Has anything come out yet?"

"Canapes are over there. Get in quick before the boys descend."

I skipped to the banquet table with its crisp white cloth and candelabras and sized up the platters of dainty appetisers. Three mouthfuls of rare steak on pastry, and my hunger-anger reduced a notch. Mum and Dad had brought in a chef for the meal. God bless good cooking.

The dining room's ornate double doors swung open, and a vision stepped into the frame. Plus my brother alongside. Lennox had stuffed his oversized limbs into a suit jacket over jeans.

Jesus. The jacket fitted him nicely.

I resolutely brought my gaze back to the platter and picked up my next snack. A shadow loomed over me, and Lennox arrived at my side. He glanced at me then at the table, reached out an arm, and plucked my appetiser right from my fingers. Then he stuffed it into his maw, winked, and strolled to the end of the room where Seb had joined Dad.

I glared daggers after him. This was going to be a long meal.

---

*A*s it turned out, dinner was a blast. The chef delivered course after course of exquisite treats: delicate roast chicken and vegetable kebabs, a delicious and filling paella, a frothy, minty palate cleanser, and a trio of individual puddings, rich in taste and with tiny flowers added as decoration.

I stuffed my face, unashamedly happy to claw back the energy I'd burned wrenching bolts in the garage. My family ate well, too, talking and laughing as the courses went by.

Only Lennox was choosier about his meal. He demolished the meat, asking for seconds, but didn't touch the sugary treats. He stuck to water, too, like a weirdo.

"Isobel, tell your brother and Lennox about your career decision," my father encouraged.

We'd just heard my brother explain his idea to spend time in Scotland, learning to fly helicopters with our Uncle Gordain. He was also considering taking a role in an investment firm in New York, so he could get a background in business that he felt he lacked.

I sighed and swiped at my mouth with my serviette. The last of the dishes had been cleared away, and a dozy state had settled over me. "I'm taking in classic cars for repair."

"Specialising. Good." My brother gave me an approving smile.

"Not modern cars?" This came from Lennox. He'd barely spoken during the meal except to answer direct questions and to compliment the food.

I raised a shoulder. "Computers."

That wasn't the whole answer. Modern cars often required brand specialism, but my singular inability to operate any computerised device beyond the basics of my phone was forever going to be my downfall.

He didn't say any more, and my brother picked up his questions. "How are you going to start up?"

"I'm launching it at the rally. I've had a few customers so far but I need to put my name out there." It all felt so minor compared to Seb's goals and achievements.

"Makes sense if you're working from here," Sebastian said.

All the while, Lennox's stare warmed my neck.

"Eventually, I'll organise my own space but I don't have that yet."

My brother furrowed his brow. "What do you need?"

Mum's garage was a showroom with tools and space for a mechanic. But I couldn't just set up shop there. I needed my own dedicated workspace with a pit as a minimum or ideally a hydraulic lift so I could get under the cars. My parents had offered me the money to build it and, after my twenty-first, I'd have access to a trust fund they'd set up for me, but for the sake of my already too-heavy pride, I wanted my business to support itself.

"Once I've earned enough, I'll invest in a purpose-built garage. I don't mind starting small until then."

Sebastian shot a glance to Lennox. "What do you say, engineer? Up to it?"

Lennox shrugged. "Nae trouble. We could throw it together in a couple of days, it'll be good practice."

My brother nodded. "Done."

At the end of the table, our parents exchanged a smile.

I waved. "Hello? What are you talking about?"

"We'll build you a workshop," Sebastian informed me. "You just tell us when and where you want it, and it'll be done. No problem."

I widened my eyes. "No, I've got this. Honestly."

My brother stood. "It'll keep us busy. You'll be doing the world a favour. Heaven help you all if the two of us are underoccupied."

I swallowed and dipped my head, a little stunned at the turnaround. I'd been slow off the ground in pushing my business idea, an odd kind of fear stopping me, but I really did want to do it. There was plenty of trade to be had for a reliable restorer, and I had experience. Aside from my own premises, what I really needed was a backer, but that was another pipe dream.

"Thanks," I managed.

Sebastian pointed to Lennox. "Thank him. He's the one who has been learning how to build shit up and smash it down. It's his area. I'll do the grunt work. Now we need to get moving if we're going to make our plans for tonight."

Lennox jumped up from his chair. The dark, inward expression he'd been carrying lifted, and excitement gleamed in his eyes. He didn't glance my way, and I followed the two of them in kissing my parents goodbye and grabbing our keys.

Anticipation had me on my toes. I'd looked forward to this part of the evening. My brother had taken me with him once or twice before on his jaunts.

Where I took my feelings out on engines and roads, Sebastian used his fists.

This would be fun to watch.

6

COMPETITIVE

*I*sobel

I followed my brother's car through the winding roads that left Belvedere and into the Peak District National Park. It would take three-quarters of an hour to hit the outskirts of Manchester and our destination.

He sped ahead, his hazard lights flashing in a taunt.

No way could I let Seb lead for the whole journey. Like the brats we were, we used to race this trip, and I was elated to see my brother hadn't changed much.

As soon as we hit the dual carriageway, I burned rubber and swung wide, overtaking his BMW and leaning on my horn to rile him. But Seb was never one to ignore a challenge. He pulled up tight behind me and haunted my back bumper. I matched his moves, keeping my position.

Every now and again, he swung out, maybe checking what was around the corner.

I drummed my fingers on the steering wheel, waiting for his play.

Then Seb took his chance. He blasted past me around a

sweeping bend. I hit the accelerator, but a lorry blocked my path, my brother's car sitting next to it in the outside lane.

I had nowhere to go.

"Fucker!" I cursed and admired him in equal measures.

I couldn't help wondering at Lennox's reaction.

I'd missed having my brother around, but it was his passenger whose face I pictured each time I left them in my dust.

We carried on our cat-and-mouse game until the roads grew busier and broad, squat industrial buildings with wide car parks lined our route. Seb indicated into one of them, and we parked in a shadowy corner. I'd borrowed an old Audi of Dad's for the journey. He had no sentimentality over cars, but still, I wished I'd chosen a different vehicle. This place begged for ours to be stolen.

"We need to find a lockup," I told my brother, hanging over my open door.

"Do I look like an amateur?" Seb took his phone from his pocket and made a brief call. Then the metal door to the industrial warehouse rattled and lifted. Seb swept his hand towards it. "Her ladyship first."

I rolled my eyes and got back into my seat and drove into the dark interior. With our cars now safe, or at least safer, we strode through the empty warehouse to the back wall. From behind a door, music blared and muffled yells emanated.

I stole a glance at Lennox. He held himself tight, his muscles pronounced through his t-shirt. Where I'd switched out my heels for a pair of Converse and added a leather jacket over my camisole, he'd abandoned his suit jacket to the car. He worked his jaw, sparing no attention on the warehouse around us.

"We're right on time. You ready?" Sebastian asked him quietly.

"Wait, you aren't fighting?" I said to my brother.

"Not tonight. Nox is taking my turn."

I blinked at Lennox. He fought, too? I had no idea. Lennox lifted his chin, and Sebastian rapped once on a reinforced panel. The door swung open, and a burly man muttered to Seb then ushered us through.

Ahead, a jeering crowd encircled a pair of men, stark white light displaying the makeshift ring. Sweat permeated the room, trapped by the low ceiling of what looked like an old office suite, and the dull thuds of fists meeting flesh resounded. The spectators crowed when one man fell, a spray of dark blood painting the floor.

The first time I saw Sebastian fight, it had nearly given me a heart attack. Except he was good. I'd never seen him lose. But Lennox... I dragged my brother aside, tracking his friend as he checked in with the official.

"Has he done this before? Does he know what he's letting himself in for?"

Sebastian's nostrils flared, the bloodlust already taking him. "He's two inches taller than me and at least a stone heavier. The man drove tanks and carried a rifle for the past several years, and the men in his unit called him Hard Nox. What are you worried about?"

I had no idea, and I tried to dislodge the uncomfortable sensation in the pit of my stomach. Seb pulled me in front of him, and we jostled into position ringside.

I couldn't keep my gaze off Lennox.

He stripped, hauling his shirt over his head, leaving him in just his jeans. *Jesus.* I swallowed hard. He'd been built at eighteen—I'd felt him with my own hands—but now, he was a warrior. Ropes of muscles bulged over huge biceps.

I'd read a romance novel last week—my favourite pastime that didn't involve cars—and came across the expression 'big dick energy'. Lennox must have a huge, swinging cock by the power coming off him.

He flexed, expanding his broad chest, then twisted at his waist, warming up. His jeans—sadly not tight enough to give me an outline—were the only permitted clothing, and the official claimed his discarded shirt then shouted for attention.

I wished now that I hadn't insisted on taking my own car, that I'd sat in the back of Seb's ride and listened in to their talk. I knew why my brother fought—it was his form of anger management and it kept him sane.

A memory formed in my mind. Lennox had told me he sometimes did crazy things. I struggled to remember his wording.

'I do daft things when I'm fired up. I cannae help myself.'

But 'daft' didn't describe the violence about to go down. I'd always thought of Lennox as the perfect, law-abiding, clan-chief-in-waiting do-gooder. I'd been wrong. Maybe we had more in common than I'd thought.

His competitor emerged from the crowd, with sleek muscles over a wiry frame. The two men touched bare knuckles.

"Fight!" came the cry.

The crowd hooted, and the men took their fighting positions, circling one another.

Sebastian dug his fingers into my shoulders and bellowed Lennox's name. I only stared. I liked fights, fair ones, anyway. Boxing and wrestling matches. But I didn't like this one. The second man didn't have Lennox's height, but he had a cruel glint in his eyes and scars over his skin.

He feinted and drove a fist into Lennox's side.

I gasped and cringed.

Lennox barely moved. But the hit seemed to wind him

up. He rocked back to avoid an uppercut then weaved and swung out, landing a punch directly to the side of the man's head.

The man staggered, half falling. He clutched his temple before recovering and jerking upright again. Lennox waited for him to take his stance and, the second he did, landed another punch to the same side of his head.

"Come on! Too easy," Sebastian taunted.

Then it was on. Bad-scars guy snarled and danced around the ring. He jabbed, taking potshots at Lennox who kept with him, muscles taut, shoulders easy. He dodged the hits but otherwise seemed to be taking his time.

"What are you waiting for?" Scars goaded. "Are you in this to fight or—?"

Lennox swung a meaty fist, connecting to his opponent's temple again.

The man moaned. For several seconds, he swayed, holding his face. Then out of nowhere, he snapped a sneaky right hook. Lennox whipped his head back, avoiding a direct hit then landed his own in the same place one more time.

His competitor dropped like a stone.

The crowd roared, but the man stayed down. Lennox stared at him and rolled his shoulders.

"A win," the official announced and raised Lennox's hand.

Fuck me.

He'd won.

The whole thing hadn't lasted more than a couple of minutes. Sebastian howled in delight, and I gaped, then we pushed our way back to the exit. A few moments later, Lennox joined us, drawing his shirt back over his head.

My brother grabbed him in a hug and slapped him upside the head. "Fucking awesome," he hollered.

Another man joined us—the official—and handed Lennox a narrow white envelope. His winnings, I presumed. Lennox handed it straight to my brother. Seb always posted his through the letterbox of a charity in the nearest town. Looked like Lennox was sticking with the tradition.

Sebastian took the official to one side, speaking with him in low tones out of earshot.

Now alone, I eyed Lennox. "Are you okay?" I asked. The hit to his ribs was the only one that had landed, but it had been a hell of a blow.

Lennox shrugged and flexed his hand. "Barely needed to take a swing."

Blood beaded on his eyebrow.

"Shit. You're bleeding," I said. That last attack must've caught him.

He wrinkled his forehead and moved an inch closer to me. "Want to clean it up for me?"

I stuck my hands firmly in my pockets and gave no reply. Then I let myself just gaze at him. "Fighting's a step up from daft things, isn't it?"

His gaze bored into mine, his brown eyes burning orange in the light, then he blinked as if getting the reference. Lennox's lip curled in an attempt at a smile. Our eye contact grew weighty, and the uncomfortable worry I'd been carrying shifted into...something else.

I swallowed but didn't break the connection, enjoying it.

My pocket vibrated. I extracted my phone and glanced at the screen. *Casey Warwick.*

"Got to take this," I told Lennox then quick marched to the edge of the room. I wasn't fool enough to go outside on my own—Sebastian's fight clubs were hardly frequented by honourable people—but I was glad of the distraction. Even if it was Casey.

I answered the call.

"Imagine my surprise when I found your begging text this afternoon," Casey started.

Instantly, my back was up. This guy was the worst. "I'm not begging, just requesting that you do what you agreed," I said as politely as my mouth would allow.

"Yeah, funny when people don't do what they promised," he replied.

Was that a thinly veiled dig at my bailing after that unfortunate kiss?

Oh, fuck him.

I closed my eyes for a second. Across the room, another fight started. "Listen, Casey—"

"Tell you what, Isobel, if you want our cars that badly, I'll give you a chance to earn them."

My shoulders raised an inch higher. "How?"

"I'm on my way to Monte Carlo for a test rally. We have a spot open in three days. Beat me, and the cars are yours."

Monte Carlo was in Monaco, a tiny country in the south of France famous for car racing. I could easily drive there in time. My competitive streak flared. "What car?"

"Nineteen-sixties MGBs. No modern enhancements. Got one?"

I did. Well, Mum did. I cast my mind over that car. It ran, but it needed a good tune-up. Which meant working on it overnight then setting out early in the morning if I was going to reach the race in time. "No problem."

"There is another way you can persuade me..." Casey added, a sleazy tone to his voice.

This time, I couldn't help myself. "Fuck off, Casey. Text me the details, and I'll see you at the starting line."

I hung up the call and stared at my phone. I hadn't raced in a while, and getting a place in Monaco handed to me was a dream come true. Plus, it would allow me to get away from such close proximity to Lennox.

This was a good thing. For sure.

Sebastian joined me, Lennox at his shoulder. "Everything okay?" my brother asked me.

"Fine."

"Want to go to a club?"

I shook my head. "You can. I have something I need to do at home."

I had a car to mess around with and a race to prepare for. I wondered if Mum wouldn't mind a night in the cold garage giving me a hand.

7

OPPORTUNITY

Lennox

Seven AM found me standing in the centre of a guest room's polished floor at Belvedere. Last night's fight had taken the edge off my frustration, but I still burned for action. Anything.

Running, snowboarding.

Fucking...

For Christ's sake. Now I was thinking about Isobel again.

I heaved the weights I'd borrowed from Sebastian over my head and ignored the slight pain from my ribs. I continued my reps, stretching out my muscles barely used in the bout.

My father was the source of my frustration, or, rather, my lack of clarity over how to handle him. I'd spoken to him the moment I'd walked off my army base, and he'd been full of enthusiasm about me coming home, working at his side, learning the ropes of running the McRae estate.

I loved that. Wanted it.

But I had my own ideas, too. Half formed but more compelling. Ones I wasn't sure Da would agree to. I'd been my own man for too long and couldn't see a way I could live under my father's rule. We'd butt heads. Argue.

I'd have to leave and I couldn't bear the thought.

Instead of getting on a plane, going home, and talking to him, I'd made excuses and joined Sebastian.

From the bedside table, my phone rang. I stowed the dumb bells, wiped my sweat with a towel, then answered the call.

"Lennox, can ye talk?" It was Gordain, my uncle.

"Aye. Is everything okay?"

"Your Da said ye were at your leisure for a couple of days, and I have a favour to ask. It's short notice."

I knew my uncle well. He wouldn't ask if this wasn't important. "Talk to me."

In short sentences, he explained the problem. Viola, his daughter, was competing in a snowboarding competition in the south of France. But her escort—required as she was only sixteen—had broken her leg on the practice slopes, and Viola couldn't compete without a responsible adult. Her mother was sequestered away, recording with her orchestra and, though her father could go, he was with a trainee pilot until tomorrow afternoon.

"I can get there for just after lunch, but her qualifying rounds are in the morning. Can ye go today? I'm sorry to ask, but it would mean the world to Viola. She'll be out of the running otherwise."

I frowned. Leaving now would mean delaying our start on Isobel's workshop. No matter. I'd double down when I got back.

"I'll go. Nae trouble."

Gordain thanked me and gave me the details of the snowboarding event. I sent a text to my young cousin then took a quick shower, dressed, and went to find Sebastian.

And Isobel. I needed time alone with her. Yesterday, my mind had been all over the place. Leaving the army after four years had always been the plan, but I hadn't counted on the mindfuck it would bring. I was reeling. Not in my right head at all.

I still had to find a way to make friends with the lass again. If I could look at her without losing the ability to speak. Maybe if she taunted me, that would help.

At Sebastian's rooms, I knocked, and the door immediately opened.

"You heard it, too?" my friend asked. Like mine, his hair was damp. "Come on, let's go see what they're doing."

"Who, what?" I paced after him down the wide corridor.

"Is and Mum. Time trials, at a guess," he answered.

Downstairs, we exited the mansion to find Sebastian's father on the steps. The first of the sun's rays hit the stone wall above our heads. Unlike the blunt brutality of my castle home, Belvedere was a grand place, designed to inspire and create awe at the wealth of its occupants. Gold leaf lined the frames of a hundred windows, and the higher ones blazed in the dawn light.

Yet my attention snapped to the green two-door car pelting around the manor's track. The scene was something from an old movie.

"What the hell is she driving?" Sebastian asked his father.

"A sixties MGB. Isobel will be racing it. She and your mother have been working on the thing all night." James sighed and scrubbed his hand through his black hair at the exact same second his son did.

Sebastian grinned and slapped his father on the chest, and his dad wrestled him into a hug. I loved the close relationship this family had. I adored my family, too, but we were more rigid. My dad barked first then asked questions later. He'd schooled Skye, Blayne, and me in self-control and expected us to know how to behave. James and Beth had raised their children to be whoever they wanted to be. Both models had their plus points.

I could see that now, though I hadn't four years ago.

The antique car took a corner then slowed as Isobel steered towards us.

"She's alive!" her mother hollered from the passenger seat.

"Congratulations, you two. Then you're going?" James asked.

The women exited the car, grins all over their faces. Isobel's glance slid over me before returning to her father.

"Yep. In perfect time, too. I need to leave in half an hour if I'm to get the Cross Channel," she said.

I drew my eyebrows in. She was leaving now? My opportunity to talk to her was growing slimmer by the second. "Where are ye going?" I asked.

"Monaco. I'm racing this baby on the Formula One circuit! But I need to drive there first, and the car has to be inspected. The actual race isn't until tomorrow night."

My mind sped ahead of me. Luckily, my stint in the army had improved my geography. Monaco wasn't far from where I was going.

I knew an opportunity when I saw one.

Beth took her daughter's shoulders in her hands and eyed her. "If you want, we'll change our plans and I'll go with you."

"Don't be silly! You and Dad have been planning this holiday forever," Isobel protested.

"Shit, I wish I could offer but I have somewhere to be tomorrow," Sebastian said.

He exchanged a loaded look with me, and I got his meaning. He'd given up his slot to fight but still needed to get rid of his angst. So he'd found something sooner. Good.

I stepped up. "I can go with ye."

Isobel gave a short, slightly high laugh. "I really don't need a babysitter. It's a straightforward journey. I'll nap after I've driven onto the train then power through. I've been to plenty of races on my own."

"You'd be doing me a favour. I need to go to France to help Viola. I'd planned to catch a late flight tonight, but we'd make it in time if we drove, aye?"

Isobel glanced at the car and paled. It would be a snug fit, but travelling together would give me time to say what I needed to say.

To address that kiss we'd shared years ago. The one I'd never managed to forget.

To cover the 'girlfriend' remark she'd thrown my way, the snipe showing me she still cared that I'd hurt her.

Let alone the sheer, unnerving thought of her being in a race. I knew this was what she did. Just like I knew she'd become a mechanic. Sebastian had casually shared her success stories, but I still had the same gut-crunching fear as when she'd been sixteen and I'd chased her to that airfield.

"That would work," Isobel replied, bringing her focus back to me. Her shoulders slumped in defeat.

Beth clapped once. "Perfect! That makes me feel so much better. And Lennox, if you see that Warwick kid while you're there, feel free to smack him in the chops from me," she said, then took her husband's hand, and they entered the house together.

My mind homed in on that name. The Warwicks were involved in this?

For weeks, Amber Warwick had been messaging me. I'd

ignored her, but that family were bad pennies. In one way or another, they were bound to show up.

I packed a rucksack and ate breakfast in record time, then snagged Seb out of hearing of his family. "Are you going to be okay on your own?" I asked him, meaning the fight he'd clearly set up.

"Why wouldn't I be? It's only a brawl." He gave an easy shrug. "Should I be worried about you left alone with my sister?"

My jaw dropped. "What are ye implying?"

"She'll tear you to shreds if you're not careful," he replied with a smirk. "Whatever you did to piss her off, undo it, will you?"

I studied him for a moment. The kiss Isobel and I had shared was our business. I didn't subscribe to the idea that families had to know each other's personal affairs. Then again, if he'd been the one to upset Skye... "Do ye want me to tell ye?"

Seb laughed under his breath. "God, no. Just fix things so we can all hang out together when you get back."

"That I can do," I agreed, and then I grasped him in a bear hug, walloped him on the back, and set out for a road trip with his sister.

8

THAT OTHER THING YOU SAID...

*L*ennox

For the majority of the journey to England's south coast, Isobel ignored me. She answered if I spoke to her, but her sentences were short, factual, and without warmth.

Fine. I deserved that.

I'd offered to drive, and she'd given me an eyeroll, so I shut up and kept to my thoughts. But by the time we reached London, Isobel was visibly flagging. She hauled on the wheel, the effort distinct.

"Did ye get any rest last night?" I asked.

"Not much. But I don't need a lot of sleep."

"Ye will if you're to be any good at racing. Pull over. Let me drive us to the train. You can kip here and take over again once we're in France."

Isobel's mouth pulled down at the sides, yet she signalled and stopped at the kerb. We switched seats, and I shunted the driver's seat back on its rails.

"This isn't like a modern car." Isobel snapped her seat belt in place, worry lines on her forehead.

"I'm a trained military engineer. I've driven and repaired tanks. I'll work it out."

"There's no power steering," Isobel continued, my credentials unimpressive to her. "Or any other driver's aid. Like, zip. There's four gears, and it doesn't like hills."

"I've been watching ye drive for three hours. I noticed."

"You've been watching me? Sounds creepy." She folded her arms.

"And ye didnae have your eyes all over me at the fight last night?" I grinned, glad for her antagonism. "Were ye being a creep?"

"You weren't even looking! How would you know where my eyes were?"

"I saw," I corrected.

It was true. My mind might've been on the action, but I could never ignore this lass.

Isobel huffed and slumped down. After a minute, she closed her eyes, and her breathing steadied.

"Sweet dreams," I murmured and concentrated on driving the slow-arsed, uncomfortable car through the morning traffic.

In odd moments, as a soldier, I used to imagine times like this. When civilian life would have me out on a casual drive. It had been a challenge to picture. For four years, I'd been going somewhere and doing something one hundred percent of my waking hours. Then I'd expected to be at Castle McRae, fully occupied.

If I didn't have this purpose with Isobel now, or, rather, with Viola, I'd be going out of my mind.

At Folkestone, I got us in line for check-in then reluctantly nudged the lass. She woke with a start.

"It's okay. We're at the station. I need the ticket to board us," I told her.

Isobel stared at me, her cheeks flushed.

For a long moment, she didn't speak.

In a weird vision, I was eighteen again and gazing into teenage Isobel's eyes. Isobel carried a fierce expression most of the time, a tiny-but-mighty attitude that warned you to fuck with her at your own risk. But that armour had dropped the moment before she'd kissed me. She didn't wear it now, either.

She swallowed, hard, then broke our connection. Floundering, she searched her bag, then she stopped and flapped a hand. "No ticket needed, it'll recognise the number plate. We just need our passports for the next bit."

I drove on, getting us through the wide expanse of the station, through immigration, and into the train's vehicle section. Once parked, there was nothing to do but wait out the thirty-five-minute underwater crossing and let the train carry us from England to France.

And talk.

"Are ye tired still?" I asked.

Isobel yawned and stretched her arms out in front of her. "Actually no, that power nap did me good."

"I'm glad. Tell me more about this race you're heading to."

"Um, it's a classic car race, hence the MGB." She patted the dash. "They're testing the road track, so it's not a televised event. I was invited by... I mean, I got the chance to attend. Not gonna turn that down."

"What has Casey Warwick got to do with it?"

Isobel's dark eyebrows drove together. She studied her nails. "He'll also be competing."

"Did he invite ye?"

She took a moment over answering. "Yes. So anyway, tell me what it was like in the army. You and Seb took such different roles. I wondered why you didn't go into the same regiment to stay together."

Nice subject change. "Sebastian focused on his weakness —he wanted to develop his leadership abilities. I joined the Engineers to go at my strengths. I'm a natural leader but I also wanted skills I'd use at home. I—" I was about to launch into my plan but I hadn't shared it with many other people.

Isobel gazed at me. I had her full attention. It was oddly reassuring.

My words came out slow. Unpractised. "For years, I've had the idea to build a winter sports centre on Mhic Raith, our mountain. Ages ago, Gordain got planning permission, but he never progressed it any further, so I know it is possible. I have the skills to build the place myself, with a wee bit of help. The costs would be minimal, at least to set the building on the ground, though I need an investor for operating costs."

Isobel nodded, a loose curl of hair springing with the motion. "That makes a lot of sense, not just for Viola but considering how many of the cousins are into snow sports. Plus it's harder in the Highlands in the winter, right? Employment-wise? We don't have the same problem. Belvedere attracts visitors all year round."

"Aye, exactly! It would give jobs to the family and to locals, and give Viola a practice facility right on her doorstep. She and Blayne would be up there all day every day if they had a chair lift and somewhere to take a breather. As it is, both have to travel elsewhere in the mountains to get their time in."

"Awesome. Then what are you waiting for?"

Wasn't that the million-pound question? I switched my attention to people ambling down the narrow train aisle, the yellow light draining the colour from their faces. Isobel's antique car drew stares, and the unnerving idea came over me that, alone, she would've been vulnerable here. Trapped in the train inside the tunnel. What if some chancer tried the door and got in with her? There were no guards around. No visibility with all the vehicles crowding the space.

"Something wrong? You've gone all square-shouldered," she said.

"Nothing." I took a breath and tried to rid myself of the notion that she was defenceless. She'd lock her doors. Probably have a secret knife stashed somewhere.

"I saw Viola board recently," Isobel said. "Dad and I went with Vi and Gordain to Italy, to this ski resort in the Dolomites where a competition was being hosted. It was beautiful. We stayed in this gorgeous cabin in a little mountain village. The mountains themselves were great jagged rocks tearing from the earth."

I sniffed. "No way would that be as bonnie as Mhic Raith."

Isobel laughed, the sound startling me. "Of course not. It was just a nice place to stay. You could add some chalets to your plan. It can be a hiking destination in the summer, too."

"I'll think about it." I grinned, mentally debating where we could add accommodation. It was a great idea, one I hadn't considered. There was the odd holiday cottage here and there on Da's land, but nothing right on the mountain.

We settled into silence again for a while and, in the picture in my mind, I tried to place Isobel on the slopes, but for the life of me, I couldn't recall seeing her on a board. "When ye went with Viola, did ye go out on the snow?"

She widened her eyes. "Do you mean skiing? No! I'm chronically unbalanced. I went on a sled ride, though."

"I can't believe all these years and I didn't know ye couldn't snowboard!"

Isobel reached over and shoved my arm. Her fingertips glanced over my skin where my sleeves were rolled up, and her touch left an invisible mark.

"You say it like it's an affliction," she said.

"It is!"

She sobered, her smile dying. "Well, I have worse, so I'm not going to worry about it."

Ah fuck. I went to speak again, but daylight shone into the carriage, and the train came to a halt. We were in France.

"I'll stay at the wheel for a while longer," I said quietly.

Isobel simply pulled the sleeves of her too-big plaid shirt over her fists and took up her position staring out of the window.

The afternoon rolled on, turning into chilly evening with the sun fleeing the landscape. We had to switch phones for the route planning, as the car had no charging facility and Isobel's backup charger had died. Conversation came a little easier, and we covered our family updates. I exchanged army stories for her racing news, but I knew I needed to do more.

I'd made her smile. I needed to see that beam of warmth again.

Sharing a space with Isobel did strange things to my heart—and my body in general. When away on missions, I'd had a lot of time to think and often not much to do.

I'd worked on how to apologise to her and how to set the record straight. A year ago, I'd gone home for Christmas— the single time I'd managed to get leave on that hotly competed-over week—only to find Isobel had been and gone. So, I'd waited until the spring and coordinated time off with Sebastian, then gone to Belvedere with him, but she'd stayed away for the duration.

I hadn't seen her at all, and the change was startling.

Four years had turned her from a troubled girl who'd dazed me into a fucking gorgeous woman. I was probably sex deprived—it had been a while—but my mind was in the gutter.

By ten PM, we'd taken the mountain road from Voiron to Grenoble, then stopped off in the city to grab food from a late-night café. We'd had supper, but I could always eat, and Isobel seemed to need endless feeding, too. On the last stretch to the snowboarding resort of Les Orres, I handed Isobel pizza slices as she drove, and tried to choose the best way of tackling our awkward past.

The MGB's headlights picked up only the empty road, so we had no distractions.

"Can I talk to ye about something?" I asked.

Neither of us had spoken in a little while, and my voice had Isobel jumping.

"Sounds loaded. If it's about anything pertaining to events of Christmas four years ago, then nope." She made an exaggerated 'P' sound on the 'nope'.

Huh. She'd been expecting this, then. "How about if I tell ye how I wasn't dating Amber Warwick?"

Isobel winced. "Ah, there you go, talking about it anyway. I have zero interest in who you have or have not dated. And I don't like liars."

"I'm not a liar!"

"A liar would say that." She waggled her head from side to side as if she'd proved a point.

I exhaled hard. "Right. I can see why you'd think the worst of me—"

Isobel pursed her lips, speaking over me. "Sure, not like a kiss-and-run behind your girlfriend's back is a big deal."

"She was not my girlfriend!" I uttered. "Why the hell are ye worrying about Amber? It's ye I need to apologise to."

"I don't care about Amber." Isobel wrinkled her nose. "Maybe I have dreamed of the day when you grovelled for my forgiveness, but it doesn't matter. We don't know each other anymore and we certainly don't owe each other anything. It's ancient history and pointless to dwell on."

My blood heated. "For four years, that night has been on my mind. It does have a point. We kissed. I liked it. Then I remembered the stupid favour I'd agreed to do for Skye."

Isobel was poised, ready to shoot me down again. But she shut her mouth with an audible snap. "Skye? What has it got to do with her?"

"Amber's her friend. She asked me to stand at Amber's side and hold her hand in front of her stepdad."

"Why?"

"To fix some issue in the family that would magically be made better by her having a boyfriend." I owed Amber nothing, but the more I thought about the request, the more ridiculous it seemed. But eighteen-year-old men aren't known for their powers of reasoning.

Silence once again descended in the dark car. Isobel fidgeted, gnawing her nail one minute then drumming on the steering wheel the next.

Far too soon, we were following the signs to Les Orres and SnowFest, the snowboarding contest. The winding, hilly roads and treacherous, snowy corners had us both fully concentrating on the route. Then we were there, outside the wood-clad hotel where Viola was staying. A whoop made it through the car's windows, and the lass herself waved from a balcony.

I'd ran out of time.

I twisted in my seat to face Isobel. "I'm sorry. I've wanted to say that for years. If I'm honest, it's eaten away at me."

She half turned but didn't say a word, shadows hiding her expression.

"Viola's about to launch herself at us. Come in, will ye? Stay the night here. I'd bet there will be space. It's too late to continue the drive now."

This got me an answer. "I have to check the car in for an inspection. I race tomorrow evening, and if I'm not there early enough, I'll lose my place."

Ah Christ. It didn't sit well with me, her driving off into the black night, back down the mountainside and out to the coast. She wouldn't reach Monaco until the early hours, and with no phone for directions, she could get lost or fall off a cliff. Anything could happen.

Misery descended. "Please. I'm worried."

Isobel gave a short laugh. "Jeez, Len. I can look after myself."

She climbed from the car, striding away to meet our only mutual cousin. The two lasses grinned and hugged, and I dropped my head back, freezing air creeping around my neck. I'd said the wrong thing, making it about Isobel's capabilities rather than the fact I wanted to be around her.

When had I ever said the right thing? I should keep my mouth shut.

Viola appeared at my door. She had the Fitzroy genes for certain, with long, dark curls spilling from under her silver-and-purple beanie hat, the Viola McRae 'VM' logo of her brand front and centre. She battered the window with her fist, and I relented and climbed out.

"You made it! I nearly gave up on you both. Thanks so much for coming." She tackle-hugged me.

I patted her back. "Nae bother. It was good timing for me."

"I heard you were out of the army! Let's get your bags and go inside. You can both tell me about the trip."

Isobel came up alongside us. "I've got to get back on the road."

Viola clapped her mitten-covered hands to her mouth. "No!"

"Sorry. I'm racing tomorrow. I have to drive to Monaco. No rest for the wicked."

"Fuck," Viola said tartly. "I'd love to see you race as much as I'd love you to see me race."

Isobel hugged her again. "Next time. I promise I'll make it."

I claimed my bag from the miniscule back seat. Like Isobel's, my phone had died, and I cursed the ancient car for its lack of facilities. As I straightened, a desperate idea sprang into my mind. "Viola, do ye have your phone with ye?"

The teenager produced it with a flourish.

I turned to Isobel. "Exactly where and when is your race?"

"Eight PM on the F1 circuit. We drive through the town." She eyed me curiously. "Why?"

"Can ye give us the details? Just in case. Vi can note it down."

Her eyes lit a tiny degree, like she had caught on to my idea. "Can I have that, Vi?"

Viola passed her the phone, then Isobel painstakingly typed something in. She reminded me of my Uncle Ally whenever he was faced with writing. "Just logging in. Every race has a driver's info area online. Mine came through to my email earlier. Ah. Got it." She took a screenshot of whatever had loaded. "If, er, either of you can get there in time, I've given you a backstage pass so you can get into the driver's circle. No big deal if you can't use it. I don't have anyone else to give it to."

She didn't meet my eye and instead just handed Viola back the phone then turned to leave. "See you, Vi. Good luck tomorrow," she called over her shoulder.

I handed my bag to my cousin and gave her a little shove. "Go inside. I'll be a second."

Viola widened her eyes but did as I bid her.

"Isobel." I jogged to the car.

Isobel halted. "Please don't tell me to drive safe."

"Wasn't going to. I meant what I said. I'm sorry for what happened between us."

She brought her gaze to mine. "That other thing you said..."

I searched my memory. "What thing?"

Colour flooded her cheeks, illuminated by the bright hotel. "You liked our kiss?"

A *whomp* of heat hit me. The attraction I'd been almost sure was one-sided turned into clear, keen chemistry. "Are ye kidding?"

"No."

"Aye, I liked the kiss. I never forgot how your mouth felt on mine."

Isobel stared at me like a bunny in the headlights.

To mark my point, I moved in on her and pressed my lips to her cool cheek.

Really, I wanted to kiss her again, properly. In the swirling snowflakes and icy bite of wind on a strange mountain, this lass singularly fascinated me. I had no clue if I'd be able to get a whole country away from the time Gordain arrived tomorrow. But even I knew when the timing was wrong. So I straightened and forced myself to take a step back.

"Please text me when ye have a working phone again." Then I added, "Not because I don't think ye are able to make the drive alone—"

"But because you're going to worry about me. Got it," Isobel finished for me, still with an odd expression on her face.

Then she was in the MGB and driving away, taking my peace of mind with her.

9

TOO. MANY. DINGS

Isobel

The MGB and I crawled across the border and into Monaco at five in the morning. I left the car at my hotel's secure parking then hit the mattress in my room like I was made of stone. That last leg had been a killer.

Truth was, I probably could've stayed with Lennox and Viola and slept on Vi's floor, but the whole journey had left me rattled. Lennox's admission and his insistence on opening that can of worms... That motherfucking kiss on the cheek.

I groaned into the nice bedsheets and tried to shut off my brain.

But no, my mind hated me. Memories taunted me of how good he smelled, of how I'd begun to crave his touch when we drove, of how his strong fingers held the steering wheel.

I'd stared at his goddamn hands and been turned on.

What the fuck was wrong with me?

I hoped he wouldn't show up tomorrow. I'd probably

crash if I caught a glimpse of him before the race. Or explode in a fireball of lust.

After tossing and turning for another hour, there was nothing for it. I gave in to want and flipped onto my back, then I stuck my hands in my shorts and let the thoughts of Lennox flood in. I moved my fingers fast over my already slick flesh. My mind conjured images. His mouth, muscles, and his no doubt massive dick... Yes!

I growled his stupid name into the room then clamped my mouth shut as if he could hear me. I'd made myself come using Lennox McRae as a sex aid. I was too exhausted to worry about the implications of that.

In no time at all, I was asleep.

*S*ome hours later, and little more refreshed, I checked in the MGB then took a stroll along the track. Ornate apartment blocks and hotels lined the tiny city's route, with the road already closed off to traffic for the afternoon and evening's races. It might not be the big, televised event the country was famous for, but it would still draw a crowd.

I'd studied the Circuit de Monaco before, having watched the Grand Prix live here with Mum, but I wanted to especially eye in the two tricky corners that caused problems for other drivers—the Mirabeau and the close-by Fairmont Hairpin.

Not that I was worried. This wasn't a speed race—the cars didn't have the capacity. It took a painful eleven seconds to reach sixty miles per hour. No, this was about being ballsy and trusting in your ride. It was hairy driving the MGB around a corner, as the opposing front wheel lifted clean off the ground, but if you became attuned to the responsiveness, and you could power on through, you could win on skill.

I knew my ride and I had faith in it. Besides, I had bigger balls than Casey Warwick, that was for sure.

"Look what the cat dragged in," a voice hailed.

I raised my gaze to the blue sky. For fuck's sake. I'd thought his name and summoned the Devil.

"Casey." I turned around, keeping my sunglasses in place.

"Didn't think you'd show." He sauntered down the street, his jacket over his shoulder, though it really wasn't that warm, and his arm around some poor unfortunate woman.

"Unlikely," I muttered. "It's possible that you'd hoped I wouldn't show, because you knew this was over before it began, but since when have I ever backed down from a challenge? Got a point to make, Casey?"

His grin dropped. "I'll catch up with you," he said to his companion. "Go on back to the Paris."

The unfortunate pushed up on her high heels and laid a kiss on Casey's jaw. She left, and Casey rubbed his face.

"Run while you still can," I mock yelled after her.

Three years ago, when I'd been high on winning and clearly out of my mind, I'd mistaken this antagonism for something else. Casey wasn't bad-looking, but he wore his family's money on his sleeve. Every sentence contained a reference to wealth—case in point, the casual hotel name-dropping. The Hôtel de Paris was one of the fanciest in town. Give him five minutes, and I'd bet I could count off a handful of other references. Shame it wasn't the summer months so he could drop in the family's superyacht.

"Been here long? We flew in this morning, but I had my MGB driven in a few days ago," Casey said.

Ding ding! His flight would have been by helicopter, and he referenced his personal driver. Two points to me.

"A few hours." I yawned.

"The team's already scoped the circuit, but I like to do my own homework, know what I mean?"

Ugh. A ding! for him having a team, but I was going to double my points for his blatant disregard of their advice.

He raised a hand to his shield his eyes, scanning the view. A shiny watch flashed on his wrist, his movement pulling his expensive shirt tight across his biceps. "Would've driven the Bugatti here, but you can't trust other drivers not to want to fuck with such a nice car."

Too. Many. Dings.

I sucked in a fortifying breath. "How about we cut the crap. I'll see you on the starting line and then after to claim my win. First past the post between us, right?" I half turned to walk away but paused, my finger in the air. "Just to check, you do have the power to make the decision on the cars, right?"

I meant for the rally. He'd know that.

His jaw clenched. "Yes. I'm a director of the company now. I can do what I like."

Good enough. I needed to continue on my route. I had roads to check and no time to waste on this blowhard. But despite my irritation, I'd had an idea, and now was the perfect moment to execute it. Time spent with Lennox, when he'd talked about his plans for the future, had made me think about my own.

"All right. Then how about we make this more interesting?" I said.

Casey raised an eyebrow.

I continued. "I'm starting a classic car repair business."

"What's that got to do with me?"

"Sponsorship from Warwick Supercars. I want it." They were one of the biggest car clubs around, and most of their members with any kind of car collection would have classics. Their backing would give me instant customers. I'd barely need to advertise.

I was actually surprised I'd thought up such a good idea myself.

Casey tapped his chin, pondering. "We could do that. That's if you win," he said. "What happens if you lose?"

I paused. Shit. I hadn't thought this through.

Casey's eyes gleamed. "You go out with me."

Ugh. Unable to resist, I raised my middle finger to him.

He pulled an 'ouch' face. "Yeah, well, you can't have much faith in your driving ability then. I guess that makes sense, considering I already beat you once."

Hell no. He didn't just go there. I clamped down on the half a dozen offensive sentences I wanted to throw back. I would not respond to his baiting. I wouldn't. I— "Fine. Be ready to talk me up to your members because your ass is mine, Warwick."

Fuck. Me and my stupid mouth.

"Kinda hoping it'll be the other way around," Casey drawled.

But I was out of there. Tonight, I'd beat him and win twice over. And my business would have a nice boost in the process.

***

I ambled along the waterfront, a strange mood descending on me. With hours to kill, I had nothing to do. For years, I'd happily travelled alone, but spending all of yesterday with Lennox had been...nice. I'd enjoyed his company, his gruff complaints at delays, and his cautious smiles and happy conversation.

I wanted him with me now. He'd texted to check in on me, and I'd replied but left it at that.

I couldn't help the little voice that told me he was still a liar.

The fact was, over the years, I'd seen multiple pictures online of him with Amber Warwick. I'd never gone searching, but I was friends with Skye, and the pictures found their way to my eyes. None of them had ever been definitive, now I thought about it, but Amber was definitely clinging to him in a few.

There was no reason whatsoever that the photos should have bothered me, but they did.

I stopped at a low wall and stared at the choppy grey sea. Then I gave in to my demons, took out my phone, and called Skye, not only one of my most favourite people in the world but likely the only person who could shed light on Lennox's romantic history.

Apart from Sebastian, and hell was I asking my brother a question like that.

The first *ring* came, and I realised the flaw in my plan. Lennox had described how Skye had asked him for a favour —the one that had him holding Amber's hand. Drat. My question dried in my mouth.

Skye answered with a bright singing of my name.

"Hello," I replied, somewhat more glumly. "I missed you and I had a minute, so I just wanted to say hi."

"I'm so glad you did! I was just talking to my brother about you."

I stood straight. "You were? Where is he?"

"Home, of course. He's been following Viola's progress and reporting to us after every race. He's so jealous that he can't be there. We heard about your and Lennox's role in helping to make sure she could compete."

Ah, she meant Blayne, her younger brother.

"How's she doing?" I choked out my words then listened to the snowboarding update.

Vi was a hot contender to win and had been courted by teams and sponsors alike. She'd be in her element.

"Gordain has been patient with replying to each text, but I think next time he'll argue for Blay to just be let off school so he can go himself."

"Gordain made it there, then." My heart leapt.

"Uh-huh. Ooh, while you're on the line, I need to ask a favour. I have to take a trip to New York. I'm applying for another internship and could use a local refresh. Are you free next weekend? Shopping, good conversation. It will mean travelling home on your birthday. That's the only downside."

Argh. I couldn't bring myself to backtrack and ask about her twin. It felt too obvious. Would he have stayed to watch Viola or jumped on the first available transport here? Could he make it in time? Did I even want him to?

Yes. I did.

As a minimum, to ask the questions I hadn't been able to last night.

Buoyed, I faced the sea breeze and stepped on along the open path. "Shopping? I'd love to. Tell me all about the new job."

Whether I saw Lennox again soon or not, at least I'd have a plan with my bestie to anticipate.

*N*ight had fallen, engines roared, and exhaust fumes scented the air. I'd been in this position too many times to count, and no nerves affected my stomach. In too many areas of life, I was deficient. I still rarely wrote by hand, I was slow on the uptake, but in this circumstance, in the driver's seat at the start of a race, my hot temper served me perfectly.

Energy coursed through my veins, and my pulse galloped, flooding my system with adrenaline.

This was my arena, and I would excel.

Two cars over, in an almost identical green MGB to mine, Casey's helmeted head pointed straight forward, and he spared no glance for me.

No matter.

He could eat my dust at the finish line.

10

PERFECT MOMENT

*L*ennox

My taxi careened around the corner, hurling me against the door. I grabbed the oh-shit handle and braced myself. We barrelled down the street, nearly colliding with a fence.

The driver slammed on the brakes. "Closed, eh?" he said, gesticulating at the road as the car shuddered around us. "You need to walk now," he added.

Fuck, I was already late, my cross-country marathon from Les Orres to Monaco a never-ending catalogue of delays. I'd grabbed a lift into the nearest city from the slowest driver in history, got on a coach that proceeded to break down, then finally persuaded a cabbie to take me the rest of the way.

Still, I'd made it. And not a moment too soon, from the rapt attention of the crowds ahead of me.

I thrust a handful of Euro notes to my speed-loving driver and half fell from the car in my rush to get to the race.

Squeals of tyres and engine growls filled the night air. I ran, dodging the barrier, and legged it down the road, my bag banging on my back. People milled, watching the race from balconies and rooftops. In my elevated position, I made out a bend of the illuminated street track, and I stopped, gawping.

Several vehicles jostled for space on the road. Two dark-green cars, each with a white circle on the bonnet— identical to Isobel's MGB—crammed in tight to take a corner.

Somehow, they both got around, not quite touching, then sped off along the brightly lit way. I scowled then exhaled in relief.

All day, I'd pictured this time with any number of unhappy scenarios. I could've missed it. Isobel might not have arrived—though her brief reply to my message had reassured me. She could crash. Be hurt.

I stomped down the outrageous thoughts and pushed on.

A few years ago, on my first assignment overseas with my brand-new unit, we'd come under gunfire. It was entirely unexpected, and we were green recruits, though we knew the drill. We'd taken up an offensive to survive and to quell the insurgents.

At that moment, I'd been able to test the edge of my darker side. I liked fighting, loved the adrenaline rush but, in the field, faced with the rare opportunity to shoot another human, my line became clear. I didn't want to kill anyone.

Maybe that was why I felt drawn to Isobel, to her spiky personality and independence. As long as I'd known her, she had never been a yes-person. Always carving her own path and taking risks. Pushing boundaries without fear.

Right now, my stomach clenched tight with worry for her.

It was almost as good as fighting myself.

I descended a slope between two hotel buildings and

spotted a race official. "Drivers' area, aye?" I yelled above the noise.

The woman glanced at the pass I'd had Viola send to my phone then pointed me in the direction of a crew-filled space, a short distance beyond the finish line.

Shoving my way through the thick crowd, I reached a security checkpoint, flashed the pass again, and got waved through. Then I was behind the scenes, in a garage area with men and women busying with tyres and pieces of engines. Support crew, I assumed.

Isobel didn't have any of this. She'd come alone. My admiration grew. Christ, the lass had more confidence than anyone I knew.

A voice on a loudspeaker barked increasing excitement, and cheers rose. At the other side of the security barrier, the cars came into view once more. A purple MGB had the lead, a blue one close behind.

I peered for a glimpse of Isobel.

There! She had third place. At least I thought it was her. I couldn't make out the number plate or see behind the windscreen. My heart galloped, and I gripped my hands into fists, willing her on.

They disappeared behind a tall building then emerged again, taking the corner at speed.

The leader skidded out with a scream of tyres on asphalt. Directly behind, one of the green MGBs braked and swerved.

The car abruptly veered right then left as the driver tried to correct its path. It wobbled, teetering on two wheels.

Then it rolled.

Metal shrieked, glass smashed, and the car slid on its roof. Another driver slowed but still shunted into it, spinning the car. The crowd yelled.

Horror choked me.

I was running.

The purple and blue cars belted ahead, over the finish line. All I could imagine was Isobel hurt, or worse. My heart pounded, and adrenaline flooded my system, spiking panic holding me in its grip.

I stormed to the security barricade, ready to jump it, and to push my way through. I didn't care if I got hit by a car. I didn't give a fuck about anything.

I had to reach her.

Just as I was about to attempt to vault the wall, the other green car zoomed by, taking third place.

I stared after it, torn.

A stream of vehicles made their way over the line and then slowed to enter the restricted area at my back. On the track, crew swamped the stricken vehicle. Where was Isobel? In the wreck or not?

I took another step but glanced back at the third-place winner in the drivers' area. The occupant climbed from the car.

My heart stopped, started again. Even with a jumpsuit and helmet on, I knew Isobel in an instant. I jogged to her, dodging celebrating teams and homing in on the lass standing by herself.

Without caution, I bellowed her name on my approach. "Isobel!"

She gaped and then spotted me. "Lennox!"

Then she dropped her helmet and was across the ground and in my arms before either of us knew what hit us. I hoisted her up and slammed my arms around her. She hugged me, her legs finding their way around my waist.

We held each other close.

The crowd vanished. Nothing else mattered. Isobel was okay. I took a long, deep breath, satisfied.

"Thank fuck," I eventually managed, my pulse still thrumming with fright. "I thought you were hurt."

Isobel relaxed back in my hold, her fingers linked behind my neck. "You came."

"I did."

"I didn't think you'd make it." Then she gave a short laugh, and her grin snapped back into place like she'd remembered herself. "I took third!"

"Aye, ye did." I had no idea if that was good or bad. I only cared that it hadn't been her in the wreck.

"That's a good thing," she said, unnervingly answering my unspoken question. "I just had to beat one person and I did!"

I still held her to me. She didn't let go either.

"Someone crashed," I managed. "Their car was just like yours."

"He's okay," she replied softly and tipped her head at a driver striding by the bay, cussing and berating the people around him.

I vaguely recognised Casey Warwick and his stepfather, but I couldn't tear my attention away from the lass in my arms.

Right now was the perfect moment for that kiss I wanted. Isobel glanced at my lips, then she wetted her own.

A familiar heat surged through me.

Someone tapped on my shoulder.

I ignored them, but Isobel stared behind me then groaned. She pushed at my chest, and I released her, placing her on the ground. Only then did I look around.

Amber Warwick stared at us, her sister, Erika, at her side. I barely knew Erika but had instinctively disliked her the couple of times we'd met. The way she glared at Isobel now had my hackles rising.

Isobel glared right back. "Oh good, the Warwick ghouls. I mean girls. Did your brother send you as a distraction so he could limp off to lick his wounds?" she asked.

Amber pouted. "I've no idea what you're talking about. If you want Casey, why don't you go find him?" Then she switched her focus to me. "Hi, Lennox. Thanks for coming. I appreciate you taking the time to see me. So kind."

Confusion had me recoiling. "I came here to see Isobel."

The lass in question rolled her eyes. "I'm going to claim my win." She turned to leave, her mouth set in an unhappy pout.

I snatched her hand. "Wait for me, will ye?"

She didn't meet my eye. "Sorry, no can do. Gotta put the car to bed then talk to a man about a dog."

Nope, she was not going to get the wrong idea. "I came here for ye, and we're going to spend time together. Dinner. In one hour."

She raised her gaze, but the sweet wonder had gone from her beautiful eyes, replaced by a more typical antagonism. "Drinks. My bar."

"Done."

"I'm staying in the Sea Lodge."

"I'll find ye." I pressed her fingers, but Isobel was already moving again, vanishing into the throng of uniformed race staff, drivers, and their families.

I'd travelled for hours to be here in this moment, and the fucking Warwicks drove my lass away.

"The Sea Lodge? Cheap hotel. Why would she stay there? Trouble with the Fitzroy bank balance, or has her dad finally cut her off?" Erika appeared next to me.

I dragged my gaze off a retreating Isobel and twisted to

Amber, ignoring her sister. The two women were clearly made in the same mould—tall-ish, with blonde hair and long faces, and draped in expensive clothes. I owed Amber nothing except the courtesy I'd give any of my sister's friends, so I stifled my irritation and lifted my chin. "What's up, Amber? I have somewhere to be, so if ye want to talk to me, now's your chance."

She blushed. "Not in a public place, Lennox."

What? "Seriously. A minute, then I have to go." I had a hotel to find and I desperately needed a shower.

Amber reached out and curled an arm around my biceps, her other hand landing on my chest. Far too close, and far too familiar. I flinched, but she clung on.

"I'm so lucky to count you as a friend. You are such a good man. I have a favour to ask, but it's quite in your interest to accept. I know Skye would want you to hear me out," she said.

Her sister raised her phone and snapped a shot of us. Twice, in the past four years, when I'd been with my sister and we'd run into the Warwicks, my photo had been taken in exactly the same way.

Fuck this. I shook the woman off and took a large step back, my hands up. "As ye heard, I have a date. Apologies, but I know what's in my interest better than anyone else. See ye around."

I strode away and didn't look back.

At Isobel's hotel, I booked a room and climbed straight into a shower, washing the grime of the day off my skin. Warm water beat down, and soap suds rushed over my body. I couldn't stop my mind from conjuring Isobel. Her hot body and slight weight in my arms. That gleam in her expressive eyes.

She'd been glad to see me.

We had a date tonight.

Instantly, I was hard, my cock jutting up, the water hitting the head.

I closed my eyes and braced myself on the shower wall, then I took myself in hand and gave my cock a nice stroke from root to tip. The zing of pleasure had me doing it again. Over and over. My whole body became sensitised. My visions changed to Isobel's naked flesh. To the determination she'd shown me and the battles we'd have if I was ever lucky enough to take her to bed.

Ah Christ, Isobel on the sheets with me bearing down on her. Into her...

My balls tightened, and I came with a yell, shouting the lass's name to the humid air.

For four years, it had been her I'd got myself off to. A liberty I wouldn't apologise for taking. I wouldn't hide it either.

Perhaps tonight, I could make that dream a reality.

11

LUCKY

*I*sobel

That asswipe, Casey, had vanished. After I'd left Lennox to fend for himself against the ghouls, a fact I felt slightly bad about, I'd sought Casey's pit crew, but none of them knew where he'd gone. His car had been dented and scratched to fuck, and he'd stormed off, apparently in a foul mood.

He'd walked directly behind us, his stepdad keeping pace, but I'd been wrapped up in Lennox and not wanting to climb down so I'd let him go. I had the vague thought that I should be talking to Warwick Senior, rather than Casey, but the guy intimidated me, so I'd ducked the issue.

I called Casey's number, but it went straight to voicemail. So I sent him a text then headed straight to my room.

Fine, came Casey's response, right as I walked in the door.

I gave a happy little dance. I'd won the race against Casey and secured the cars for Mum's rally—whoop!—and I'd grabbed my business a ringing endorsement—double whoop!—but I had a date tonight, and fuck, that blew everything else out of the water, a fact that startled and warmed me.

I showered the sweat and menthol away—the scent added to race suits to keep them fresh—and dressed then styled my hair, thinking of nothing but Lennox.

I didn't date often. I'd had a few boyfriends, mostly casual, over the years, but I'd never wanted to settle down or commit to anyone. I had my own life to lead, plus the idea of letting anyone too close, letting them see my flaws...

You couldn't give your loved one a printed birthday card or avoid writing them a note forever. You couldn't easily explain how hard it was to keep your temper when minor things went wrong.

No. Not for me.

Lennox was somehow different. I liked him. A bolt of happiness had shaken me to my very bones when I'd laid eyes on him at the track. It couldn't have been easy getting there in the time he'd had. He'd done it. For me.

I peered into the mirror, carefully applying a sparkly blue line above my eyes. I'd gone to way too much effort—thank God I'd adopted Skye's mantra of always having eveningwear packed when in places like this. My figure-hugging black dress was held up by spaghetti straps and a clever drape. The neckline skimmed my boobs, my super-sexy bra pushing them front and centre. Then, to top it all, my killer heels showcased my legs through a split in the dress.

The shoes would bring me closer from my usual five-two to Lennox's mighty height.

Lipstick was a no-no—I'd forget I was wearing it and swipe it over my cheek—so I dabbed on gloss, and there, I was done.

A final critical glance had me sucking in a breath. I'd

never look like Amber or reach her level of loveliness. It wasn't self-pity, I simply didn't have the poise. But Mum always told me beauty was in the eye of the beholder. Perfectly attractive people were nothing without chemistry.

Lennox and I had bucket-loads of that.

I grinned, imagining his reaction. I couldn't be any more different to earlier. Then, I'd had my hair tied back and most likely grease on my face. He'd gazed at me like he wanted to devour me. Now...

I took a quick photo of myself and sent it to Skye. *Good enough to eat?* I texted.

Scrumptious, she replied. *Who's the lucky guy?*

I doubted her twin would have told her anything about me, so I'd save that piece of juicy gossip for another time.

What happens in Monaco... I wrote back, and Skye sent me a series of outraged emojis.

I left my room with a hopeful step.

The lift slowly dropped down. Nerves that had been absent when I'd been behind the wheel turned into elephant-sized butterflies in my stomach, and I entered the darkened bar, scanning for Lennox's broad form. *Please be here. Please.*

Patrons sipped cocktails while others danced to the thudding club music. Couples embraced in corners, neon lights swirling over the crowded dance floor.

Lennox sat alone at the bar, a tumbler in his hand.

Almost instantly, he spotted me. The man's jaw dropped, and he placed his drink down and stood from his barstool. His eyes widened, and his mouth morphed into a laugh. I bit my lip and forced my feet to move until I was in front of him.

Lennox's gaze soaked me up. "Fuck, Isobel," he said, his voice gruff. "Just... Give me a second."

I hid my smile and took the seat next to his. "Whenever you're ready."

He scrubbed his hand over his face, still staring. I stole his drink and downed it. It was whisky, and it burned my gullet. I gave Lennox a wink.

He sat heavily in his seat. A dangerous glint lit his eyes. "I had all kinds of chat lined up, about the snowboarding and about watching ye race. Ice-breakers. But I'm stuck on how ye look. Woman, you're beautiful. Ye would be if ye came down in your leathers but when ye put your mind to it..."

"Thank you," I managed. How did he make me feel like this? A shy, sweet thing. Not my usual brash self. "You're extremely hot yourself."

Lennox had rolled up the sleeves of his dark-grey dress shirt, displaying strong forearms for me to lust over. He raised a hand to gesture to the bartender, and his muscles flexed.

My insides clenched. Man, I had it bad.

"Same again?" Lennox asked me.

"Uh-huh." Even my damn voice was breathy.

We sized each other up, waiting on our drinks. They arrived, and I necked mine, needing the Dutch courage.

"Did Viola get through her qualifiers?" I asked.

Lennox's gaze wandered my body. "Mmh," he replied.

I assumed that meant 'yes' but, like him, I was struggling to summon words. My breathing got heavier and my skin more sensitive, almost as if I could feel his touch.

"Was it a hassle getting here today?"

He brought his attention back to my face. "Terrible. But utterly and entirely worth it."

I hopped to my feet, the pressure getting to me. "Dance with me?"

Surely he'd refuse. Did he dance? I couldn't remember ever seeing him do so. But Lennox was full of surprises. He threw back his whisky, rose, and took my hand. Then he led me to the dance floor.

In the middle of the crush, we faced each other. On instinct, at least on my part, we collided, greedy clutches possible now our stops were off. His knee parted my legs, and his hand splayed over the middle of my back, over my bare skin. I pressed my hands to his chest, he was too tall for me to loop my arms around his neck, and...we danced. Close.

The DJ switched things up, and the bass thumped in a new, faster beat, but we kept it slow, moving against each other with our own rhythm, exploring the other's body. Lennox slid his hand up my spine and into my hair, and his fingers caressed the nape of my neck. Oh God, how did I not know that was an erogenous zone?

I pawed all over his biceps. Hard, solid muscle met my exploration, and a chain of miniature bolts of desire burst through my body. Little fireworks of need.

It was strange how we could do this—come together without hesitation. Walk right through the usual polite advances. Earlier, when I'd flown to him and jumped into his arms, it had been the most natural move in the world.

I pressed my cheek to his chest, and Lennox tucked his head over mine.

His lips touched my hairline.

I shivered and raised my face to his. Our gazes linked.

The powerful, hypnotic sway of the music had nothing to Lennox's draw. He wanted me. It was there in his heated look and in the way his possessive hands kept me near. But he'd had this same expression, at least the start of it, when we'd kissed the first time.

I was too far gone to wonder if the outcome would be the same. Could I trust him? Maybe. I wanted to, but still a frisson of fear mingled with the fire in my belly. I had unanswered questions, about Amber, about honesty.

Fuck it. They could wait.

Previously, I'd made my sexual encounters all about that one deal—sex. I'd never cared to hear that I was pretty or how much the guy liked me.

No one had ever looked at me the way Lennox was right now.

Utterly confused, I brought Lennox's face to mine then gave him a soft kiss. A test.

Hunger roared.

He made a low noise, audible despite the pulsing music. Slowly, he nudged my face and returned my kiss. Ah God. Unlike when we were teens, Lennox was in no rush. His lips grazed mine, passing over with the barest of pressure. A second sweep took just as much care, serving to tease me. His gentleness was a surprise. As if he wanted to savour me, rather than wham-bam, see ye later, ma'am.

To add to my growing fervour, Lennox's thumbs made circles on my spine, then one hand wandered south, and he seized my hip. He ground his hard dick into my core, and I gasped, unable to stop myself. At the same time, he kissed me in the way I needed. His tongue demanded entrance, and I welcomed it, giving him my mouth while I clung on to his body. He tasted of whisky and long-held dreams.

Our dirty dancing had ended, and an outright seduction had taken its place. I'd closed my eyes on the first returned kiss but I couldn't help but be aware that we were in public. Our intimate moment had witnesses.

I wanted this man all to myself.

The rush from beating Casey coupled with the utter joy

of having him waiting for me, and I pulled away, breaking our mouths apart. Lennox blinked and focused. His mouth curved into a wicked smile that had me swallowing.

"My room," I said, hoping he could lipread.

Lennox's nostrils flared, and his gaze searched mine. Then he inclined his head and released me from his tight hold. He kept close as I weaved through the dancers, out of the bar and into the brighter lobby.

Breathless, I zoomed to the lift. It had been maybe twenty minutes since I was in it last. How things changed.

"Hold up." Lennox tugged my hand.

"Why?" I jammed my finger on the 'call' button then glanced up at him. If he stopped this, I was going to cry. I'd become hornier from one tiny kissing session with him than...ever. "Don't ask if I'm sure, or if I'd like to talk instead."

"When have you ever done anything you didn't want to? No, I need this," he said and swooped to claim my lips once more.

I surrendered immediately. Lennox McRae wanted to kiss me, and hell yes, was I going to let him.

The *ding* at my back broke our moment, but only for as long as it took to get into the lift and press the number for my floor. Thank fuck the box was empty. Lennox collected me in his arms and pinned me to the mirrored wall, ravishing my mouth with his. Before, when he'd picked me up, I'd strangled his waist with my legs, but my dress wouldn't allow it now. I was at his mercy and could only cling on for dear life.

No hardship, except I never gave up this much control.

The door opening had us breaking apart and darting down the hall. I slammed my key card over the reader, and we stumbled into my bedroom, grasping, holding, needing.

Lennox's hands were everywhere, at my backside, digging into my hair. He kissed my throat, and I rolled my head to give him access, loving his attentions.

"Shirt off," I demanded.

Lennox withdrew and undid a couple of buttons before pulling his shirt over his head in one go.

Lord above. I stared, mesmerised by his solid, massive form. At the fight, I hadn't let myself lust too hard—one glance and he or my brother would've seen it on my face. There were no restrictions in place now.

Lennox had the body of a warrior, with perfectly honed abs and that V of muscle I could never remember the name for. But he was far more real. Rough blond hair dusted his chest, thickening into a happy trail that I needed to follow. His muscles were those of a hard-working man. Cut by his time in the military and through the snow sports I knew he loved.

What a man.

I found my zip and rid myself of my dress, stepping aside in just my lingerie and heels. An odd sense of worry descended, nerves again, unfamiliar and unpleasant. This kind of exposure had never mattered, I'd never cared.

A single peek at Lennox's awed expression, and the nerves fled.

"Isobel," he growled. "Isobel." Once again, he took my waist. He pressed his forehead to mine. "Ye are so beautiful, do ye hear? Every inch of ye. But this?" He took my black satin bra strap under one finger and rubbed it with his thumb.

"My lingerie?"

"Aye." He dragged the strap down my arm and rumbled approval, palming my breast. "Isabel Fitzroy kissing me and inviting me to her room? I'm the luckiest bastard alive. But ye in lingerie? That's the jackpot. Enough to bring this man to his knees."

He cocked his head like he'd had an idea, then Lennox sank to the floor and skimmed my curves with his huge hands. I bit my lip in glee. He homed in on the tattoo that curled under my breast and around my side. I'd had it done years ago, bribing a tattoo parlour owner to ink me with a swirling pattern that reminded me of speed.

He found the other that circled the top of my thigh. A garter-style lacey frill with a dagger on the inside, the point facing down.

"This is fucking sexy, too," Lennox said.

Then he hooked his fingers under my thong and drew it down my legs. I stumbled, trying to kick it off, and grabbed on to his shoulder.

"I thought you liked my underwear."

"I like what's underneath better." His hot mouth landed right over my clit.

I squeaked and held his head, in no small way stunned that this was happening. He groaned and licked me, using the flat of his tongue to open me to him, and all of my confusion vanished.

Oh. My. God.

"So wet. All for me," he half snarled.

"Keep doing that," I ordered. "Never stop. Fuck!"

Lennox made a noise of agreement then nudged me backwards until my legs hit the bed. He picked me up and threw me onto the mattress, landing between my spread legs and starting up where he left off. His eager mouth was joined by steady hands, holding me open. His leisurely licks had me writhing. Then he slid a finger inside me.

Pleasure bloomed, fierce and new. His thick finger sent ripples through my body.

"More," I begged.

He obeyed, adding a second finger to stretch me. Then he rose to watch my expression, toying with me.

"You look so fucking hot right now. Laid out for me. Play with your nipples."

"Put your mouth back on me."

"Do as I say then ask nicely."

"Please! A billion times, please," I pleaded and slipped my hands into my bra to take my breasts. I rolled my hard nipples, working my hips in time.

Lennox watched, fascinated, then gave a dark chuckle and got back to work. He sucked my clit, fucking me with his hand, and in no time, I was sweating, an orgasm coiling as tight heat inside me. Lennox set the pace, seeming to know exactly what I needed. His fingers hit my G-spot over and over, and I moaned, so close.

"After ye come, I'm going to fuck ye until ye scream my name," Lennox said against me. "Until my touch is the only one ye want. Do ye hear?"

I gasped my answer, and he gave me one final suck. I shattered, spiralling as waves of pleasure took me under. My core tightened and released around Lennox's clever fingers, and I groaned low and long. Oh God, I needed this. Had I come last night? That was nothing like this. It had been years, surely. Vaguely, I heard Lennox swear, then his mouth was on mine, giving me a taste of myself while I saw out my aftershocks.

"Jesus, you have skills," I mumbled.

"I have far more than that to show ye."

I opened a lazy eye then pushed up on my elbows. "Trousers off. Now."

Lennox's wild gaze held mine. "Do ye have condoms?"

I went to speak then snapped my mouth closed. "No."

"Shite." He closed his eyes for a second. "I do, but they're in my room." He ducked and gave me another long, drugging kiss. "Don't go anywhere."

I could've stopped him. His dick had more than one way of getting action here. But I really, really wanted to have sex with him. "Run. All the way. Then run back."

"I'm in room four-oh-six. It's one floor up. Time me, I'll be under a minute."

I snickered, and he grinned and kissed me again. Then he climbed off the bed and claimed his shirt from the floor, reinstating it and depriving me of one hell of a view. At the door, he took a deep breath then jumped up and down on the spot twice.

"What are you doing?" I asked with a giggle. A goddamned *giggle*.

"Trying to get my blood back to my brain." He stared at me. "Fuck," he said again, then he vanished on his quest.

I rolled, bundling myself in the quilt, unable to stop my grin at how things had turned out. He said he was lucky, but I'd won.

All my misgivings fled.

I jerked, suddenly awake and chilled in the middle of my bed.

Alone.

An awful dream had claimed my rest. The Warwicks had waged war against me, posting mean pictures online and being vicious. It was a childish nightmare, one borne of the bullying I'd suffered at Erika's hands and no doubt brought to the fore by seeing them today. Or perhaps from letting Lennox inside my armour.

Shivering, I rose and glanced around the room. Where was he? He'd said he'd be a few minutes. I must've been out of it for hours.

On autopilot, with my brain frazzled from too little sleep and too much excitement, I left my bed and used the bathroom, brushing my teeth and washing as if it were morning. Well, soon it would be, and I'd have to check out and go home. I stumbled about, packing my toiletries away, then busied around my bedroom, doing the same to my clothes and shoes.

Still, Lennox didn't appear.

I dressed and straightened out the bed, still shaky from the dream and my weird semi-awake state. A thought pushed through the murk. I bet he got back to his room and fell asleep.

Right. Couldn't leave without him. I was his ride home. Lennox had told me his door number, so I grabbed my key card and left, jogging to the lift. In the corridor, a couple trundled their cases, presumably checking out, I guessed. It must be later than I thought. Or earlier, rather.

The lift arrived, and blearily, I entered it.

"Ha! Rough night?" a woman said.

I glanced up and found myself face to face with Erika. For fuck's sake. In the mirror beyond her, I caught a glimpse of myself. My curls were a rats' nest and my eyes dark, my hastily thrown-on jacket askew. I dragged my fingers through my hair and tidied my collar.

"None of your business," I muttered.

The lift descended, and I sighed and pressed the 'up' button.

"Bet you thought you were in with Lennox McRae, huh?" Erika tried again. "I knew he'd see sense."

"What?" I bit out.

"He always goes back to Amber. They've been that way for years."

I recoiled. "Lennox and Amber aren't a couple."

Erika widened her eyes at me, her perfect lipstick mouth forming an O. "You don't say? That'll be a surprise when they wake up together tomorrow." She laughed at her own joke.

The doors slid open, and Erika exited. "I hung out with them for a while, but they wanted me out of the way." She took her phone from her purse then held up the screen, her other hand holding the lift door.

The picture showed Lennox and Amber entering a bedroom together. Amber's sequined red dress had fallen from one shoulder, and Lennox—in the same grey shirt he'd worn on the date with me—was in the process of fixing her strap. An intimate moment. Then Erika scrolled to the next, with Amber clinging to Lennox in the race pit.

I winced at it.

Erika released the door. "If you ask me, there'll be an engagement announcement soon. See you around!" She breezed out of sight, and the lift closed then started up once more.

I shrank into the corner, fighting a sudden headache. It wasn't possible. Erika lied as a favourite pastime. Still, I couldn't help admitting my doubts.

I blinked at my own reflection, a wealth of hurt unfurling.

He'd left me and gone to her?

At the fourth floor, I blindly exited the lift.

Don't jump to conclusions, I told myself. But my brain didn't work that way. Fighting nausea, I tried calling Lennox, wanting to be reasonable but knowing I would yell the second he answered. But no answer came, and my phone died in my hand.

I found myself outside room four-oh-six, glaring at the door.

Were they in here? Talking, or worse? I rapped a knuckle on the wood. Nothing happened. I slammed it with the flat of my hand... And the door popped open.

Without hesitation, I stormed into the grey room. The empty bed was unruffled, and Lennox's bag sat on the table, a few items of his clothing draped on a chair.

"Lennox?" I called. No lamps were lit, and the bathroom was dark.

I advanced another step.

In the dull glow through the window, I spotted a small box perched next to his sports bag. A black-and-gold jewellery box. I collected it and snapped it open. A new-looking ring glinted, the single, clear stone reflecting the light.

A diamond solitaire. An engagement ring?

I'd already concluded that none of this made sense, but now, anger churned my belly. Whatever the fuck was going on, Lennox hadn't told me the whole story. Amber had expected him—she'd said so in the pit. Then the images... The ring...

I despised lies. I hated being left out of the picture.

Already out of my rational mind, I snapped. My final thread of control lost.

A short cry fell from my lips, and hot tears pricked my eyes. I snatched the pen and pad from the corner desk and sloppily wrote Lennox a note, not caring who the fuck saw it.

ASSHOLE. RING'S IN THE SEA. SWIM FOR IT. BYE.

With my misshapen letters and random capitals, there

was no doubting who wrote my charming words, but, this time, I wasn't going to sign my name and make it easier for them to ridicule me.

Them.

Lennox and the Warwicks. One happy crew.

Taking his fucking ring with me, I bolted to my room and snatched up my things. Then I checked out, retrieved the MGB from the garage, and shakily drove to the beach road.

Darkness turned the sea black. With no working clock, either from my dead phone or from the MGB, I guessed it wasn't as late as I'd thought, but my mind was set on my course of action, and there was no going back now.

The salty wind whipped my hair into my face.

With as hard a throw as I could muster, I carried out my threat and tossed Lennox's engagement ring into the sea. Fuck him. Fuck me for believing him.

I drove away with wet cheeks and didn't look back.

12

LONELY VIGIL

*L*ennox

In a fury, I left the hotel, storming into the street. Dawn had broken, angry red and yellow streaks shattering the sky. I cursed the time I'd wasted.

"Isobel!" I bellowed down the road.

She was long gone, I knew it. I bunched my hands into fists and hoisted my bag over my shoulder.

A car pulled up, parking illegally. Casey Warwick climbed out and sauntered across the pavement—I instantly recalled what Isobel's mum had said. She'd asked me to smack him in the face if I saw him. That was highly appealing right now.

He raised his chin at me. "I've come to pick up my sister. She ready?"

"How the hell should I know?" Despite myself, I asked him a similar question. "Have ye seen Isobel Fitzroy this morning?"

He tidied his hair in his reflection in the hotel's glass window. "Done a runner, has she? She did the same to me once. Not a cuddler, that one."

My blood boiled. She'd slept with this muppet? That was the fucking living end. I about-turned and stalked up the hill.

"Lennox! Wait!" Amber's voice called behind me.

I didn't look back. If it hadn't been for the appearance of her and her sister last night, none of this would've happened. I had no more time for that family. Never again.

I snatched up my phone and tried Isobel's number yet another time.

It didn't even ring. It was switched the fuck off.

"Rah!" I howled, startling seabirds from their perch on a wall. I jogged to a taxi. "Airport. Fast," I commanded and chucked my bag into the back seat.

If she thought she was getting away with this, Isobel had another think coming.

---

*B*y the time I'd sulked through my flight and landed at Manchester airport, I'd finally cooled down. My phone ringing had me in a panic, but it was my mother.

"Lennox, where are you?" Ma asked.

"An airport."

She paused. "Which continent?"

I blew out a breath, my mood lifting a fraction. I paced through the arrivals terminal, heading for the exit. "Ours. I'm in Manchester." Then I added for no good reason, "Chasing after a lass."

Ma went to speak then stopped. I could almost hear the cogs of her brain whirring. "Oh!"

I adored my mother. She was brave and fierce, but under an elegant veneer. She'd set up her own successful wedding planning business which in turn helped my sister develop her own career as a dress designer. Yet she'd always been there for us and for Blayne. I'd helped out at countless weddings, watching as she worked, swan-like, effortlessly managing the highly strung brides and grooms around her.

My hot head clearly came from my da.

I needed my mother's steady advice now.

"I don't think you've even mentioned a woman to me before," Ma said. "Certainly not chasing one."

"Aye, I have. Once before."

She chewed on this for a second, connecting the dots of where I was and what I'd said in the past. She didn't know that we kissed but she knew I'd upset her best friend's daughter. And pursued her across the Cairngorms. "Not Isobel?"

"Aye," I said again, eloquently. "She threw a fit and ran out on me."

Ma giggled. "Beth is going to have kittens. We always thought it would be Skye and Sebastian, never you two."

"Ma! Focus!"

"Sorry, so why did she get upset?"

I stepped outside of the terminal, a wintery breeze cutting into me. "A misunderstanding, I guess."

"My poor boy. I'm going to ask you a question, but don't take this as judgement, just a hint at a potential solution. This misunderstanding, could you have done anything to prevent it?"

"No!" I reconsidered. "Maybe."

Actually, there was a whole lot I could've done, but how could I have predicted what was going to happen that evening? The Warwicks had no reason to be in our hotel. Isobel had no reason to mistrust me. But still... I ground my knuckles into my eyes. "Fine, I see what you're getting at. What do I do now?"

"I take it you've gone there to find her and make things better?"

I nodded, though she couldn't hear me, so I grunted as well.

"Calmly clear up exactly what happened and bring her out of the dark. How long have you two been dating?"

"We're not."

"Uh-huh. Then clear that up, too."

I had no idea what I was doing with the lass, I only knew the impulse that I'd had to apologise and then... Well, my desire to be around her eclipsed rational thought.

"I shouldn't get close to anyone," I said to Ma. "My head is all over the place now I'm out of work."

"I'm not surprised. You're under pressure and you've never worked well without boundaries. Do you remember your father used to give you lists of jobs every weekend? It's because you didn't cope with free time. It unnerved you and you'd be pinging off the walls. Don't beat yourself up for feeling unsteady when you're not on solid ground."

"That's exactly how it feels." Ma understood me better than anyone. I swallowed hard. "I had an idea I could do something on the estate. Make a job for myself, but my own business. Not Da's."

"An excellent idea. Which brings me to my main reason for calling. Can you make it home tonight?"

I sighed. "Probably, or at the latest, the morning."

"I'm taking your father away for a few days on a surprise break. We leave in the morning to join Beth and James on their holiday. Skye will be here, but I'd like you to be, too. It's half term, so Blayne is out of school, and I'm worried if he's not fully supervised, he'll break something. Either a limb or some ancient part of the castle. Come home, work out your plan, and keep your brother alive. Sound good?"

It did. Mostly.

"I'll be there," I agreed.

Then I told my mother I loved her and got into a cab.

⸻

*A*t Belvedere, coaches and cars lined the public car park, and I directed my driver away from the tourists, down the no-access road to the private area of the grounds. We reached the security gate, and I paid my fare then walked the rest of the way on foot.

The garage doors were open in a long row, and my heart leapt. But it was unreasonable to think Isobel could be home already. At best, she'd be here midway through the evening, so there was nothing for me to do but wait.

I stomped across the icy grass and hailed the groundskeeper. "Hey, Mr H."

Mr Hinchcliffe, who must've been eighty if he was a day, dropped his shammy and raised his hand to his eyes. There was no one else in the garage, and I stuck my hands in my pockets and mooched in.

"Young Lennox. Are Sebastian or Isobel with you?" Mr Hinchcliffe asked, peering behind me.

I was six-five and eighteen stone. Despite the fact I was twenty-three, no one else saw me as young anymore. "Naw. Seb's away for another night. Isobel's on her way, though." Sebastian had finally replied to my multiple texts confirming he was alive and coming home tomorrow.

I kicked the wheel of the nearest car. "Give me something to do, aye?"

Mr Hinchcliffe sized me up, his thick grey eyebrows

merging in the middle. He'd known me since I was a boy and readily accepted that I was there alone. "Oh dear. How about you start with a couple of oil changes and we'll see if that improves your mood."

He set me to my task, and I took out my temper on filters and wrenches.

---

*C*hilly day turned into a freezing night. The day trippers left, and Mr Hinchcliffe retired to his cottage. His wife, who ran the indoors staff, brought me a sandwich and a flask of soup, and I kept up my lonely vigil, finally giving up my post at the one remaining open garage door to seek shelter inside a car.

Despite the bitter cold, I must have passed out, as I woke to the rattle of an engine and bright lights filling my windscreen. I snagged my phone and checked the time. Nearly 5 AM. Christ.

The lights died, and Isobel climbed from the MGB, a dog-tired slump to her shoulders.

I had no clue, not one iota of an idea what I was doing. Ma had told me to be calm and clear, but now, faced with the lass who'd blown up on me at the first opportunity—again—my blood pressure shot through the roof.

I cracked open my door and stepped out. Isobel jumped, her torchlight flashing around.

"Who's there?" She peered into the dark interior of the garage.

"The big, bad wolf," I answered.

"Lennox," she replied, her voice dull.

"Aye. Remember me?" I had a host of things to say but I

couldn't start a sentence. I rounded the car, choking on my words.

Isobel collected her bag from the MGB and killed her torch, tossing it back inside the car. Out of her heels, she was tinier than ever.

"I'm not apologising," she said. "You can stand there glaring at me all you want, but I don't care about the value or the waste."

I followed her outside. Moonlight fell on her, silvering her curls.

"What do ye think I want an apology for?"

"Your ring."

I gripped the back of my neck, my fingertips digging into my skin. "I don't own a ring. I never have. You mean the ring ye found in my room and flipped out over? Is that the one?"

Isobel shrugged and shut the garage door. She turned her back and slogged towards the mansion.

My strides ate the ground. My long shadow chased me. I caught up with Isobel and got between her and the house, my hand out. "Don't walk away from me. I've waited all day and all night to see ye."

She stopped short and raised her face to mine, her features twisted in hurt. "Yeah? Well, I woke to an empty room and news that my guy had climbed into bed with someone else. Someone he's been on and off with for years and lied to me about and probably wants to marry." She dragged in a shuddering breath. "Then I drove for twenty-four hours, broke down in the middle-of-fucking-nowhere France with a dead phone, and I just want to go to my bed. Please, Lennox. I'm tired, hungry, and pretty fucking blue."

Her voice broke, and my anger ebbed, shifting to a rawer array of emotion.

"It was all a stupid mistake," she added. "You and I

shouldn't have happened. I don't want it, and you should leave."

"Stop," I said.

"No. You made yourself clear. You left me."

"Did I?" I sought her eyes, but she looked away. "How long do ye think I was gone from your bed?"

Isobel made an off sound. "What does it matter?"

"Twenty-seven minutes. I know, because I checked the time when I left then tried to call ye when I returned."

She shook her head but didn't move again.

"I left your room, and fucking Erika Warwick was on my floor. She followed me, begging for help with their fucked-up family. There's more to that story, and I should have told ye everything, but it didnae matter. It was all ancient history and no concern of mine. When I pretended to be her sister's boyfriend that Christmas, it was because she'd fallen out with her stepdad and he and her mother were on the rocks."

"You already told me this. What does it matter?" Isobel said quietly. Tears glinted on her cheeks, and she shivered violently.

The MGB had no heating, and it was well below zero. She drove all that way, alone, and had to seek then wait out a rescue in the cold. My heart wrenched.

I dropped my bag and shed my jacket then carefully placed it around her. "Christ, woman. You're half frozen. Let me come inside with ye now and explain."

"You're lying. Twenty-seven minutes is impossible," Isobel muttered and shouldered past me.

Stubborn arse that I was, I snatched up my bag and stuck with her.

We entered the house directly into a large kitchen, the huge, old fireplace at one end juxtaposed with modern shelving and shiny ovens. Isobel dumped her things, discarded my coat to a chair, then set her phone to charge on the tiled counter. Then she hauled open a fridge, spilling a patch of light around her. She extracted a covered bowl and glanced back at me.

"Did Hinchie feed you?"

It had been a long time since I'd eaten, and that was after going without food all day. I'd been too het up to contemplate a meal. My hesitation over answering earned a snort from Isobel.

"She must have done, but you're starving again, I bet." She fetched a second bowl from the fridge and took both to a microwave, shut them in, one on top the other, a plate between, then set the machine going.

I watched her, working through what I needed to tell her next. In my role in the military, I'd been trained to think fast and make my ideas known. None of that had prepared me in the slightest for handling this kind of situation. Where my heart was more involved than my head.

Isobel flicked on the undercounter lights, popped a hip against the side, and took the initiative. "Where did the ring come from?"

"I told ye that Erika found me. She followed me into my room and handed me the box. She told me it was an engagement ring to be used as a prop. I didn't even see it. I don't give a single fuck that it's at the bottom of the ocean."

Her shoulders lowered an inch. "A prop?"

I kept going. "The favour was to stage a proposal, which, if ye are to understand that, means ye have to know the background. That Christmas, when you and I first kissed, Amber had come out to her mother, but her stepfather had blown up. Amber is a lesbian, ye ken? Her stepfather is a militant homophobe. So she backtracked and lied then needed an alibi. Skye asked me to help—my sister, she's a sweetheart to anyone in need—and even though I didn't like it, I agreed."

Isobel's eyes widened. "Amber's gay?"

"Apparently."

"And instead of challenging the guy or kicking him out of the family, they all chose to lie?" She shook her head, her curls tumbling loose from her hair tie. "How far was this going to go? Were you going to walk her down the aisle?"

I stepped in and placed my hands on the counter either side of the woman, caging her in like a wee frightened animal. Then I brought my face to hers, my temperature rising after sitting in the frozen garage for so long. "I wasn't going to do anything. Erika asked, I told her where to go. She burst into tears and said her sister was devastated and there was no one else they could trust. I left to return to ye, but fucking Amber appeared in the hall, weeping and falling on me. I guided her back into her room where she asked the same question her sister did. I had them both, one in each ear, telling me how they'd have nothing if their mother's marriage failed. Erika ducked out, Amber had a kind of panic attack; it was a nightmare."

Isobel glanced down, so I took her chin and forced her to look at me.

"Why you? Why not someone else?" she said.

"I've no clue and I didnae care. I walked away. Again. I came back to ye, but ye wouldnae answer my knock. I had a missed call, but your phone was off. So I sat on the damn floor and waited for ye to wake. I fell asleep and when I came to, it was dawn and ye still didnae answer. I traipsed back to my room and found your note."

I pulled it from my back pocket, the paper folded neatly and puzzled over extensively.

My lass had problems writing. I'd had no idea.

Isobel snatched it then ducked under my arm. She took the note to the cooker hob and turned on the gas. A flame *whooshed* to life, and she stuck the note into the fire.

It caught instantly.

"Ouch!" she yelped and danced backwards.

The burning paper fluttered to the floor. I leapt on it, stamping it out. "Are ye trying to burn the place down?"

Isobel nursed her hand. With a sigh, I grabbed her arm and led her to the tap, standing over her so she couldn't bolt.

She held her fingers under the cold water and swallowed. "Sorry for what I wrote."

"Huh. So ye are sorry for something, then. For the record, I am, too."

She turned off the water then grabbed a towel and switched her attention to the dishes rotating in the microwave. The scent of tomato sauce warming met my nose. My mouth watered.

"Is that spaghetti?"

"Yup. Hinchie usually cooks enough for me and Seb if Mum and Dad are away."

We were thawing, Isobel and me. She was descending from her high horse, and I was ready to jump off mine. Maybe after we ate, we could talk this through properly.

Finally, the food *dinged*. I took the towel from her hands and batted away Isobel's attempts to help.

"Get cutlery. And grated cheese," I ordered.

"So bossy," Isobel muttered, but still she obeyed.

Across the other side of the expansive kitchen—designed to cook banquets, I imagined—was a wooden table. I carried the dishes there and removed the plates. Isobel joined me and took the seat opposite.

We continued our ceasefire, guns silent while we ate. In turns, we piled handfuls of cheese on our spaghetti and stuffed our faces. The colour returned to Isobel's cheeks, though the dark rings remained underneath her eyes.

When we'd finished, I took the dishes to the sink and washed up. Isobel dried them and put them away.

"You never dated Amber?" she finally said.

"No." Then the wrong words came out of my mouth. "Did ye date Casey?"

"What? No!"

"He implied that he'd slept with ye."

"He's a fucking liar. I kissed him. Once, and never to be repeated. Not that it's any of your business."

It wasn't. Yet I was a mixture of aggravated and relieved.

Isobel watched me for a minute. "Not that I don't believe you, but there are pictures of you are Amber together. Hence why I asked."

I furrowed my brow. "Where?"

"Online. She's been sharing them for years. And her sister has. She showed me in the hotel. I'll find it now." Isobel moved a step away, presumably to retrieve her phone. But she paused and stared at me for a long moment. "I tried to find you, and to call you. But Erika told me where you were, and I flipped out. I thought I'd been asleep for hours, so everything else piled on top of that to make a disaster. I blow up easily. It's a major flaw in who I am."

Erika? For fuck's sake. That family had a lot to answer for. "This has been one hell of a misunderstanding."

Isobel gave a sad shrug and continued across the kitchen. "Story of my life. I told you we were a mistake."

My heart sank. "Didnae feel like a mistake to me."

"No? Five minutes of fun wrapped in days of frustration and hurt, does that seem worth it to you?" She picked up her phone and stared at the screen. Then she swore.

"What is it?" I asked.

"Sebastian. He needs me to collect him from the airport."

We exchanged a confused glance.

"Does Seb often ask you for rides?" I asked.

"Never. He'd rather walk." Isobel's fingers flew as she tapped out her reply. "I need to go. His last message says his flight lands in an hour."

God, and I needed to get back to Scotland. What shite timing. "I have to go home," I told her.

It couldn't end like this. The road trip, the flirting, the dash to get to her. Yet weariness rolled into defeat. Isobel didn't want to admit it, the same attraction I felt. In the cold predawn darkness, whatever had drawn her to me had died.

"I can give you a lift to the airport. Or you can stay here and Seb will take you later. Your call," Isobel said, oblivious to my misery.

"I'll come now and get the early flight," I muttered.

We left the house and headed back through the bitter night to the garage. Isobel snagged the keys to her dad's Audi and gestured for me to get in.

"Which car is yours?" I asked. I'd seen her drive a couple of different vehicles from the Fitzroy fleet, but nothing stood out as clearly hers.

Isobel glanced at the shiny row. "None, specifically. I drive whichever I want. But I never really claimed my own."

Huh. She was car-mad but didn't have one of her own? Now wasn't the time to unpick that, she was wobbling on her feet. I wrinkled my brow. "Want me to drive? You must be exhausted."

"I'll live," she replied and got behind the wheel.

We set off. On my phone, I booked the next flight to Inverness then stared into space and brooded.

Everything was wrong. The frigid air between us.

Isobel's hard-as-nails act. Even if I thought she was full of it, I couldn't force her to see me.

Even if I wanted it. I couldn't be sure of anything right now.

All too quickly, the bright lights of the airport appeared in the distance.

"For what it's worth," I said, "I'm really sorry for not getting back to ye in time."

Isobel swallowed. Her fingers trembled and she hit the indicator. "It wasn't your fault. And the rest was all me."

"Are ye sure you've had enough?" There. Heart on the line. Take it or break it, lass.

She rounded the corner into the short-stay car park then brought the Audi to a halt and killed the engine.

In unison, we unclipped our seat belts, but neither of us got out of the car.

Isobel went to start a sentence but stopped. Then she tried again. "I don't want a boyfriend," she finally uttered.

"Good. I don't want ye to have a boyfriend either."

The corner of her mouth lifted in a pretence of a smile, but it faded just as quick. "I'll never be a good girlfriend. There's too many things wrong with me."

"What are ye talking about?"

Her focus fixed on the dash. "You don't want to open that can of worms, believe me."

Fine. I wanted to know everything, but another time when we weren't both fighting exhaustion. I changed the subject, needing to give her a heads-up. "I spoke to Ma about ye."

Isobel groaned. "You did? That means I'll get the third degree from my mother when she next calls. What did you tell her?"

I let a fond smile broach my lips. "Not much, but she'll

assume what she likes. She gave me some advice which I'm trying to follow. I know these past few days have been challenging, but at points within them, I've felt so fucking happy. That's because of ye. I never forgot your kiss. It kept me warm over the years. I'm going home now because I need to take care of my brother, but really, I want to stay in this car and keep talking with ye."

"I have no idea why you like me. None." Isobel rubbed her eyes with the side of her hand. "I don't have a magic kiss, and my personality sucks."

"Want me to tell ye how wrong that statement is?"

"No." She gave a small, stressed laugh. Then her phone dinged. She squinted at the screen. "Seb's touched down."

I glanced at the time. "And I need to check in. Come on."

We left the car, and I pulled Isobel under my arm as we crossed to the terminal building. She kept with me, and her hand snaked to grip the back of my jumper under my coat. Something in that tiny action had my chest aching.

Inside the doors, we halted, needing to separate.

Isobel shuffled back a step. "I don't know what to say," she said.

"Me neither."

She peered up. "Thank you for coming after me. Or ahead of me. Whatever. I'm glad we worked out what went wrong."

"So am I. And in terms of what happens next, ye decide. I'll go home and stomp about like a bear with a sore head until I hear from ye. But it's in your court. Just so there's no ambiguity, I wish this hadn't ended. Ye set my heart racing, and I'm pissed off that we didn't get to take things further."

She chuckled, and the heavy exhaustion on her features lifted. "Tell me about it."

The Tannoy crackled and announced the closing of the Inverness flight.

Isobel pressed up on her toes and kissed me on the cheek.

"Call me," I ordered. "Get your phone fixed and answer one of the fifty missed calls and ranting messages ye have from me. As a minimum to tell me about Seb. I want to know how his fight went because all I've had from him is single-word answers. But I want to hear from ye more."

Then I really had to go. With a last, desperation-edged gaze on her tired, gorgeous face, I tore myself away and jogged to catch my flight.

13

THE BIGGEST FUCKING IDIOT ON THE PLANET

Isobel

A wreck limped out of the arrivals line. No, not my pride. My brother.

The bright airport light drove shadows over Sebastian's face, but it didn't hide his black eye and split cheek. He raised a hand but then winced, hefting his bag on his shoulder.

"Oh holy fuck." I ran to him and gaped.

"Looks worse than it is," he mumbled.

"Were you hit by a truck?"

He made a sound like he was trying to laugh, but it came out as a pained grunt. I took his sports bag and guided him towards the exit. I couldn't help a glance over my shoulder. Fifteen minutes ago, Lennox had left to return to Scotland. I was the biggest fucking idiot on the planet for letting him walk away with nothing more than a promise to call.

Actually, Sebastian was probably the bigger idiot of the pair of us.

We got to the car, and I manhandled him into the

passenger seat. There, he closed his eyes, his jaw tight where he was obviously in pain.

Fat chance of getting him to drive. He could barely move. Exhaustion had the edges of my vision red. My heart beat out of time, and I dropped into the driver's seat for yet another slog.

Once we'd cleared the airport and were out on the open road to home, I glanced at my brother. Bleary-eyed, he regarded me.

"Want to talk about it?" I asked.

"Not much to say. I had a fight. The other guy was a surprise."

"Did you lie on the ground and let him wallop you?"

Sebastian clutched his ribs and pointed at me. "She's so funny! You should go on stage."

I stuck my middle finger up to him and didn't hide my smile.

"Lennox wants you to call him," I said. "And Hinchie is going to flip when she sees your face. You're lucky Mum and Dad are away."

No reply came. Sebastian slept.

---

*A*t Belvedere, I shook my brother awake then helped him into the house and to his rooms. He fell onto his bed with a barely concealed sigh of relief. I stripped his shoes and his jacket then found him aspirin and water. He woke enough to take the painkillers but instantly dropped back into a deep sleep.

Blood congealed on his mouth. His cheek and forehead swelled, shiny.

I could've done more for him. Probably should've. But I was finished.

I laid on the rug by the side of his solid wooden bed, and the world disappeared.

---

*H*inchie, our housekeeper but to all intents our grandmother, too, woke us some time later. After my weird experience with Lennox, where his twenty-something minutes felt like hours, I couldn't trust my judgement anymore.

Besides, Hinchie was yelling and flapping at us both.

With her Derbyshire accent thickening by the minute, she bemoaned Sebastian's stupidity in fighting and mine in driving without rest. We sat up and nodded along to the lecture, me on the floor, somehow now with a blanket over me, and Seb against his white pillows. He was still dressed in his jeans and shirt, his black hair dishevelled and his red and purple bruises startling.

Fuck it, what was I doing on the floor? I clambered onto Seb's bed and shoved his feet aside, like I would've done when we were little.

"Ow," he complained.

Hinchie wrung her hands together, her chin wobbling. "What hurts apart from your poor broken face?"

"Nothing's actually broken," Seb said, kicking me. "It's flesh injuries. It'll fade in a week or two."

"And you!" Hinchie came back to me. "You broke down in the middle of nowhere in a foreign country. No way of getting help. You could've been murdered and no one would know a thing about it."

"You broke down?" my brother asked at the same time I said, "How did you know that?"

"Lennox McRae called the house and asked after you both," she said, smug.

I searched my pockets for my phone. We'd got home at around eight this morning. It was eight PM now. "Jesus. We slept twelve hours." The phone powered down again in my hands. I cursed at it. "This phone is broken."

"Lennox called twice," Hinchie said, her eye on me. Then she switched back to my brother. "Have you put anything on those bruises?"

"I've not even looked in a mirror." He rubbed his broken cheek then stopped, grimacing.

Mrs Hinchliffe flattened her lips. "I've got arnica. I'll go and fetch it now."

"Thank you," he called.

"We love you," I added.

She left us, and I stared at the broken device in my hands. "Lennox wants me to call him."

Seb rolled up and reached for his dresser. He produced a phone from the drawer, took mine, swapped the SIM, and pressed through whatever options were pinging up. It was second nature for my family to take on tasks like this for me.

He handed it back. "Should be good to go. Did you and Lennox make up?"

I thanked my brother with a thumbs-up then found my contacts—all present and correct. Then I sucked in a breath and pressed Lennox's name to place the call. "Kissed him. Ran out on him. So, not so much," I replied.

The call connected, ringing.

"Fuck's sake, Is. Shouldn't we have a rule about sleeping with each other's friends?" Sebastian groaned.

"I didn't sleep with him. Not technically."

"Far too much information," my brother drawled.

"Isobel," Lennox answered, his deep voice familiar and warm.

A sharp pang resounded in my heart.

"Hey. We've both been asleep until now." I tucked my legs in, making myself into a ball around the ache. "Seb's alive, you can speak to him next. I told him I kissed you."

My brother tossed a pillow at me. Then he swung his long legs off the bed and stood, staggering. "I'm not listening to this. Tell him we'll catch up later. I need a shower."

He exited to his bathroom, and I clutched the phone a little tighter.

"Christ, woman." Lennox chuckled. "Ye really have no filter, do ye?"

"I've had precisely no time to think, due to being unconscious, but I know I'm sorry," I told him. "I fucked everything up. It's a common thing for me."

I felt it all now. Contrite as fuck, stupider than usual. Hindsight was a wonderful thing.

Lennox made a soft sound. "Ye had a big reaction, that's for certain. But then look at me. I was in a hell of a state. I camped out at your house, yelled at ye, wouldn't leave when ye asked me to."

Ah God, no. He'd been sitting at home all day, blaming himself.

"Stop. Don't even go there." I leapt from the bed and skipped out of the room, able to head to my own bedroom now I knew Seb was alive and well. "This is all on me. I told you that."

Mrs Hinchcliffe ambled back along the hall, a clear bottle in her hand.

"Hang on a sec," I said to Lennox then I put my hand over the receiver.

"Seb's in the shower," I told Hinchie. "I'm about to change and clean up."

"I've a lamb joint and roast veg waiting downstairs for you. Are you hungry?"

"Yes. A million times, yes." I made big eyes.

"I'll leave your brother this then I'll go plate up your tea. Be down in fifteen minutes."

My rooms were the opposite side of the hall, a few doors away. I let myself in and put the replacement phone on loudspeaker. "Lennox? Sorry, I need to wash and change, too. But I want to keep talking to you. Tell me what you've been doing today."

Lennox choked. "While you're there getting naked? Do ye think I'll be able to concentrate?"

I laughed into the empty air of my living room. "Taking my jumper off," I informed him.

"Gods above," Lennox muttered.

"Top's next, and then my bra."

"And now I'm hard and I'm meant to be going out this evening with my brother."

"Oops." I grinned, my cheeks warming. The effects of a good night's sleep had worked wonders on me. The effects of talking to Lennox worked in entirely different ways. "Want to tell me about your evening plans instead? I just want to hear your voice."

"Not sure I can get the idea of ye stripping out of my mind." He shuffled, as if getting more comfortable. "Ye rang me, I'm guessing from the minute ye woke?"

"Pretty much. Weirdly, I miss you. Probably from spending so much time together."

He drew a breath, audible down the line. "I might have thought about ye once or twice today."

I carried the phone into my bathroom and pulled the cord for the light. "Is that why you kept calling Hinchie?"

"Maybe. I caught a glimpse of Ma's calendar when I got home. It's your birthday on the weekend."

It was. The day I got back from New York with Skye. But I didn't have any plans to celebrate. I'd been alive for almost twenty-one years, but my actual birthday was on the twenty-ninth of February. A leap year. We celebrated on the twenty-eighth for the three years I didn't get a birthday, but it had always felt very apt. Like I was only a quarter of a person and I didn't really deserve more. I hummed a neutral response and leaned into the shower, switching on the water.

"I ken that ye have plans with my sister, and probably other stuff happening around the day. But would ye like to come here before? Or I can come there when I'm free and start on your workshop?"

A thrill chased through me. "You know that you're insane for wanting anything to do with me?"

"Hush. Is that a yes?"

I chewed my lip, toeing the tiles at my feet. "I haven't found the perfect place for the garage yet, so put a hold on that, but I'd really like to come to the castle. Please don't make it about my birthday, though. Just a visit."

"Come as soon as ye can. Bring your brother, too, and we'll make a party of it. Skye misses ye both. I've got an army buddy coming to look at my building idea. We'll go snowboarding with the kids then we'll get time alone, too."

"Alone time, huh? You've thought this through," I said, fighting the urge to keep telling him to save himself. I loved his idea.

Scotland, me, him, and the whole McRae estate. The cousins to have fun with.

Getting Lennox alone again.

Lennox sighed. "We have unfinished business. From the moment I walked away in the airport, all I wanted was to about-turn and find ye again."

"I wanted to come and find you." I said, even quieter now, my heart racing though I stood still. Shower steam clouded around me and misted the slate tiles. "I told you I miss you. I do now and I'm talking to you."

He made a grumbling sound. "Says the lass who doesn't want a boyfriend. Tell me, over the years, how often has that first kiss we shared been on your mind?"

"A lot. It was my first kiss."

Silence met my ears. "Fuck, Isobel, just... Fuck! I had a whole speech lined up about following this draw between us, then ye throw that in?"

My throat clogged, and I swallowed. "Back then, I got upset every time I remembered the kiss. My first should've been special. But now I know why you were with Amber, it feels different. Maybe it was special after all."

"I wish I'd told ye the facts at the time instead of letting ye suffer. I was angry and in over my head."

"It's a good thing you didn't tell me. I would never have kept the secret to myself. I hate lies."

Another voice sounded on Lennox's end of the line.

"Five minutes," he yelled, I guessed to Blayne.

"We both have to go." I wrapped my free arm around myself, suddenly not wanting to end the call. Not for the shower my body screamed for and not even for Mrs Hinchcliffe's epic roast lamb.

"Work out when ye can get here. Tomorrow's good for me, aye?" he added.

I grinned and closed my eyes. "You're crazy."

"Crazy is one word for it. Call me soon, sweetheart."

Then he was gone. He'd called me sweetheart.

Sweetheart.

I wasn't sweet and I wasn't all that sure I had a very good heart, but I liked that word from his lips.

I stripped off the rest of my clothes and stepped under the water for a much-needed soak. The hot water sluiced over me, carrying away the dirt but not helping with my stress.

I had reasons why I didn't want anyone close. But hanging out with Lennox, 'following the draw' as he put it, that didn't need to be anything more than fun.

I forced away the thought that I was kidding myself. If we could let ourselves be drawn in, then he could draw out, too, when he was done, just as easily.

14

SO DIRTY

*L*ennox

Seb finally returned my call after midnight. I'd brought Blayne home an hour ago—we'd only gone to Castle Braithar to see Viola, back from her trip and triumphant with her first-place trophy—but there was no way I was sleeping.

"How bad is it?" I asked him.

"I copped a beating. It was due," he answered, his tone flat.

"You need to give me more than that."

"I was KO'd after a lucky punch. They had to pull the guy off me. Fucking embarrassment."

A chill ran through me.

Since the age of seventeen, both Seb and I had fought. It had started in military cadets and continued when we became ranking officers. But the fight I'd had last week, where I'd taken his place, had been our first that wasn't military-organised.

Or the first I knew about, anyway.

Military fighting rings existed to occupy combat-ready

soldiers when there were no operations to be had. Senior officers turned a blind eye, permitting the violence so long as rules were followed. It stopped the adrenaline and bloodlust from coming out in other, less healthy ways.

Gambling on the bouts was strictly forbidden. Use of lethal force was the same. A knockout, as Seb's had been, meant an instant end to the fight.

But his opponent hadn't heeded the rule.

"Seb," I started.

"I know. Don't. Mrs Hinchcliffe has been on at me all day. She called Mum and Dad, and our gran. Isobel keeps making jokes, but even she is worried."

I stiffened at the mention of Isobel, but I needed to focus on Seb. There was only one person he'd really listen to. "On the subject of sisters, Skye wants to see ye."

"I can't see her like this," Seb muttered. A photo capture sounded down the line, then my message app pinged. I found the pic. It was of Seb's face, black and blue.

"Fucking hell." I stared at the screen.

"Skye won't forgive me," he said.

"She's aware that you're hurt. If ye don't come here, she'll come to ye." My sister loved Sebastian. I had no idea what form that love took, as they led separate lives, but she would take his being injured hard. Unlike Isobel, she despised fighting.

Sebastian swore. "Isobel told me about your invite. We'll come. Maybe in a couple of days. Isobel has some work to do on Mum's rally, but she's already looking at Inverness flights rather than driving."

"Grand." I didn't want to talk to him about Isobel. I hardly knew how to think of her myself. "Are ye going to tell me why ye took this fight?"

"Another time, Nox. I need sleep. Just... Don't worry

about me, all right? It was a mistake. I'll take more care."
Seb yawned. He needed rest to repair his broken body, and I
needed to plan a weekend for my lass.

I bid farewell to my friend, then got on with the job in
hand.

---

*O*n a chilly lunchtime, I paced the great hall's
flagstone floor, throwing the occasional log on the
fire and muttering to myself. Isobel and Sebastian were due
this afternoon, and I was counting down the minutes until I
could leave to fetch them.

I was so fucking happy to be home. Even just a few days
in the Highlands had refuelled me, and I was all about
setting goals and creating a new purpose. I'd spent hours
out on the estate, roaming free and able to finally relax.
When Da returned, I intended to have a full plan to work
through with him.

I also wanted Isobel here. Badly. For all kinds of reasons,
not limited to having her in my bed.

"Earth to Lennox, are you receiving?" my wee brother's
voice interrupted my reverie.

Not that 'wee' was the right word. There was nothing
small about Blayne. At sixteen, he was almost my height,
and I had the idea he hadn't finished growing.

"What?"

"Granddad's on the phone. He wants to talk to ye." He
tossed me the castle phone, and I plucked it from the air.

"What time are Seb and Isobel arriving?" Blayne asked
before I could answer the call.

"An hour. I'm leaving for the airport in ten."

"Good. Maybe after they get here, you'll chill." He saluted—badly—and dropped into a chair.

I frowned at him and put the phone to my ear. "Hello."

"Lennox! I spoke to your mother this morning, and she told me you'd left your unit and were a free man. What a relief."

I gave a short laugh. Ma's dad, Maximus Storm, had been a doting grandfather all my life, never minding his own business and always giving advice. He also hated the military and had bemoaned my decision to enlist. Like me, and Da, he was a big guy and a force to be reckoned with. "I'm a civilian again."

"I want you to come work for me," he said, no messing around.

"Work for ye? In what capacity?"

"Pick your role. If you aren't interested in the business side of things, like your Aunt Scarlet, then you can take over managing one of the production companies."

"That's extremely generous of ye."

"Not at all," Granddad said, a proud smile clear in his voice. "I want more Storms working for Storm Enterprises. This is a family business!"

One to which he was supposed to have retired from years ago, but he maintained ownership as well as a directorship role.

"Your sister has already refused me," he added.

"You asked Skye?"

"I did. A couple of years ago. But she's always been more interested in her dress design. She gets that from her grandmother, of course."

Granddad continued, listing the various companies I could take a role in and the sort of work I could do. He barely paused for breath. "You've moved around so much in the past four years. Why not make a home in London? Try it out for a while. It's a good opportunity and it'll keep you occupied. I know you must be bouncing off the walls with nothing to do each day. Tell me you'll at least think about it."

Blayne eyed me from his slouch in the wooden high-backed chair. Yesterday, we'd gone boarding, and I'd told him about my plans to build a centre on the mountain. If I acted fast, it could be done over the summer. I had an engineer friend coming today to help with the tactics, and I had endless energy for getting it done. But two facts remained inescapable. Da had to agree to it, and I needed to find funding.

If I couldn't get both, my grandfather's offer was a valid alternative.

"Thank ye," I said. "It's kind of ye to think of me." It was a good opportunity, and I was lucky. But living in London didn't fill me with excitement. It would take me farther from the Highlands I adored.

When I got off the call, I sat heavily opposite my brother. He gazed into the fire, his expression downbeat, then he raised a single eyebrow at me.

"Did Granddad offer ye a job?"

"Aye."

"Will ye take it?"

"I'm not sure. What's with the gloom?"

Blayne sighed. "Now you're back, I want ye to stay for a while. If ye work for Granddad, you'll move again."

I reached out and laid my fist into his shoulder in a gentle thump. "Ye never told me ye missed me."

"Are ye kidding? Both you and Skye vanished, and for four years it hasnae been the same. Even when ye come back, it's short-lived." He shrugged, seeming self-conscious. "I'm just saying it would be nice to have ye around."

I gazed at him for a moment. Something was up. "Is there anything particular ye want to talk to me about?"

Blayne planted his boots on the floor and clambered to his feet. "Naw. Not really. Are we going? I want to speak to Isobel."

"About what?" I followed him to the door, tapping my pocket to check for my car keys.

"Just something she can help me decide," he said enigmatically.

We drove to Inverness airport, and I tried again to get my brother to open up, but the teenager was having none of it. He chose the music instead and DJ'd for me as we travelled.

Then we were there, in the arrivals hall, and my pulse beat hard in my throat. I had no idea what to do with myself. I couldn't pace the room, though my limbs were infected with energy. Should I grab Isobel into my arms when she walked up? I wanted to.

But our family would be watching, and I had no idea where she and I stood. We'd flirted on the phone. Isobel had called me to say when to expect them but also just to chat, too, wanting to know if I'd heard from the Warwick sisters about their ring. I'd related how I'd explained to Amber that it had been lost, giving no more detail than that, and that I'd ignored her since. It had Isobel laughing. She'd admitted that she didn't know if it made her happy to have me protect her or annoyed that I'd stolen her glory.

One thing for sure was that she maintained that she didn't want anything permanent in a relationship. Which made me...what, exactly?

I was not a fan of being out of the loop on decision-making. This weekend, I had to settle my feelings one way or another.

A stream of people emerged from the other side of the barrier, bringing noise with their chat and their trundling suitcases. Seb rounded the corner, a beanie hat down to his eyes, his black hair peeking out. Dark-red marks flared on his cheek, and a purple bruise claimed one eye.

Blayne grinned. "Sebastian! Look at your face, man! Badass."

I stared past him. Where was Isobel?

He reached us, and Blayne wrapped him in a careful squeeze. Then it was my turn. I gave him a cautious bearhug and examined his bruises, some small relief in the fact he held himself upright without flinching.

"Not as bad as you expected, right?" Seb said. "The swelling's gone down, and the cuts have dried up."

"Ye look hard as nails," my brother said, approval in his tone. "That face will scare old ladies in the street."

My gaze snagged on the arrivals entrance one more. A final person jogged around the corner. Not Isobel. No one else appeared.

"My sister..." Sebastian started. He pulled an apologetic expression. "Well, you know how she is."

Well, fuck.

She hadn't come.

"Aye, she didn't make it. It's okay," I said, my stomach dropping. I jammed my hands in my pocket and turned to the windows.

"Um, Lennox?" Blayne said.

"All right. I get it. We better go," I managed, though inside, I wanted to storm off and be on my own. Not trapped in a car fighting disappointment I couldn't share.

"Nox!" Sebastian said.

"What?" I barked, spinning around.

Isobel stood right behind me.

"Hey, you," she said, a devilish glint in her eye. Then she leapt at me.

Just like in Monaco, I caught her and gripped her slight body in my arms, bringing her in. She wound her legs about my waist and took my head in her hands.

Unlike then, there was no long gaze or hesitation on her part. Isobel leaned in and laid her lips on mine.

Holy fuck.

My heart swelled, I inhaled through my nose, and I kissed Isobel back. No shame. No worry about being seen. Isobel grinned against my mouth, stopping the kiss from going too far—a good thing as I was lost.

"I freaked out when I got off the plane. I'm no good at waiting and I'm terrible at hiding my feelings."

"And ye were feeling like kissing me?"

"Mhm." She made big eyes. "For days. Kind of obsessively. What a lunatic, right?"

I chuckled, happiness burning through my hurt. "What did ye do, hide around the corner?"

She gave a resigned sigh. "Pretty much. I stopped and talked to a flight attendant about engine maintenance on planes. I think he thought I was mad."

We beamed at each other.

Blayne cleared his throat. "Not that this isn't lovely, by which I mean massively awkward, though I understand why you've been in a miserable mood now, but can we go? People are staring at Seb."

"Seconded," Sebastian grumbled.

I released Isobel and took her hand, keeping our connection. We left the airport and, at the car, she called shotgun, laughing off the complaints from our brothers. Then I was taking her home.

All through the journey, we shared glances. Talking was impossible, for me at least, and she didn't say much either. No matter, as Blayne kept up a steady chatter. He wanted to know all about Sebastian's fight, as did I, and he secured time with Isobel to have his secret chat.

Finally, we were at the castle, and I had her bag in my hand and was dragging her through the great hall to the corridor to my tower.

"Seb, you've got your usual room," I called over my shoulder, hastening.

"So long as it's far away from you two, I'm good," he answered back.

We climbed the spiral stairs in breathless anticipation. As soon as I had her in my apartment, she was in my arms once more. I slammed the door closed and pressed her to it.

"What else was on your mind when ye thought about me these last few days?" I asked, and I kissed her neck.

Isobel tilted her chin to give me access. "Fucking you. Endlessly."

"Shite." I lifted my head to gape at her.

She pointed at herself. "No filter, remember? Plus I want to get there before I mess things up again and you hate me."

"That won't happen."

"Oh, it will. It's my speciality. Even if I try my hardest."

Her pained, honest expression broke my heart.

"It won't go wrong because I won't let it. No misunderstandings. No hiding what we feel. This is going to be fucking amazing."

"If you're so sure then take me to your bedroom," she said. "No one will miss us. We'll hide up here for a while."

I closed my eyes and brought our foreheads together.

Snug against her core, my dick had grown hard as steel. "I'm an idiot. I have a friend coming. He'll be here any minute."

Isobel paused for a second then wriggled down my body. "Fine," she said. "I'll economise. I've been dreaming about doing this."

She turned me so my back hit the door then knelt at my feet and undid the zip of my jeans. I stared, letting her manage me.

Isobel freed my hard-as-rock dick and gave a dirty chuckle. "Lennox McRae, you have a beautiful cock."

With delight in her eyes, she fisted me, then without another word, took me between her lips.

"Fuck," I drawled, widening my stance, utterly obsessed.

Isobel slid me deeper then drew out again slowly, like she was savouring me. "Talk me through what you like," she said. Then she sucked on my end and wrapped her fingers around my shaft.

A groan erupted from my lips. "You're doing it. You, here. Anything."

She used her tongue on the underside, keeping up her steady movements with her hand. Her hair fell in her face, and I wound her soft curls around my grip. I didn't want a single thing stopping me from seeing my dick disappearing inside her mouth.

Isobel tutted. "You can do better than that. You wanted to fuck me a few days ago. Don't tell me you haven't imagined this exact scene when you've been alone in your bed since. Fast or slow, hard or soft? I want to make this perfect. Talk me through it."

A spike of need shot up my spine. "Grab my balls," I said in a rush, dragging in a rapid breath.

She did, her slender fingers cupping me before tugging gently.

Oh fuck.

"Jesus, lass." I groaned again, my breathing coming in hard rasps.

Isobel chuckled, the effect dazzling.

With her clever mouth and hands, my woman gave me one of my fantasies on a plate. And I was ready to give her what she wanted in exchange. My dirty talk flew from my mouth.

"In my imagination, you'd be in your knockout lingerie or even better, naked, and sucking on me. I'd get an eyeful, and it would turn me on even more. Then, before I was done, I'd lay ye out and drive inside ye, fucking ye senseless until we're both crazy."

Isobel growled appreciation, not stopping.

"But I'd take my time. I wouldn't come until ye had at least a handful of times. You'll be begging for one more, and we'll be trying every which way to get ye there."

I'd never been into any kind of sex other than straight-up, get-the-job-done fucks but, with her, I wanted to try everything.

Live in my bed for days.

Learning her body and what made her scream.

Have her all over me, doing whatever she wanted.

My orgasm built, stealing over me until I had no place to go and nothing to do but be in this moment. Isobel seemed to know, and she moaned, picking up the pace. That moan...

"Then, lass, when I finally come inside ye, we'll both yell the place down. The whole fucking estate will hear."

There wasn't enough air in the room. My eyes closed of their own accord, and I forced them open, needing the sight of her, her black curls in my grip. Isobel's expression shifted to amused and clearly turned on.

I was so close.

Sweat broke out on my brow.

"Lennox?" a voice called from downstairs.

Fuck!

"Down in a minute!"

"Shall I come up?" the man said. Artair. My old army friend.

"No! Go away!" I yelled, strained.

Laughter floated up the spiral staircase.

Isobel came off my dick and placed her hands on my thighs, her fingertips digging in. She took a breath. "Uh-oh. We can always come back to this later if—"

"No, no way. Fuck him. He can wait, I can't." In desperation, I took her face in my hands, ready to beg.

She gave a dark laugh and enclosed me again, keeping my gaze. Now, I kept hold of her head and guided her moves, thrusting into her mouth. She followed my actions, eyes gleaming, mouth warm and welcoming. She grasped me, massaging, stroking and, in seconds flat, my balls were tightening.

"I'm going to come," I uttered.

She kept going, sucking hard. I drove my shoulders into the door, smacking it into the frame.

Frantic, I gave her one last warning. "Gonna come! Isobel!"

Then I roared, my orgasm hitting.

My mind shattered, brilliant sparks of light bursting in my vision. Pleasure shot through me, emanating from one point. From Isobel and her actions. My body racked, and my muscles clenched. Isobel stayed on me, seeing me through. A good thing, as I had gone blind.

The aftershocks kept on going. I was out of it, lost to everything.

Oh holy fuck, oh God, this lass.

Then she climbed to her feet. I grabbed her, alive again, and kissed her cheek then her throat, grabbing her arse for good measure.

"That was mind-blowing. I've never come so hard."

"Live wild, Lennox. If we're going to be fucking, we're doing everything we can think of. Dream up the sexiest things you can imagine and then, tonight, we'll do them." She laid her mouth on mine.

I tasted myself on her tongue.

So dirty.

A short while later, we were ready to leave. Isobel went to open the tower door, and I stopped her and took her mouth once more. Hard, and with meaning.

"We're not just fucking," I told her.

"No?"

"No way."

We were on, and this was just a start. Nothing was going to spoil this. Not one damn thing.

15

I WAS IN SO MUCH TROUBLE

*I*sobel

We descended Lennox's tower and entered the winding corridor at the bottom. Lennox smirked, like he couldn't keep his happiness off his face, and he slung his arm over my shoulder, holding me close.

I was smug as I could be. Having him at my mercy had been a trip. No, it was giving him pleasure that had me spellbound.

That and his filthy mouth.

Who knew? Lennox had a dirty side to him. We had so much to explore.

In the great hall, sitting or sprawled in seats by the open fire, were our brothers plus a man I guessed to be Lennox's friend. Sebastian was glowering at the third man.

All three raised their faces at our approach, and the stranger leapt to his feet.

"McRae!" he hollered.

Lennox dropped a kiss to the top of my head then strode over to him. They exchanged hard hugs, and I joined Sebastian, leaning over the back of his chair. My brother stopped his scowling and raised an eyebrow at me. I knew what he was thinking. On the plane ride, he'd asked if I was dating Lennox. I'd said no, which was the truth. We hadn't agreed any labels other than what Lennox had just said. The more-than-fucking statement. Whatever that meant.

I only knew I had a hefty crush on him.

"Put that torn up eyebrow away," I told Seb. "And mind your own business."

"Isobel. Come meet my friend." Lennox put his hand out for me.

I joined him, slipping under his arm, a little surprised that he wanted to introduce me.

"This is Artair. He was a military contractor, and we worked together last year. He's going to lend his expertise on my building project."

I reached out and shook Artair's hand. Like almost everyone, he towered over me. His dark hair was weather-tousled and slightly too long on top, and his brown eyes held humour. He had the same lean, broad-shouldered build as my brother, but that was where their similarities ended. Where Sebastian was usually sullen, Artair had a far happier set to his features. An easy smile slid into place as he regarded me.

"Artair, is that Scottish for Arthur?" I asked.

"Aye. But the Scots version is better," Artair said, his accent slightly thicker than Lennox's gentle Cairngorms brogue. "And you're the famous Isobel. I've heard all about you."

I blinked at him. "You have?"

"Ye race, is that right? Nox showed us a video of you winning a rally. You took the champagne, chugged it, but walked off before they could interview you. This was a year ago, aye?" He glanced at Lennox for confirmation.

Lennox palmed his cheek, his gaze bouncing around the room. "Not sure I remember that."

"Aye, ye did. Oh shite, man. Am I embarrassing you in front of your woman?" Artair's grin grew.

Instantly, I liked this guy.

Lennox rolled his eyes, but the tips of his ears distinctly pinkened.

I snorted a laugh, though astonishment caught my tongue. I knew the race he meant. It was one of the rare times I'd entered a televised meet, and it had been awesome. Probably the highlight of my amateur career. And he'd known about it?

With a sigh, Lennox gestured towards the door. "Anyway, we should get going if we're going to make the most of the afternoon. I've got the kit we need already loaded up. Gordain, that's my uncle, he'll be here any minute, and we'll head up the mountain together."

The castle entrance swung open. Skye stepped inside, unwinding her scarf from her neck. She gave a happy laugh and danced over to me. We hugged. Then, her gaze fixed on something over my shoulder.

Skye froze.

I released her, expecting her to have spied Seb and his bashed-up face.

But no, her attention was locked on Artair.

The moment drew out, and the air practically crackled.

My friend opened then closed her mouth then recovered, setting her features to neutral and polite. If I'd have blinked, I might've missed that. Lennox was saying something to Blayne so he couldn't have noticed. But then I glanced at Seb.

My brother has seen it. His glower was set on Artair once more, fierce and undisguised.

Skye breezed past me. "Hi," she said to Artair. "I'm Skye, Lennox's sister."

"Aye, lass," Artair replied. Like her, he had a wide-eyed, awed thing going on, and his easy manner had been lost.

Neither of them said another word, just gazed at the other.

"Skye," my brother barked.

She jumped and turned, finally spotting him in his tall chair. "Sebastian," she said. Her gaze swept over him, and her gentle expression filled with frustration.

My brother leapt up and took her arm. He led her a few steps away, and Skye pressed her fingers to her mouth, her previous wonderment dying as she took in his bruises.

Over the past few days, I'd got used to him being black and blue. But it did look shocking on first glance.

The rest of us shuffled past, grabbing coats from the small cloakroom next to the door. On passing, I patted Skye's arm. The two of us were travelling to New York on Sunday, and I was looking forward to spending time with her.

"We'll catch up later," I told her.

"You bet." She smiled at me, but strain still held her features tight.

"I'm staying. I'll see you all later," Sebastian said, but unhappiness weighed heavy in his tone.

We left them to it. I suspected this might be a step too far for Skye in however she saw my brother. It was none of my business, but I felt bad for them both all the same.

Lennox took his position at my side, and we exited the castle together.

"Has Seb met your friend Artair before?" I asked, thinking about that antagonistic look my brother had worn.

Lennox rubbed his chin. "Aye, once or twice. I don't think they like each other. I dinna ken why."

"Next question: I had no idea you followed my races. What's that about?" I said. I'd tried to picture the scene. Him, in his barracks, finding footage of me and...watching. Then proudly sharing it with others. My heart swelled.

He glanced at the people ahead. "Can ye pretend ye didnae hear that?"

"Why would I?"

He stopped, and I stopped with him, giving ourselves a small degree of privacy in the distance between us and the others.

Lennox gazed at me, his attention warm. "I'm trying not to scare ye away."

"I'm here, aren't I?"

He just stared then leaned in and gave me a swift kiss. "We'll see how ye feel after I've put ye through the wringer today."

"What?"

"Once we've handled the site plans, I'm taking ye snow-boarding."

I gaped at him. "You're joking. I thought you liked me. Do you want me to break my neck?"

He only laughed.

A van took the car park entrance, and the occupants leaned on the horn. They came to a halt, and Viola wound down the window, waving madly at us. Her dad was in the driver's seat, and Cait and Cameron, two of the other teenage McRae cousins, were in the back. All in snow gear, all making noise and whooping up the place. Blayne slid open the van door and hopped in with them. Lennox led me to his Land Rover, and his army friend got into his own car. We set off for the mountain.

I was going to die on my ass in the cold snow.

---

*O*n the mountainside, Lennox parked up on an area of rocky ground surrounded by drifts, and we jumped out. Frosty air hit me, the temperature a significant drop from outside the castle. I clamped my arms around myself. I wasn't going to die from falling—I wouldn't make it that far. In a minute, I'd be an icicle.

"Go to the van. Viola has clothes for ye," Lennox told me then swiped me on the backside to get me moving.

I jogged over, and Viola slid open the back door.

"I have questions!" she said, shutting out the well-below-freezing air.

Cait, the only other person still in the van, palmed the seats, an excited gleam in her eye. "Ye can't be dating Lennox. No way."

Even with her eyes wide in a tease and a bobble hat wedged on her head, Cait was possibly the most beautiful human I'd ever seen. Viola was pretty with her long dark tumble of curls, and Skye gorgeous with her height and always-stylish ways, but Caitriona was simply stunning. A porcelain doll with perfectly symmetrical features. Her dad, Ally, used to be a model, and she'd had more than one approach from agencies, but he'd refused outright to let his sixteen-year-old daughter even consider that career.

I arched an eyebrow at her. "I see the gossips are out in full force."

"But Lennox!"

"What's wrong with him?" I gazed through the window where he was greeting Gordain and calling something to Artair. Lennox was the image of a man in control. I liked that. I liked knowing he had his shit together, even if he wasn't entirely sure how to make his plans work. He was out here pushing boundaries and trying stuff out. So different to my crappy attempts at setting up my own business. I was working from my Mum's garage. He was breaking earth.

Viola wrangled a pair of thick ski pants from a bag and handed them over. "There's nothing wrong with him. He's great. He's also incredibly bossy. It's hard for us to see him as a nice boyfriend."

"Maybe I don't want a nice boyfriend," I replied, and hauled on the pants, pulling them over my leggings. I inched my tunic dress up around my waist. The more layers the better. "Besides," I continued, feeling the urge to defend Lennox. "That's his personality. He's larger and louder than everyone else by nature."

"I guess he needs to be. He'll be running the whole estate and clan one day. All the tenants who live in the village will come to him with their complaints," Cait added. "A hundred people work for Uncle Callum, so that'll fall on his shoulders, too. In that world, it all makes sense. It's probably why he's grumpy all the time."

"My dad has enough of it being laird," Viola said. "I can't imagine what the clan chief will get."

She passed me a padded jacket. I thanked her on autopilot and shed my thinner coat and put it on, but my mind was miles away. Lennox would be chief of the clan and owner of a castle. He'd be important—he already was—just like my brother.

Lennox would have a wife and lots of kids, and they'd be pillars of society. I imagined that future, needing the image. It wasn't far different from where he was now, except maybe minus the fighting. He'd fill the role perfectly.

The girls chattered around me, but I barely heard it. I

traded my shoes for chunky blue-and-grey snowboarding boots that I laced snuggly into place with a toggle fastening.

Then the door trundled open in front of me, and the man himself stood in the frame. "Are ye ready?"

Viola plopped a warm hat on my head. "She's all set."

I reached out, taking Lennox's arms to jump down. Now, the cold barely touched me. Only my hands and face were exposed. I took a proper look around. Mhic Raith had a stark beauty, with its white slopes and craggy peaks. Beyond, glens delved down to reveal hints of glistening, frozen-edged lochs. Castle McRae was concealed on the other side of the mountain, and I liked that. The fact that Lennox could run a business but not spoil his view from home.

A flock of tiny birds investigated our vehicles.

"Ooh, snow bunting." Viola yipped. "Take note, Is. They don't freeze up here, so you won't either."

"Thanks for that. And for the clothes loan," I called back then caught the pair of gloves Viola tossed.

Lennox helped me slide them into place. He ducked and laid a chaste kiss on my cheek. "Ye are seriously cute in this kit."

"If I fall over, I'm padded enough to bounce. You look like an arctic explorer, all rugged and tough." I peered at him, trying to see the different kind of man he'd have to become. Lennox the chief. Lennox the husband and dad. Lennox the sensible, all the wildness bolted down.

An odd feeling had displaced the warm excitement of the morning. I'd been nervous on the plane, dying for him on the drive to Castle McRae, now I was...confused again. I shoved back the sensation, inwardly frowning at it for daring to spoil my fun. Then I took Lennox's arm and tipped my head to where his friend and Gordain pointed out features on the mountain.

"Are we going to plan out a building or what?"

Lennox grinned, and off we went. The snow crunched under our boots, and to our right, the four teenagers hefted snowboards from the cars and began their journey to the mountaintop, pulling themselves on a rope in the snow.

"How far does the road go?" Artair asked.

"In summer, ye can drive almost to the top. But it's a track, not a road so could be a struggle for lorries," Lennox answered. Then, complete with hand gestures and air sketches, he outlined his vision.

Lennox described a wide, round building at the summit, with wraparound windows and full facilities for winter sports. A ski-lift would take people from the bottom of the slopes, and floodlighting would extend the hours of use.

There would be a café, a shop, and transport to bring people in from Inverness and the bigger Cairngorms towns.

This was no half-baked idea. Uncle Gordain added his own thoughts from time to time—he owned half the mountain but, luckily, he approved—and Artair made positive sounds about construction potential.

I got into it, absorbed in the detail. Lennox's animation had me excited, and he asked my opinion, as if what I thought mattered to him. He even talked up my idea of using the place as a hiking centre in the summer, and how to adapt the ski-lift to allow walkers a fast ascent.

The sun shone, breaking through the grey cloud layer and, down the valley, the cousins boarded, howling with each well-taken swerve.

Artair returned to the car and collected some kind of tripod measuring equipment. He strode up the mountain and left us alone. Gordain did likewise. Maybe Lennox had subtly asked them to give us a moment.

He took a deep draw of the freezing air and planted his hands on his hips. "What do ye think?"

"Of your building? Amazing. Awesome. You should one hundred percent do it."

"Aye?" He smiled, glancing away to the expansive view before coming back to me. "It'll keep me busy, but I'll be available, too, for work on the estate in whatever needs doing."

"Is that what you want? Both?"

He wrinkled his brow. "Aye, now I think of it. I've never really had a choice about inheriting this place and my Da's responsibilities, but I don't mind that so much. It's the sharing of them that would be my problem. I need some parts of this to be mine alone."

"I get that. Two people can't both be the boss. Particularly not two alpha males like you and Callum."

"Exactly. I need this for myself or I dinna think we'll manage together. Or maybe I'm still unsettled from being out of the army." He took my arm and guided me across the snow field, heading for a ridge. "I had this other crazy idea while we were talking. Do ye remember telling me about an alpine village ye stayed in? Wooden chalets for tourists."

"Yes! When I went to watch Viola compete."

We reached the ridge, and Lennox pulled me in front of him. An icy wind blew, but in Lennox's arms, I was cosy. He pointed to a cluster of foothills below. Between them glistened the river that ran past Braithar and fed the loch.

"I liked your idea. Ye see there, the gap in the trees near the river?"

I squinted at the pretty spot. "That would make a gorgeous place for a house."

"Aye, it would." He turned me then, so we were face to

face, and a satisfied expression came over him. "Thank ye for confirming it."

"Are you thinking of building there?"

"Perhaps. We can talk more about that later."

"Can we? Why, what are we going to do now?"

Lennox eyed me. I backed away.

"I told you, I can't snowboard. It's beyond me."

"Ye can. And ye will."

I opened my mouth. "Don't try to tell me what to do, Lennox McRae. It'll get you nowhere—"

Before I knew what had happened, he'd pounced on me and scooped me up. "If ever a woman needed telling what to do, it's ye, Isobel Fitzroy."

Despite myself, I laughed. "Jerk! Put me down."

He slapped my backside. "Never."

I was in so much trouble.

Lennox carried me over his shoulder, tramping through the drifts. Then he seemed to think better of it and swung me around so I sat in his arms, facing him. Our favourite position.

There was a light in his brown eyes now, a sparkling kind of joy that had me staring. Snowflakes dusted his thick hat, and a few rested on his eyelashes. A bolt of emotion hit me out of the blue. Lennox was so fucking handsome. He liked me, though God only knew why, and I liked him.

Really liked him.

More than a crush.

"What are you looking at me like that for?" he said, low and sweet. "Ye should be scared about what I've got in mind for ye."

"Oh, I am," I said. But it wasn't over sliding around the mountain on a piece of wood.

I was afraid of something else altogether.

*A*t the summit of his mountain, I let Lennox clip me onto a snowboard. He showed me how to start, stop, and how to fall. Viola bounced on her board alongside, cheering me on before losing interest in my pathetic attempts and tiny successes, then it was just me and him.

Without the use of my feet, and with my hands having no purpose apart from flailing, I was wildly out of control. In a car, the machinery around me became an extension of my body. I could sense and adapt direction and speed. On snow, strapped to a board, I was at the mercy of other forces.

I never did this. Since I'd ditched school, I'd stopped letting myself be vulnerable.

But when Lennox praised me, or applauded my failures and called them practice, I wanted more. I wanted to make the big man happy and have more of his smiles aimed at me.

So I allowed it, his management of me.

We played on the mountain, until the sun neared the horizon, darker skies looming in the west.

As soon as I could make it happen, I had us both take a tumble in the crisp snow. Lennox rolled me on top of him, protecting me, and I wriggled up him and landed a kiss on his mouth. He gave a small huff of surprise but instantly moved his cold lips on mine.

Too many layers of clothes divided us. We had on helmets and sunglasses that clacked together, but this kiss was the only way I had of describing the new feelings inside me.

Lennox seemed to know. He rolled us again and reared over me. "You're enjoying yourself, aye?"

I raised a shoulder, dislodging snow. "Every time I fall, you pick me up. It definitely could be worse."

"I like picking you up."

"Huh, then I'll fall more often."

My guy pulled me up so I was on my knees, then removed his sunglasses. I did the same with mine.

"Wait until I get ye home, sweetheart. When I strip this gear off ye and take ye to my bed. See then how happy ye make me."

The exhaustion from the snowboarding lifted, and my body zinged alive. "Can we go now?"

"Race ye to the bottom."

16

FANTASY

*L*ennox

Getting off the mountain took far too long. We piled in the cars, shedding the bulky snow clothes. Gordain had already left, so the kids caught rides with us and my friend. Then Viola wanted to stop off at Braithar so she could grab a bag and stay over at Castle McRae. By the time we arrived home, Isobel was practically vibrating on her seat.

We shared excited grins and ducked inside the great hall.

"Ah, Lennox, just the man. Do ye have a minute?" a polite, wavering voice came.

I tore my gaze from Isobel and found an elderly man waiting inside the door. I instantly recognised Mr Campbell, one of Da's ghillies who worked on the estate, also a tenant. Da always invited people to wait inside the great hall, out of the weather, and with Da away, I was acting in his place.

I hid a frustrated wince and tipped my head at the man. "How can I help ye?"

"Nothing to fret about. Just a wee problem with the roof

at my cottage. It's leaking. If ye have a spare minute, I'd appreciate it."

Fuck, fuck, fuck. My balls ached and, in my mind, I was already upstairs, undressing my lass, but no. Life had other plans. I forced a smile and clutched Isobel's hand in an apology. She squeezed me back.

"That sounds urgent," she said with a kind smile for our interrupter.

"Aye, lass," Mr Campbell replied with a sigh. "It's been a worry for a while. It might be snowing today, but it'll be fair dreich in the spring, and we dinna want my walls crumbling."

Of course he had to save it up for now. I cast my mind over his cottage, trying to picture the roof. "Got a ladder out there? Any spare tiles or felt?"

"Naw. Not a thing," the man said happily.

"Let's get the car loaded up then," Isobel said. "There's a stack of tiles in one of the outhouses, right? Or there was a few years ago. I remember seeing them."

She started for outside once more, and I followed, miserable and bereft though grateful that she was coming along. A quick check on the tiles someone had piled in the kitchen shed showed us they were the right ones, and we were away, Mr Campbell in tow.

At his cottage, I ran up the ladder I'd hastily brought on the Land Rover's roof rack, while Isobel and the tenant waited below. He directed my search and I found the problem: two cracked tiles over a joist, letting in water. The felt would do for now so, thank fuck, it was a simple repair. I called down my findings, and Isobel brought me the replacements, one at a time.

With the first, she pinched my arse on her way back down. With the second, she handed it over then paused and took in the view, the last of the day's light a warm orange glow. Mr Campbell lived in a clearing in the thick forest that climbed the side of Glen Durie, a valley that skirted the mountain. Snow dusted the fir trees, and a thick silence reigned, punctuated only by chinks of tile on tile.

"Where I live is isolated," she said. "And so is your castle. But this takes the biscuit."

I straightened, sitting on the roof. I liked having Isobel here with me. It felt right for her to be around. "How do ye like it?" I asked quietly, gesturing at our surroundings.

"I fricking love it. My head is buzzing half the time. I imagine it's nice to come here and decompress."

"Aye, it's peaceful enough," Mr Campbell interjected from below, his hearing apparently undiminished by age. "We're a mile out from the castle, and I like my own space."

I leaned to see him. "Why is it ye walked to the castle today?" We'd given him a lift back with us.

"Car wouldnae start." He sniffed.

Isobel's eyebrows raised, then she carefully descended the ladder. She questioned my tenant, then their voices grew fainter. The crank came of the garage opening, and a bright light clicked on then Isobel's voice returned, excited. Mr Campbell had an antiquated Morris Minor, I'd seen him drive it any number of times.

I grinned to myself, picturing Isobel getting stuck in on the old car, then got on with my own job. When I was done, I replaced the ladder on my roof rack and went to find my lass. In the damp interior of the garage, her phone torch in hand as an extra light, Isobel poked about in the guts of the engine.

"You need to get this rust cleared out or it'll mean expensive repairs," she said.

Mr Campbell grumbled, his arms folded. "I cannae pay

for that. This car has run for forty years. I'm nae going to replace her. It's only me and Dougal who use her now."

Dougal, his Scottie dog, had wandered out to join us and now sat at Isobel's feet, gazing at her adoringly, just like I was.

"I'll do it," Isobel said, dusting off her hands. Then she glanced at me quickly. "I mean, if I'm around again any time soon. I'll happily do the work for free. Without it, it's going to cause you far greater problems."

I strode right over and grinned at her. She was a sweetheart through and through. Mr Campbell had interrupted us, but she was already making plans to help him further. "Is that what's wrong with it today?"

"Nope." She grinned. "Just a simple problem of running out of fuel. Mind if I borrow some of yours?"

I gestured for her to go ahead—I always carried a spare can in the boot—then gave Campbell a quick account of the works needed to his roof. It would go on the list of tasks Da and I would get to when the weather improved.

We left him a happier man than we found him, with a patched roof and working car, and I drove us back to the castle like my arse was on fire. It wasn't far, but when I next glanced over, Isobel slept in the passenger seat.

Snowboarding was exhausting, but I wondered how much she'd slept in the past few nights. I'd dreamt of her. Maybe she'd stayed awake thinking about me.

Carefully, I carried her from the car into the castle and to my rooms. She barely stirred when I put her on my bed except for curling into a ball.

Tiny. Heartbreakingly beautiful.

I should've returned downstairs. Blayne was throwing a party. He'd claimed it was for Isobel's birthday until I nixed the idea, but it was still going ahead. Since forever, the gang of cousins had slept over at the castle—they all lived on the estate anyway—but Skye could handle the mayhem they'd cause.

There was nowhere I'd rather be than here, even if my woman lay fast asleep.

Isobel had already taken off her jacket in the car, so I removed her shoes and drew my blanket over her. Then I stripped and took a shower in my bathroom. I braced myself against the tiled wall, half hard, half hungry, a lot weirded out.

Earlier, as we'd all stood together, talking about the mountain build, I'd had this startling vision. Of a house, and a family.

Isobel had been dead centre in that fantasy.

The same had happened when we spoke with the tenant. I could imagine her living on the estate, happily getting stuck in to making sure the place ran and the people were happy.

I'd wanted to tell her about it but I might as well ask her to marry me or something daft. She'd run faster than I could speak.

Or maybe she'd surprise me and add a dog or a couple of kids to my happy family picture.

Aye, no big deal, just her spending the rest of her life with me. I snorted to myself, letting the water beat down on my shoulders and neck.

"Something funny?" Isobel said.

I spun around, right as she opened the shower door. Fully clothed, Isobel—awake, upright, and in front of me—walked under the hot shower spray and into my arms.

Her action shocked me, but I didn't hesitate. Neither did she. Our mouths met in a hard, bruising kiss that had been hours in the making.

Isobel took my biceps, feeling me up, and I grabbed the hem of her short dress, wrenching it over her head. I stole a glimpse down and—oh fuck, yes—a delicate scarlet bra was revealed. Thin velvet stripes of material hugged the upper curve of her breasts, and her nipples pushed through the fabric, their dark circles plain.

"Red," I muttered insensibly.

Isobel laughed and ducked to remove her leggings. They went the same way as her dress, out the door and into a soggy pile on the floor. She closed us in and gazed up at me.

Water cascaded down Isobel's curves, soaking her.

I forced my lips to move. "I'm about to lose my mind, so if I forget to tell ye how utterly beautiful ye are, it's only because I've lost the ability to speak."

Isobel shivered. I cupped her cheek and laid my lips on hers, at the same time, crowding her to the wall. I loved Isobel's size, how petite she was to my brawn. It gave me a sense of power, as if I could protect her by sheer force. Right now, I intended to take my time with her.

At last, we were alone. No one would interrupt us or force us to leave. She was mine and I was hers. Even if the castle burned down, my tower would stay standing. This was on.

Our tongues danced together. My blood rushed south.

Isobel gave me control.

She held on as I loved her mouth, gasping when I kissed my way to her neck then down her body. I palmed her breasts, wrenching aside the cups of her bra to reveal her nipples.

I dropped to my knees, better to worship her.

Christ did Isobel have a gorgeous body.

"If I break any of your underwear, I'll replace it," I muttered, ogling her.

Isobel laced her fingers into my hair. "You can do pretty much anything to me right now and I'll let you."

"Good to know."

I enclosed her nipple in my mouth and sucked, rolling it with my tongue, doing the same with my fingers on the other side. Isobel moaned, and the sound had me harder than ever. I held on to her waist then let my hands wander to her hips, following the curves to grab her arse. I traced along the line of her thong to where it delved between her legs.

Gently, and admiringly, I stroked over the lacy fabric. Then, with a wrench, I tore it off her, snapping the side.

"Jeez," Isobel squeaked. She reached behind and undid her bra. It fell away from her breasts, leaving her gloriously naked.

Fuck, yeah.

I should've taken a second to appreciate her, but no, I was a goner. I drew her leg over my shoulder and landed my mouth right at the juncture of her thighs. I licked her clit then hungrily moved on to her folds. The taste of Isobel was my new addiction. Tart and sweet, fucking glorious.

"Lennox!" She yelped, holding on to my head.

"What, woman? Like this?" I speared her with my tongue then followed with my fingers, readying her.

"Yes. No. Do you know what I want?"

"Tell me." I kissed her clit and waited on her.

The water rained down around us, steam billowing.

"I want you to fuck me. Here and now. I woke up needing you inside me. I've wanted nothing else for a week. Please."

I raised my head and gazed up. Her cheeks were pink from the heat, or maybe from me.

"Your wish is my command." I stood and darted from the

shower, snatching a condom from the box in my cabinet and covering myself before the cooler bathroom air even touched me. Then I was back in front of her, in our wet wonderland.

Wordlessly, Isobel took my shoulders, and I lifted her so she was in my arms. We couldn't do this standing and facing each other—our heights wouldn't allow it—but there were plenty of other ways.

Now, she was nicely lined up, and my hard dick bobbed, ready and waiting.

"Every time I carry ye or hold ye in my arms, I imagine doing this," I said.

Isobel gripped me, her eyes wide. "I know. I do, too."

I lowered her, pressing her back to the wall, and lined myself up. I'd been so desperate for her, imagining this moment.

Her legs constricted around me. I notched against her tight heat and pressed home.

Holy fuck.

My cock sank deep inside. Then deeper, as I gave her time to adjust. I wasn't a small guy in any way. Isobel groaned, and I barely held myself together. A couple more inches, and another, and I was there, buried in my woman.

But I couldn't hold still for long.

Heat snaked up my spine, and I began a slow roll of my hips, pinning Isobel in place. She breathed hard, clutching onto me, and I took her mouth in another kiss. Shorter now we both needed more air.

Earlier, she'd demanded that I describe exactly what I wanted her to do when she blew me. I understood why. I wanted this to be everything she'd imagined.

I stared into her eyes.

"Like this?" I asked, marking my statement with a hard hit.

Isobel groaned, dropping her head to my shoulder. "Fast. Fuck me fast and hard as you can. Make me come here against the wall. Where I can't do anything but hold on."

No problem there. I was wound up and ready for speed.

I clamped her to me and upped the pace, sliding in and out in long thrusts. In a minute, I was fucking her like a madman. No holds barred. Full throttle. With one hand to the wall and the other holding her arse, I pounded into Isobel. I'd wanted this for so long and now I had her.

"Mine," I growled, no let-up in my onslaught.

She gasped and tightened around me. "There. Keep doing that. Oh fuck, Lennox!"

Her grip on me increased, and her nails bit into my skin. Isobel howled.

Inside, she pulsed around me and, in my arms, she shuddered, coming.

I slowed, and my frenzy simmered, and she saw out her shocks on my rigid dick. I was nowhere near ready to finish yet.

"That was one," I said, kissing her damp hair.

"Hell yes," she murmured, her voice blissed out. "Now put me down."

I pulled out of her and let her slither to the floor.

"Look at you, all crazy-eyed and wild." Isobel ran a finger over my cheek. "Don't worry, I'm not going to neglect you."

She trailed the finger down to my nipple and pressed it. Her mouth followed, her tongue lavering me. "Do you like that?" she asked.

It was okay. Anything she did was. But my preference was farther south. "Keep heading down," I said.

Isobel sank to her knees. She grasped my cock and

removed the condom in a flick of her wrist. I leaned over to shelter her from the shower spray—wouldn't want her to drown—and watched as she mouthed my end, flicking her tongue over the ridge.

God. I hauled in a breath, bracing myself. With my earlier blow job, it had been a race to the finish, now I wanted to savour every second.

I slowly fucked her mouth, shallow little movements. Isobel closed her eyes and alternated between sucking and licking me.

"Touch yourself," I ordered.

She did, and the sight had my balls tightening.

Then I had a better idea. My shower had a second attachment—a fast spray on a small head. I snatched it from the wall and turned it on. Spray jetted out.

"Use this." I handed it to her.

Isobel raised her eyebrows. She took the shower head and aimed it at herself. First over her breasts, the water beating on her nipples.

I caught my breath, enjoying the show almost as much as the action of her mouth on my dick. Then she went lower, directing it between her legs.

Her moan hit me square in the hormones.

Isobel moved her hand in small circles, in time with sucking me. I gripped my hands behind my neck, an elbow holding my position at the shower wall. Water hit my back. It was also hitting Isobel right on her clit.

So fucking hot.

Fuck. I needed to get back in there. I jerked up and hit the button to kill the shower. Then I grabbed Isobel from the floor and brought her to her feet. She staggered and grinned, then jogged to keep up with me in my haste to leave the shower.

"Where now?" she asked.

I snagged a towel and draped it around her before snatching up one for myself. "Bed."

We kissed, tumbling out of the bathroom and through my apartment's octagonal hall and into my bedroom. Isobel fell backwards onto my grey quilt. I landed between her legs and put my mouth right back on her pussy. Under my tongue, she was swollen and slick.

Isobel gripped my hair and directed me exactly where she needed me to go. She spread her legs wide and pushed up on her forearm, watching me. "You could win awards at this. Just, oh God! Like that."

I slid my tongue inside her, massaging her clit with unhurried circles. Letting every little sound she made tell me what to do.

Then I switched my tongue for two fingers, then three, and worked her G-spot, moving my mouth to suck on her clit.

Soon, she was moaning again and jacking her hips in time with my actions.

Then she stilled and dropped back, her pussy spasming around me.

I fucking loved this. Adored making her come. She was so responsive to everything I tried.

"Bring your dick here," she said, her tone a sexy rasp.

I shook my head 'no' and kissed her stomach then the tattoo under her breast. I took her nipple in my mouth next, lingering for a minute for the sheer pleasure it gave me.

Finally, I brought my mouth to hers for a long, dirty kiss. Isobel rolled to her side and took my dick in her hand, but I paused her.

"What?" she asked.

"I'm so fucking close to coming. Trying to decide how

and where to do it." I pushed her onto her back again and reared over her. I took her hands, then stretched them above her head, loving how she looked, bared to me, ready and willing. "Between your tits. In your mouth. Buried deep in your tight cunt. Maybe in your arse."

Fuck, the thought had my heart pounding double time.

Isobel took a deep breath, as if considering the options. "I told you earlier that I'm game for anything. What turns you on the most?"

"All of it." Her doing as I said. Letting me in.

"If you want my ass, you need lube."

"I don't have any. Never done it before." And fuck, now I hated that she had. She knew what to do.

Isobel tried to hide a smile. "You should see your face. Hey, caveman, neither have I. I read about it, though. Maybe next time?"

I grumbled agreement, almost too turned on to talk.

Shifting so I was kneeling either side of her, I took my dick in my hand and gave myself a couple of strokes. Isobel watched and licked her lips. Keeping her hands pinned, I leaned forward and dipped my cock into her mouth, trying anything that came to mind.

I moved my hips with her sucks and breathed hard, getting increasingly wound up.

Then I released her hands.

"Push your tits together," I said.

She did, a grin on her face.

Now, I pressed my dick between them, my balls hitting her chest. Shite, that was sexy, the erotic image of her round breasts encasing me. I thrust slowly, mesmerised by how her tits bounced. But we'd rapidly dried from the shower, and the friction of dry skin on dry skin wasn't ideal.

"Maybe need lube for this, too," I said.

"I guess so? All things to try out in the future."

I moved back down her body and took her knee in my hand, opening her up. Isobel lay there, letting me stare at her with no embarrassment.

"You're so fucking perfect," I choked out. "So pretty."

She didn't reply, but she closed her eyes and stretched her arms out farther. A clear invitation for me to do what I needed to do.

I fitted myself between her legs again and rubbed my cockhead in her folds, loving the moan she gave up when I glanced over her swollen clit.

"I want to make ye come again while I fuck ye. Like this. So I can see your face," I admitted.

Then I slid lower and pushed inside, just a fraction. *Christ, aye to this.*

"Um, condom?" Isobel said, not opening her eyes.

"Shite. Sorry." I leapt up and found another condom from the box left on the bathroom floor. Then I was sheathed and ready.

"Maybe another time for that, too," Isobel said.

Fuck. I got back into place, sat on my haunches, and drew her legs around my hips. Slowly, I entered her.

It had felt more sensitive without the condom, but this was still incredible. This time, I wanted to savour the sensation so I set an unhurried rhythm. Simultaneously, I worked her clit. It was irresistible, giving Isobel pleasure. She charged me up, giving me a raw need to claim her, even while I was fucking her.

She arched, pushing harder against my dick and my hand, but still she let me do the work. Surrendered to my control.

Power surged through me.

My muscles locked, and my breathing came hard.

Isobel drove her shoulders into the bed and, for a further time, clamped down on me. This time, she wasn't alone in coming. I threw back my head and let myself feel it all. Her throbs and how she trembled.

My own orgasm hit in slow stages.

My balls pulsed, and my last few thrusts became staggered. I roared Isobel's name, shocked by the force as I came deep inside her. A wave took me under, an explosion of lust and deep, long-held feelings. Finally, we'd got there.

My hunger for this lass was unending. My need for her couldn't be sated.

I collapsed down onto her body, and Isobel held me close, banding her arms and legs around me. I shuddered, trying not to crush her but lost to all sense.

"This is just the start," she whispered. "Think about everything we can do."

But I was far beyond that point. I'd skipped a few months and made a scene with her by my side, still mine.

There was absolutely no chance I was telling her that until I was sure she felt it, too.

17

YOU'VE GONE NUTS

*L*ennox

Hunger eventually drove us from my bed. Living in the tower, my own private space away from my family, had always suited me, but it was three rooms plus a gym on the floor below. No space for a kitchen. It made a great bachelor pad but it wouldn't work for much longer.

I wanted the house I'd envisaged. I wanted the woman, sitting at the end of my bed, fixing her air-dried curls into a clip there, too, taking half the responsibility of designing the rooms and the space.

Isobel glanced back and winked at me. "Where have you gone in your head, big man? You have the dopiest grin on your face."

"Miles away. Are ye ready?"

She jumped up and smoothed her dress. Luckily, her bags were in my room. Otherwise she'd be wearing a t-shirt of mine downstairs.

"Actually, I have a request," she said, eyeing me.

"Anything."

Isobel's cheeks pinkened, and she eyed me. "A couple of years ago, I saw a picture of you at a wedding. Sebastian showed me."

I cocked my head. "Aye. One of our tenants. I remember. What of it?"

"You had on a kilt."

I stared at her then, slowly, got her meaning. "Ye liked what ye saw? It turned ye on?"

Isobel pressed her lips together. Her flush grew. "I was so pissed off at myself because back then, I hated you."

"Ye don't hate me anymore." My grin spread, delight filling me at this new revelation. Had to hand it to kilts; lasses loved them.

"Nope."

"And you'll like me better if I changed into it?"

She dipped her head, and I strode to my wardrobe and found the garment. I stripped my jeans and boxers and kept my gaze on her as I wound the kilt around my waist and fastened it, just a black t-shirt on top. Then I stepped back into my heavy boots.

"Oh boy," Isobel uttered. "Big dick energy."

I snorted and slung my arm around her, leading her out the door. "What does that mean?"

"Something else I listened to in an audio book. None of your business."

We left the tower to strains of thudding music, coming from the great hall.

"Blayne's having a party," I said. "I forgot all about it. It was meant to be for ye, but I convinced him not to. Now it's just a bash."

"Fun!" Isobel squeezed my hand, and we rounded the corridor...to chaos.

Three dozen or so teenagers occupied the ancient space,

draped over the furniture or dancing. Someone had set up lights, and indie rock music blared.

My parents had parties here all the time, but those were usually more genteel. Neither Skye nor I had ever had the time to invite gangs of mates around.

"Hey!" Blayne yelled. "Uh-oh, the kilt is out. Lennox has gone all chief on us."

I rolled my eyes at my brother. For a smart kid—and he was always top of the class in every subject—he said some daft shite.

He sprinted over, bringing the attention of the room with him. "Isobel, now you've stopped doing...my brother," he said, his comedy timing spot on. "Can we talk?"

Isobel grinned. "Sure. Lead the way. Somewhere a bit quieter?"

She pressed up on her toes and kissed my cheek then disappeared into the dining room with Blayne. On the way, my brother snagged two bottles of beer from a cooler, popping the lids off using the stone wall as a lever.

I worked my jaw.

Blayne was sixteen. While I was sure he'd drunk alcohol before, it hadn't been on my watch. I scanned the room for my sister. Skye was nowhere in sight.

Cameron, my Uncle Wasp's son, sat with a lass, their heads close. He was only fifteen, but I couldn't see alcohol in his hands. I bypassed them, ignoring the other kids. I couldn't ignore the beer bottles scattering the floor. Nor the stench of cigarettes and vaping. I fucking hated smoking.

Near the fireplace, Artair propped up the wall.

I raised my chin at him. "Hey, man. Sorry for leaving ye."

He waved his bottle of water at me. "No worries. I had a blast today and I would be where you were if any woman would have me. I was just waiting to say goodbye before I headed home."

Artair lived on an island in the Inner Hebrides, off to the east. I had a suspicion he more than lived there, maybe even owned one, but he'd never said.

"Do ye need anything more from me on the build?" I'd already shared with him the plans.

"Nah, I'm good. Let me know the start date, and I'll work out a schedule. Depending on the weather, it shouldn't take six weeks to get the bones of the building made."

"I'm grateful." I was. Though Artair had been a contractor and not a serving soldier, having him around brought on a strong sense of missing my unit, even if leaving had been the right decision.

He gave me a bro hug, readying to leave.

"It's nice to see you happy," Artair said with a slap to my shoulder. "You're calmer now you're a civilian. Your girl-friend won't take shit from you, aye?"

Isobel hadn't agreed to be my girlfriend, but I raised my eyebrows at the second part of his statement. "She's a force to be reckoned with."

Did she make me calmer? I'd been more wound up than ever this past week. Then again, I hadn't wanted to fight.

I walked my friend to the door.

"Ah, wait. Have ye seen my sister around?" I added before he went.

Artair's forehead creased. "Aye. She was having words with Sebastian. She packed him off somewhere else. Braithar, I think she said. Your sister didnae go with him, though."

He gave me another slap to the back then left on his long drive, and boat ride, home. I closed the heavy door behind him and grumbled to myself. Skye and Sebastian were rowing. That wasn't good.

I tried the kitchen. Viola and Cait sat on the counter. They greeted me with grins and bright eyes.

"Are you and Isobel getting married? Can I be maid of honour?" Viola asked, putting her head on her hands and fluttering her eyelashes.

I gave her a look. "What are ye doing hiding in here? There's a bunch of kids out there and no one in charge."

"Blay's in charge. They're his friends."

Cait furrowed her brow. "One of Blayne's older friends asked me out earlier."

"Aye?" In my head, Cait was still a child. Not that I was my cousin's keeper, but the thought of her, Viola, or Blayne dating didn't sit comfortable with me. "Plenty of time for that when you're older."

"Oh, don't worry. I told him I was sixteen, and he ran a mile. Besides, I have no interest in men. Or women. Or anyone, really."

"You don't?" Viola cocked her dark head. "I do. But all the guys around here seem to think I'm aloof, and the ones on the snowboarding circuit change every year. Maybe someone older would be better?"

"What have we got going for food?" I muttered and moved away.

Cait nodded emphatically to Viola. "Oh! More experienced, too. That's what you need."

Jesus. I jammed my fingers into my ears. "Don't want to know. Stop talking."

They laughed, and I stomped away.

The crowd in the great hall was getting rowdier. Two boys scrapped, and their friends urged them on. I paused at the edge, debating intervening, but their swings were lazy, and both laughed when they connected.

I didn't want to ruin Blayne's party. Everyone called me bossy, but I wasn't always. Isobel was my main accuser, and I wanted her to only think good things about me.

Actually, I wanted to find her then carry her plus a mountain of food back to my room, but she was with Blayne so that would have to wait. I grumbled to myself, travelling past the rabble to climb the inner staircase to the bedroom wing and Skye's room.

A young couple blocked my path, kissing their way up the stairs.

"No. Great hall only," I barked at them.

They blinked at me then turned midstep and trotted back down again.

At Skye's door, I knocked, but there was no answer. I swung open the door, cautiously, but she wasn't in there. The guest room that Seb used on his visits was around the corner, and I tried that on the off chance, but no, it was empty, too. I texted my sister then headed back to the stairs.

I stood at the landing, careful of the fall of my kilt, and gazed out over the great hall. Blayne and Isobel reappeared, chatting. He had his arm casually slung around her shoulder, and she elbowed him, pointing out something across the room. Then Viola and Cait joined them, making a happy group.

Growing up, I'd never paid much attention to Isobel. She was just another one of the kids, though only two years younger than me. Now, I saw a whole different person. She was unlike anyone else I knew. So utterly real and honest.

Warmth crept through my veins. Isobel was fucking amazing. I wanted to talk to her, laugh with her, and bury myself in her until it was time for her to go, then set a date in the very near future for our next meet-up. But there was far more to my feelings than that.

As if she could sense me, my lass peeked up. Our gazes linked.

Dark, glittering promise shone in her eyes.

My boots drummed on the stairs, and I hit the flagstones at the bottom, driving forward bulldozer-style.

I arrived in front of her, and Isobel grinned up at me.

"Hey, you." She tilted her head. "You okay there?"

I was and I wasn't. Heat and panic mixed in me, though I had no clue why.

Isobel seemed to understand. "Catch you later," she said to my brother. Then she took my hand and led me to the kitchen.

I stood there helpless while she raided the fridge, then I scooped up the supplies she found. Isobel escorted me back to my tower, all while harbouring a small, secret smile every time she glanced at me.

As soon as we were behind closed doors again, I discarded the food and drink bottles to the coffee table in my lounge and pounced on my woman. Isobel seemed to share my need, and urgency had us stripping each other in record time. The single lamp in the living room lit our desperate moves.

"Keep the kilt," she requested.

Frantic, I pushed her onto the couch and ran to snatch the box of condoms from the bathroom. Then I was back in my happy place, between her legs with my mouth fused to hers, my kilt rucked up and my dick raring to go.

She stole my air and claimed my heart. Years ago, I'd called her a menace. She drove too fast and made me crazy. Isobel was a rollercoaster ride, and I could barely hold on for dear life. I'd break stuff for her. I'd tear myself to shreds for her.

"Stop thinking so much," she told me, and reclined nude on my cushions.

Damn, I'd never be able to see this sofa in the same way again.

Then she took my hip and brought my hard dick to her soft core. I slid inside with an unconcealed yell of relief. It hadn't been an hour since we'd been doing this before, but the flood gates had opened.

"I never want to stop fucking you," I said, gritting my teeth and working my length in and out of her. The kilt was in my way now, so I undid the belt and tossed it to the floor. "Get used to living in my bed."

Isobel moaned and met me blow for blow. She didn't answer me but she urged me on, grinding into me.

In no time, we were panting. I caught her chin and had her look at me. Unlike before, I wasn't trying to hold off coming. We'd be doing so much of this, there was time to try out every connection we could imagine. But this wasn't about getting off either. It was a start.

"I'm yours," I said. "Ye hear?"

Isobel's forehead creased in a frown. "Lennox?"

"Aye?"

"Harder."

I grinned and did as commanded. Tonight, we were going to talk. Whether she liked it or not. But first, this.

Isobel closed her eyes and moved a hand to her clit. She gasped, sending me delirious, and then we were both coming. Her first spasms kicked off my orgasm, and I growled, resisting the urge to go still until she'd finished. Then I was there, and my balls emptied into her.

My muscles gave out, and I dropped down. My breathing

came short, and my mind was at peace. Contentment settled through the swirl of chemicals, bright lights, and serious fucking surety.

"Am I crushing ye?" I managed.

"No," she said, quiet. "Well, a little. But I like your weight on me. Weirdly."

Not weird at all. Still, after a while, I shifted so I was at her side, just breathing and feeling. Letting myself soak up the mindfuck of happy feelings. My hard-on softened, and I pulled out then quickly disposed of the condom. Isobel held out her arms, and I wrapped myself around her.

"We need to eat. And talk," I murmured into her hair.

She grumbled. "Yes to eating. No to any heavy chats. They are banned."

Throughout the day, I'd come to a realisation. Claiming Isobel wasn't going to be easy. She resisted all but the physical emotions I'd offered her.

Still, I knew her.

"You like me," I said. "I know that to be true so I'm going to tell ye some facts."

She shoved at my chest, but I didn't budge, caging her to the couch.

"You're mine and I'm yours. If ye don't want a label beyond that, then fine. I dinna give a fuck. But ye are in here." I took her hand and placed it on my chest, right above my heart. "No amount of complaining is going to change that."

"Fine. I've made a home inside your mighty pectoral muscles. Can we eat now?"

Instead of worrying about her lack of enthusiastic reply, I just gazed at her. I let the moment draw out and set my expectations. She was afraid of this, of intimacy. I couldn't force her to tell me she wanted me, too, but her actions said everything.

She'd come to me, she'd got on a snowboard to please me, she'd helped my tenant and made plans to return.

A huge grin took over my lips.

I had the idea that once Isobel made up her mind about something, or someone, they were there to stay.

"Stop grinning at me like that," she said, though her own mouth curved. "I'm about to die of starvation, and you're smiling like a crazy man."

"Totally crazy," I admitted.

I let her up, helping her stand.

"Don't finish that sentence," she warned. "You're not crazy about me. That would make you legit insane in the head, and I don't want to be the one to tell your parents why you've gone nuts."

I broke out in a laugh and guided her to my bedroom. We dressed, me in a t-shirt and boxers and her in another of my shirts plus her own underwear. The sight of her in my oversized t-shirt had me pinning her to the wall and attacking her mouth.

"Food," she said after some seriously sexy kissing. "More of this after we've recharged."

"Deal." I kissed her on the nose, and we started on the food.

While we ate, I stuck on a movie. Isobel half watched it but more, I caught her stealing glances at me.

Fine, lass. Work it out however ye want.

"I'm flying out with Skye tomorrow," she said suddenly.

"Aye, for her research trip to the States."

Isobel giggled, the prettiest sound. "We're going shopping. I guess you could call it research because she's applying for her internship soon, but I'm just going along for the ride."

I was going to miss her. The realisation had me frowning at the sandwich I'd thrown together from the cold cuts.

"Do you really have a thing for lingerie?" she asked casually.

"You in lingerie. Not the underwear itself."

"Uh-huh. Do you have a favourite?"

I blinked, considering it. "Anything I can get off ye fast."

Isobel poked me with her toes. "I'll bear that in mind."

With the food demolished, I took my lass to bed. I had another day of her at my side, then she'd vanish.

I had so much shite to do. Finally talk to my da about the build, then get on with pushing the project. More, I needed a next date with Isobel in my diary.

"What day do ye get back from the US?" I asked her softly. Evening had turned into night, and we were naked again, a third or fourth round of spectacular sex leaving us content in a pile of tangled limbs, my blanket and the heat blazing from me keeping us snug.

Isobel raised a lazy shoulder. I'd done the impossible: exhausted her.

"We're there three days."

"Come back here. Or I'll come to ye." I kissed her arm, trailing my lips up.

"Maybe," she said.

"Not good enough," I muttered. But I wasn't going to push. Instead, I sighed, tucked my head against hers, and closed my eyes.

Isobel and I were a thing now. No matter how long it took her to realise.

18

A LION

*I*sobel

In the lead-up to a race, I typically didn't sleep much. My head would be full of the speed I'd need to take the corners and ticking over the mechanics or performance of the car I was driving. The anticipation wasn't uncomfortable, though. I got by fine on a little sleep and a lot of preparation.

Contrary to that, when I'd been at school, the buildup to tests or exams had me nauseous. I still couldn't sleep, and I'd be doing the same rehearsal, but with fear enclosing me in its claws. I'd sweat, pace, and be unable to concentrate. Even when I'd had private tutors at home, the moment of testing always did me in.

I crumbled under examination. I nearly always did well in driving.

What I couldn't work out was, while lying in Lennox's bed, wrapped up in his huge, naked body after a night of incredible sex, was which side of the camp my brain was on when it came to him.

Lennox didn't make me feel sick, that was for sure.

But I knew with absolute certainty that I'd fail the test he wanted to put me through.

He'd told me, face to face with no room for denial, that he was mine and I was his. I really fucking liked him saying that, even if it staggered me.

Even if it was wrong.

I wasn't the woman Lennox would end up with. He just didn't know me well enough to realise that yet.

Sure, we'd been in each other's company a lot over the past couple of weeks, but the worst he'd seen of me was my shitty handwriting.

Huh. No. He'd also witnessed my temper. And my awesome ability to try to avoid tough situations.

But I hadn't been forthright with my full story, and the more I mashed it up against his, the worse we fit. I didn't want to hurt him.

He was too fucking amazing to string along.

"I can almost hear your brain whirring," Lennox said, squeezing me. He stretched out his arms then banded them around me once more. "How long have you been awake?"

"Don't know. A while."

Dawn's light crept through the small arrow-slit windows in his tower bedroom. There were no curtains or blinds over them, so I guessed he never slept in.

I sat up and pointed, clutching the blanket to my bare breasts. "How do you take an afternoon nap if it's light in here?"

Lennox followed my finger. He considered the row of little windows as if he'd never seen them before. "We'll cover them. I'll screw in some hooks if ye like naps."

These little plans he was making. I sighed and drew my knees up, shuffling out of his arms. "Don't change anything for my sake."

"I am yours and you are mine," he said slowly. "I told ye. That means I'll change anything for ye."

This was getting out of hand. I needed to lay out the facts.

"Lennox, can you sit up a minute?"

He did, a frown marring his handsome, sleepy brow.

"Where do you see yourself in a few years' time?"

His lips tweaked. "Is this a job interview?"

"Seriously."

He took a deep inhale. "Ye know I've struggled coming out of the military? That's because I need something to do. All the time. I'm nae good at being idle. The snowboarding centre will be my focus. That'll keep me sane while I pick up managing the estate alongside Da."

"Right." I chewed my lip.

"And I'm going to build my own house," he continued. "On that spot I pointed out to ye yesterday. I'll need to get that idea worked through, but it's a goer. I can't live here for the rest of my life."

"Can I tell you how I picture you?"

He gazed at me. "Aye. Do. I'd love to know."

"A leader. A respected part of your community. With a pretty wife and sweet, clever children. People will adore your family. They'll think you're perfect because you will be. You'll build a lovely house and fill it with your happiness."

Lennox took my face then kissed me, his lips soft. "Want to know what I see when I visualise that house? A workshop not far away. A garage for a skilled mechanic to run her business from. Plenty of work in Scotland besides Campbell's Morris Minor."

Hurt, swift and jagged, sliced through me.

I winced. "Don't. Please. Can't we keep this for what it is? We're attracted to one another maybe because of that first kiss thing, or maybe because you're... What did you call it? Confused from being out of the army? But we aren't going to get any further than this."

"Why not?" His tone darkened.

"Because I'm not like you! I'm not ever going to be in a role like yours. I'm not smart. I won't be that pretty wife. You're here making all these plans while I'm barely coping with the idea of setting up my own business. In my parents' garden. Do you see?"

"No. I have no idea what you're talking about."

"You know I can't write? It's a condition called dysgraphia. I had years of physical therapy to get to the crappy stage I'm at now. But that's the easy bit of my brain. There's a whole list of my failings in a report somewhere. The educational psychologist my parents took me to called it a non-specific learning disability, but that's crap, right? I'm just stupid. I do idiotic things all too often. If I'm tired, I can't tell the time. If I'm up against facts I don't like, I see red and fly off the handle. That isn't me being petulant, it's just what I am. So how do I fit into that picture we just drew of you?"

Not the nice wife. Not the mother of clever children.

Lennox watched me, the smile from his lips gone. But he didn't speak. Instead, he actually listened, as if he was taking me seriously.

I wavered, wondering at myself. Did I want him to yell or did I want him to give in?

"Okay," he said simply. "I understand."

A dangerous chill slunk into the air between us.

I stared at him, for once, not just in utter lust, though his strong fighter's body was laid out like a feast. "Is there any more to your sentence?"

Lennox snapped out a hand and caught me around the back of my neck. Then he dragged me to the mattress and reared over me. "Nae right now. Ye told me your history, and I'm glad for it. I hate that ye suffered, but it's up to ye to work out what you're doing with all this snarling. But first, ye have to handle the fact that you've royally pissed me off."

I shivered, hopelessly turned on by his rough move and dominance. Lennox bent down and laid his mouth on my neck. Not a kiss, but a bite. A testing of his teeth over my jugular. Like a lion would do to his mate to show her who was boss.

I moaned, instantly wet.

Lennox took rude grabs of my breasts with rough hands, and he pinched my nipples then moved lower, seizing my legs and parting me to give him room for what he wanted. His mouth took mine in a hard, ravishing kiss.

I took it.

I let him.

Then his fingers were at my core and skating over my clit and through my folds. He drove two inside me, and I arched up, so fucking turned on.

His mouth curved into a savage smile. Then he lifted off me and yanked me so I flipped over to my front.

"Dinna ye move, woman," he warned me.

I buried my face in the sheets and closed my eyes. Every inch of my body had lit up, every nerve ending begging for his touch. I trembled, waiting.

A foil wrapper tore, then Lennox knelt between my legs. He spread them wider, around his thick thighs, and laid his hands on my ass, lifting my hips so I was facedown and ass up. He caressed my cheeks and parted them and ran his thumb down my crease. He used his dick next, rubbing the head up and down me, getting himself wet and stroking himself though he was harder than steel already.

All of this was for him. The fact that I was getting off wasn't of interest to him.

Fuck, it turned me on.

Without warning, he entered me with one, swift thrust.

"Ye give me this shite about how we aren't right," he said, his voice a jagged-edged snarl. "Ye give all this chat, but it's bollocks, aye? So hear me. I'm going to fuck it into ye so next time ye see me, ye won't question right or wrong."

He marked his speech with ferocious thrusts, each hitting a pleasure centre deep inside me.

I cried out, wildly excited.

With that, he pulled out and lifted me into his arms. He changed position to sit at the top of the bed, against his oak-panelled headboard. He had me on his lap, facing him.

Now I was on top.

I'd ridden him in the night, but it had been pitch-black, and we'd been too lazy to turn on the lights. Now, his attention was fully on me. He remained perfectly silent as I adjusted my balance. Then he put his hands behind his head, gripping his own neck.

"Show me what ye now know, Isobel," he said.

I had no idea what he was asking for. But I bent down and kissed him, at the same time sinking on his dick. He didn't kiss me back but let me do the work. I began a slow ride.

He had free rein of my body but he seemed to be trying to prove something. His fingers interlaced behind his head and he held his huge body taut.

Still, I kissed him. Fucked him.

I should have stopped. I should've let him go. But this was too perfect. I kept up my unhurried rise and fall on his dick and, eventually, Lennox's hands landed back on me. He held my breasts and drew out my nipples. Then he gripped my ass, running his fingers beneath, feeling over where we were connected. He played with me, seeming to know exactly what to do to turn me on more.

All I had to do was keep moving, keep making love to him, and he added the rest.

My ass, my breasts, my clit. Each in turn got his attention until I could barely take it.

Then he broke our lips apart and put his mouth to my ear. "Mine," he said. Then, "Yours." Each punctuated with an upwards thrust of his hips.

I shattered, coming, and seeing stars. My control vanished, and Lennox took over. He claimed my mouth, kissing me through my climax and gave a broken cry against my lips when his own hit.

I'd never known anything like it. Like him. I sprawled on his chest, the closeness, the warmth sinking in. He held me and didn't let go. His heart beat under my ear, a strong and tender sound that belied the harder edges of its owner.

Anger still brewed in him, I could sense how he held it back.

"When ye choose the site for your workshop," he eventually spoke in my ear, "it'll be fine Scottish soil I break to build it for ye."

A thudding came from the stairs. "Lennox!" Blayne yelled.

Lennox growled discontentment and snatched the blanket over my nakedness.

The apartment door rattled. I slid off Lennox, making sure I was covered.

"Dinna ye dare come in here," he called.

"I wasn't about to. Gross. But I need your help," Blayne whined. "I just woke up, and ye should see what some fucker has done downstairs. Lennox!"

Lennox closed his eyes briefly. "Two minutes," he replied.

He left the bed and stripped off the condom, then tied it up and discarded it to the bin. From his dresser, he wrenched out jeans and a sweatshirt and quickly dressed. Then he prowled back and knelt on the bed. Free of hesitation, as if he knew he was about to lose the right, he stooped and found my willing mouth again.

I kissed him, with force, showing him that I, too, had teeth.

Then, without another word, he was gone.

---

*I*n the great hall, Skye and Lennox stood side by side, Blayne in front of them. Both had their hands on their hips and identical frowns. Even though they were entirely different in shape and size, the two had never looked more like twins than they did now.

I peered around them to see what the fuss was about.

I'd taken the world's quickest shower then dressed and ran downstairs, not wanting to miss out on the drama.

Oh boy.

Across the floor of the great hall, green spray paint marked out a... I tilted my head. A giant dick.

My jaw dropped, and I gaped at Blayne. "Who did this?"

He shrugged, sheepish. The kids from last night had gone, but the evidence of his party remained in strewn cans and bottles. And the huge green penis.

"I just woke up and it was there. No one I know does that sort of shite. Christ, my head hurts," Blayne complained. He ran his fingers through his messed-up, dark-blond hair and winced.

Skye sighed. "How much did you drink last night?"

Lennox only glowered. He didn't look at me.

"I don't know. It's not like I've never been drunk before. I'm not a kid," Blayne muttered.

"Aye, ye are! You're sixteen!" Lennox spluttered. "Case in point: ye couldnae control yourself and ye couldnae control your friends."

Blayne grimaced and stuck his hands in his pockets. "I'll clear up. Just stop yelling."

Lennox inhaled through his nose. "Get in the kitchen. We need soap, hot water, and scrubbing brushes."

The two brothers marched away.

Skye sought my gaze and rolled her eyes. "Da would freak if he came home and saw this."

"Lucky he isn't back until later. You know, Seb and I used throw wild parties at Belvedere," I said. "It's a rite of passage."

She nodded and stooped to collect pieces of broken glass from under a chair. "Lennox and I never did it. That's probably why he's cross at Blayne. Da was always harder on us than our brother."

I got stuck into helping. We found boxes in the store room and collected up the recycling while Blayne and Lennox scrubbed the green paint. Every now and then, I snuck glances at Lennox. His gaze never came to meet mine.

One by one, Viola, Cait, and Cameron emerged from the bedroom wing, yawning. They gazed wide-eyed at the scene. We soon had them pitching in.

My brother never showed, though. Nor had I seen him last night.

"What happened to Seb?" I asked Skye, out of earshot of everyone else.

Her mouth turned down, and she pushed back a stray

lock of yellow hair from her eyes. "I sent him to Braithar. A while ago, he talked about taking helicopter flying lessons. You know Gordain offers an intensive course? I told him to do that. It's a whole month of keeping busy." Then she added, even quieter, "Better than getting his face beat in anyway."

I heaved a sigh. "Good. It'll keep him occupied."

"That's right. And in the meantime, you and I are flying out tonight!"

"Can't wait," I said. And I meant it.

Things with Lennox had got intense quickly. He'd been too hasty in the things he'd said, and space would clear his head of my mess.

Maybe the same applied to me. I still stubbornly clung to the thought that he wasn't for me. But as the day drew on, after lunch with the cousins and a run into Inverness for specialist paint remover—which finally got rid of Blayne's giant green dick—I became increasingly uncomfortable.

My defiant, smiling, false front couldn't stay in place.

Lennox and I had barely spoken. He'd pass me without a single touch, but all the hairs on my arms would rise. I'd avoided him, wanting to get away from the feeling I was making things worse.

Yet nothing diminished the absolute need I had to be around him.

Even in his tower, as I packed my bags alone, readying to leave with Skye, I did it reliving the kisses, the tight holds, and the painful closeness we'd shared. I was addicted. He was my drug. My body ached, needing a next hit, though my mind knew I shouldn't want it.

He didn't come up to the room, no matter how long I lingered.

Finally, it was time to leave.

I trudged down the spiral steps, my bag over my shoulder and my heart in tatters.

Lennox waited at the bottom.

"I'll take ye both to the airport," he said.

"Thanks."

"I want ye to think about me, while you're away."

I stared at the gaps in the stone floor. "You need to come to your senses, which means I need to get out of your head."

"Naw. It's the other way around."

"Aren't you listening to a word I say?"

Then Lennox did something startling. He caught my hand and hauled me against him. His expression had turned serious and...emotional. Unlike any face of his I'd seen before.

"Yours." He pressed my fingers to his chest. Then he laid his on the skin over my heart. "Mine."

This wasn't the kind of nonsense spouted when overrun by sex hormones.

It was real.

We were dressed, and nothing clouded his view. I couldn't hide from this.

It was all I could do to stand firm under his scrutiny.

"You're mad," I choked out.

"Wrong. I'm still fucking fuming, and that's my problem to deal with. Ye heard what I had to say, now go and do what ye need to do," he replied, that dangerous tone back in his voice.

Lennox released me then escorted me back into the great hall. His sister was waiting, and the three of us got into his car, and he delivered us to the airport. There, he kissed her on the cheek but only gave me one long, pointed look.

Then we had to leave and, once again, Lennox walked away.

19

FRUSTRATION

*L*ennox
Da called me into his office. My parents had arrived home late last night, and Blayne and I had shown them the extremely clean flagstones and told them what happened. Weary from travelling, they seemed happy enough that it was fixed, though the air in the great hall still smelled of paint, spilled beer, and cigarettes, and Blayne still moped, complaining of his hangover.

I felt their disapproval. If there was one thing I hated most in the world, it was disappointing my da.

Now, in the cold light of the next morning, Da waved me in and gestured for me to sit. I dropped into the leather chair.

We were too alike, Da and I. I knew something was bothering him. It only grated on my ragged nerves.

"Blayne has decided to leave school," he said.

"What? Why?"

"He wants to be like Viola and become a pro-snowboarder."

I pinched the bridge of my nose. Blayne was good, but

he wasn't a competition winner. "I hate to say it, but he isn't ready. Not yet. Viola is a different class of athlete. Besides, she hasn't given up her education. Gordain and Ella have tutors for her. Like Isobel had when she left school."

Da huffed. "He said that Isobel told him to go for it. Apparently they had a chat, and he took from it that leaving school was a grand idea."

For fuck's sake. I pulled a face. "Ye know she wouldnae have said that. She left school because she had problems. Blayne doesn't have any, other than thinking boarding is more fun."

"Aye. I agree. But he's insisting. I dinna want to come down on him like a ton of bricks but I also have no intention of letting let him waste his time." My father regarded me for a long moment. "Which brings me to my next point. Blayne told me you'd revived your idea to build on the mountain."

I squared my shoulders. When I'd been eighteen, we'd had a brief conversation about this, and he'd told me to wait until I could manage it on my own. Now was the time. "I need a project, and a winter sports centre will be good for employment and good for the kids. Both Blayne and Viola would be able to use it. I have the idea sketched out—"

Da held up a hand. "Not now, aye? Ye see where Blayne's mind has gone. If ye place a training facility in his reach, there will be no excuse. We'll never get him into a classroom again."

I stared at my father, at the resolute set of his jaw. "It's more than a place for him to play. And if ye want to, we can ban him from there other than at the weekends."

"Sorry, Lennox. I have need of ye elsewhere. For now, at least." On the wall of his office was a huge, wood-carved map of the estate. Da leapt up and strode over to it.

I knew this map well. I'd studied it as much as I'd walked the land it covered.

"There are half a hundred other projects ye can work on." Da pointed out an expanse of boggy land far to the north, describing how part of it needed draining to keep the footpaths usable. Then there was farm management, fences and walls, cottages that needed repairs for their tenants, including Mr Campbell's roof. The stuff we'd been doing for years.

With enthusiasm, he trod on my dream and gave me a task list, just like he'd done when I was a teenager.

Was this my future? Isobel might've been wrong or right with the way she'd seen it, because I did have to become an estate owner, like my father. I needed to find a way to work alongside him. But did it have to be like this?

Da spoke on, and I considered my alternative—to go into business with my grandfather. London. An office, probably.

I didn't want that either. No. I'd carved out a path and now I wanted to follow it.

I interrupted Da with a raised hand. "Stop for a minute. I know ye think it'll be bad for Blayne, and I do want to take on management of the estate, in time, but the mountain project isn't a pipe dream for me. I've worked hard on it. It's a phone call or two from being underway, and in a few months, after the snow's gone, the building work could be complete."

I tapped on the mountain on the map. "I want to do this first. Hear me out."

A while later, I left my father's study. I'd made my case and, to his credit, he'd listened. But he hadn't approved it, and he'd made the point that the money for the build still needed to be found. I knew this. Even with free labour from my old unit, I'd still budgeted for materials, specialist trades, and then a year of operation before I turned a profit. It wasn't an insignificant sum.

Accordingly, a dull edge of frustration bore down on me. I was pissed off that Blayne had almost scuppered my plans and unfairly annoyed at Isobel for encouraging him. More so, after a day, she still hadn't been in contact, and that bugged the fuck out of me.

All my sureness about her having feelings for me crumbled, I'd been convinced because she'd freaked out so much. Now I wasn't so sure.

Whatever we had between us balanced on a knife's edge. Abroad, and obviously not thinking about me, she could decide to call a halt to it all.

The idea had my gut churning.

Then Da's reaction to my plans had left me even more unsettled. Though he'd eventually listened, there was no guarantee he'd say yes.

Isobel had implied I didn't know my own feelings, and I couldn't deny the fact that I was spinning. Maybe she'd been the one of us making sense.

I stalked back to the tower, needing to be alone.

Emotions whipped wildly at me.

Everything felt off. I was the wrong shape, and trying to fit into multiple places but failing. With my da, who wanted me to pull one way while I pulled the other, with my lass who couldn't tell me that she wanted me at all.

This had been my problem forever. It was why I'd got

into fighting, so I could offload my excess of energies into the world. Otherwise they built in me, leaving me pent-up.

Wanting to fucking break things.

Just like I was now.

For a couple of hours, I stewed in my annoyance in my apartment. The ghost of Isobel taunted me. My bed smelled of her. My couch only brought memories of what I'd had but might never see again.

My phone rang. Sebastian. The wrong fucking Fitzroy.

I snatched it up answered the call. "Aye?"

"Nox. You around for a drive tonight?" Seb asked. He was still staying at Braithar.

My spine tingled, and my muscles primed. He wasn't offering a casual couple of hours behind the wheel. If he'd arranged a fight, I needed to be there.

Fuck it, I needed in.

"Name the time," I replied.

20

WEDDING DRESS

*I*sobel

A gentle knock came at my hotel room door. I opened it, and Skye entered, her eyes wide in concern as she peered at me. Yesterday, on the flight to New York, I'd developed a migraine. It had been the worst flight of my life with no painkillers and no ability to properly rest. I'd slept long and hard to recover once I'd hit my bed.

"How are you now?"

"Normal, I guess?" I flexed my neck. "I haven't had one of those since I was a kid."

I used to get migraines all the time, growing up. But they'd stopped after I reached my mid-teens, and I'd assumed they'd cured themselves.

"Too much big thinking." Skye tapped her own forehead.

I burst out in a startled laugh. "I'm in no danger of that. Hang on a sec. I'll grab my things and we'll get out of here."

I shrugged on my blue peacoat and shouldered my bag. Skye went straight to the window. We'd booked into a hotel in central Manhattan with easy access to shops and sites.

Outside was a sheer drop fifty storeys down to the busy city roads.

For a woman raised in rural Scotland, Skye loved the city. Even now, she gazed in wonder at the view. Her mother, Mathilda, was half English and half American, and Skye held a US passport and had studied over here.

We left my room and headed to the ear-poppingly fast lift. It was waiting, so we walked right in.

"What have you been up to this morning?" I asked Skye.

"I scoped out the office I might be working in, if I'm lucky. Then I called a friend for a chat over lunch."

"Which friend?"

"Amber Warwick. She's been blowing up my phone for days so I thought it time I called her back."

I'd just pressed the glowing white button for the lobby and I froze, finger out. I hadn't had any time with my friend to tell her what had gone on over the past couple of weeks. This trip was going to be our catch-up. I guessed her brother hadn't mentioned anything either.

"Whew." I blew out a breath and straightened. "I had a run-in with the Warwick family not long ago. Did she mention me?"

Skye blinked. "No! Though I said you were here with me. She asked us both to drinks when we got back home. I thought it might be fun."

I wrinkled my nose. The plunging lift sent my stomach in a whirl.

Skye echoed my expression. "Or not? You know, she did go on about Lennox a lot." She trailed off, as if remembering the secret she had with her friend.

"I know about Amber and Lennox," I said. "He told me."

"He did? It's always bothered me, what I asked him to do. I felt so sorry for her at the time, less so now as I get the impression I was played." She tucked away a smooth length of blonde hair. "Can I tell her he's off the market? It would be nice to stop her attempts at using my brother."

Skye wanted to know what I was doing with Lennox. Hell, I did, too.

The lift dinged and let us out. Skye put her arm through mine, and we strolled through the lobby and out into the brisk winter day. A chill wind had us hustling for a cab.

"Macy's, please," Skye directed.

We were going to scope out a number of wedding dress designers in the Garment District, as well as go shopping for ourselves. We huddled in the cab, and I pondered her Lennox-sized question.

"Can we do a brotherly information swap? I'm worried about Sebastian and I'm hoping you can tell me something good," I asked.

Skye sighed. "I'll happily talk about him, but he and I... We're not a couple. We never will be. I don't think that's what you want to hear."

The seat leather squeaked in complaint under my elbow as I shifted to gaze at my friend. "God. I always thought the two of you would get married. You've always been so close."

"I love him and he loves me. That isn't the problem. But we're not *in* love." She dropped her head back on the seat, and our cab pulled out into the slow traffic. "I'm part of his problem. He hates the fact that *we* never happened. I care about him so much, but do you know we've never even kissed?"

I'd been so wrong about them. I'd imagined a dozen reasons why they hadn't got it together. A lack of the right kind of love was never one. "I assume you two were kind of beyond that stage. Stealing kisses and sneaking off."

Skye blew out a heavy breath. "Nope. Imagine kissing Sebastian. You, I mean."

"Gross!"

"Exactly. That's how he once described the idea of kissing me. Like he'd be laying his lips on his sister."

Ouch. "I'm so sorry." I reached out and took her hand. "That was a shitty thing for him to say."

"But honest. And I felt similar, too. It's all my fault, I think."

"How can it be your fault?"

Skye shook her head, dismissing the question. "All this was before he joined the army and I went away to university. He said that once we were the other side of his service and my studies, we should try..." She wrinkled her nose delicately.

"Try... What?" My brain caught up. "Sleeping together? Ew."

"Exactly! He repeated the idea the other day, and it was awful. I could see in his expression how he hated the thought. Like it caused him physical discomfort and I repelled him."

My flipping brother. "Then why the hell was he suggesting it?"

"You know better than I do how stubborn he is. He's got it in his head that we should be a couple because our families always wanted it, and we always said we would when we were little, so he's determined to see it through. He's believed it since childhood, therefore it should happen."

"Even if it makes you both miserable? I've got to be honest here, you sound trapped. Both of you."

Skye paled. For a moment, my confident, put-together friend appeared vulnerable. "I've felt that. And I told him so, which hurt. Badly. Yet once I spoke the words, it was freeing.

Both of us have spent years feeling awful because we slept with other people. Last week, Sebastian asked me if I'd ever fallen in love. I haven't, and he thinks there's something in that. Like if we keep holding out for each other, something will change."

This was a fucking tragedy. "He's an idiot."

Skye gave a wan smile but didn't agree.

"What did you make of Artair, Lennox's friend?" I asked, my mind leaping back to the heated look they'd shared at Castle McRae.

She slid a glance my way. "Why do you ask?"

I chewed my lip. "Because the two of you saw each other then burst into flames."

Skye snorted. "We did not. It was nothing. Just fleeting eye contact."

"Does that happen often?"

"No. Never," she admitted. "Fine. I might have thought about it. Him. But I don't even know the man. What keeps going over my mind is the fact that I'd finally decided to cut Sebastian free, then the very next eligible guy I saw, boom, fireworks. It was just a reaction, don't you think?"

I shrugged. "No idea. I'm just pointing something out here. I've never seen you look at anyone that way before. Stuck on him and unable to turn away. You never stared at my brother like that."

"Exactly!" She waved a flustered hand. "Sebastian and I have no chemistry. None. I see him like my brothers, except moodier and surlier. The sort of woman he needs would be someone who could tolerate that or even enjoy it. The fact that I had a lightning jolt of attraction for a stranger says everything."

Her cheeks pinkened, and her gaze distanced. "I don't even want a relationship. Not for a long time. Once I have my career underway and a healthy amount of time has passed, maybe I'll be ready. Then, I'll be hunting down the punch-in-the-gut big feelings that you and Lennox have, where you can't keep your hands off the other person. Where a man will revolve around me the way my brother orbits you. When that happens, I'll know. He'll be the one."

She blew out a weary breath, but I'd gone still.

It was so strange, hearing her assessment of mine and Lennox's...relationship. She'd only seen us for the past couple of days at Castle McRae, and even then, we'd been fractured and prowling around each other.

My mouth moved of its own accord. "I have no idea where I'm at with your brother. I can't even tell him, or myself. All I know is that I care about him, but it won't work out long-term. Whatever we have now is temporary."

"Why?" Skye refocused on me.

"Because!" I struggled to continue my sentence.

"Because isn't an answer."

"I have this idea that I'm not right for him," I admitted, forcing myself to be honest. "Whether I'm correct or wrong, it's in my head, and you know what I'm like when I fixate on something."

"Huh." She raised a knowing eyebrow. "So you're sleeping with him and then you're going to break up with him when you're done?"

Ugh. I didn't want that. "It's weird talking to you about it. You and him have the same eyes."

She batted her lashes, a cute action despite the sadness still surrounding her. "Seriously, though. I've never seen him intense about a woman before. I like you two together. You fit well."

That could not be true. "Really? Am I what you pictured when you imagined your brother settling down?"

Skye's gaze took me to pieces. "You're talking about settling down. That speaks volumes. No one else's view counts other than yours and his. Answer me this: If it's not you, who do you see him ending up with?"

Manhattan's busy streets passed by outside the window, and I brought the responsible-Lennox image to mind. Huh. Weird. "Amber Warwick. How odd is that?"

Skye's look changed to incredulous, but the cab pulled over, our journey done. We paid the fare and set off on our quest.

Skye had attended a prestigious fashion college and now intended to specialise in wedding gowns. High-end beautiful creations that took months of work and cost a fortune. She put her heart and soul into her designs, and each one was exquisite. All with Skye's unique and feminine style.

"What's our plan?" I asked. From our place on the pavement, there were ten bridal shops within throwing distance.

Skye forced brightness. "You're the bride. You'll try on a couple of dresses, and I'll ask casual questions to help me understand the market here. Is that okay?"

"Lead the way." I liked shopping. I liked being nicely dressed. I'd never in my life pictured myself in a wedding dress, but it would be fun to try. An image flashed before me of my own wedding, of saying vows and kissing the man I loved. I swallowed.

"Don't use my title, okay?" I added to my friend. *Lady Isobel* had never suited me.

Skye agreed and directed me into a classy boutique. Immediately, two assistants swooped, scoping us out.

"This is my soon-to-be sister-in-law," Skye said with an amused smile just for me. "Isobel has no idea what kind of dress she wants to marry my brother in, so we'd love your advice."

I rolled my eyes at her the first chance I got, but it was Skye's afternoon, and I was just along for the ride.

A few hours and half a dozen shops later, I emerged from the changing room with yet another ivory gown draped artfully around me. This one had a heavily embroidered bust which was a little too tight and pushed my boobs up under my chin. The sample dresses were all spacious, I guessed so anyone could try them on, and the assistants used clips to tailor the fit. Too much, in this case.

I walked to the plinth and stood on the rotating platform. Skye eyed me critically then took a picture with her phone.

"Again, a veil would accentuate the bride's dark hair, or a tiara would set off an updo perfectly," one of the assistants remarked.

Skye questioned them on the latest trends in what their brides were doing with their hair. I sipped my champagne. It was nearing five, and we'd need to leave soon.

Yet I couldn't quite drag myself away from my reflection.

I had plenty of nice dresses at home. Mum and Dad frequently hosted smart parties and even a ball, once or twice, where we'd all dressed to the nines. But I'd never even considered what I'd look like in a wedding dress.

I'd simply never imagined wanting to get married.

Now I had an image in my head and I couldn't let it go.

Just like I'd done with the image of Lennox and Amber.

"Isobel?" Skye's voice brought me out of my stare. "Unless you want to order that dress, we should leave now."

I hopped down and changed back into my jeans and shirt. We left the store, and Skye towed me with her to a coffee shop. She joined the long queue and summoned a reflective smile.

"Thank you for today. That helped me no end. I'm so

impatient to get into this business. It'll do me good to fight for something instead of just constantly battling with myself, and I know I can do well. Many of these stores are missing the mark with their customers. They are overly formal. There's a huge gap in the market for a bride who wants to be able to eat and not be a princess, but also have a one-off, knockout dress. Execs, CEOs, ladies with ideas of their own."

"You're going to nail this internship."

"I hope so. I've studied long enough, and it would be the perfect début." My friend's eyes narrowed. "Are you flagging? Is your head hurting again?"

I played with my bag strap. "No. I'm a little thrown, though. It was strange seeing myself like that."

"Oh yeah?" She took out her phone and found a picture. "Like this?"

On her screen, a happy, pretty version of me beamed. In a long, cream dress, with my eyes sparkling, I barely recognised myself.

The woman in the image was confident. I could imagine her knowing her own mind. She'd be fearless.

And she was me.

"Can you send me that?" I asked.

"So you can forward it to Lennox?" She poked at the device. "Sent."

"To me or to him?"

"Both of you."

I swallowed. Would I have sent it myself? Maybe. Maybe not. But I wanted to know his reaction to that shot. I drew a heavy breath. "I should call him. I will, tonight. But he's pissed off with me, and it's my fault, as always."

We inched forward in the queue.

"Don't be silly. Lennox could drive a saint to distraction

with his restlessness and stomping about. I bet he did something to deserve it."

"Actually, no. This is all on me. I know why, too. I'm starting to see the bigger picture."

A rush of clarity hit me. I'd been hiding behind the odd, long-held vision I had of Lennox and Amber, the one that had been indelibly printed on my mind when I'd seen them together at age sixteen. Back then, I'd been creating a horrible view of myself and I'd bundled them into that image.

Fixating. I was good at that.

I needed to change all of it. And I had an idea of where to start.

My phone buzzed my pocket. I extracted it. *Mum.*

Skye waved me off, and I found us a table.

"Hey!" I said.

"Where are you?" Mum chirped.

"New York City helping Skye with research. Hold on, I have something to show you." I quickly sent her the bride shot and returned the phone to my ear.

Mum was silent for several seconds. "Oh, Isobel," she said, her voice soft and full of wonder.

I gave a pleased smile and wriggled in my chair. "Bet you never thought you'd see me dressed like that."

"I did, maybe not for a few years. But you'll fall head over heels at some point and we won't see you for dust. I've always known it."

I blinked. "Really?"

"Uh-huh. And definitely before Sebastian."

I chewed on that while Mum bemoaned my brother's bruises yet again. She'd already tried probing me with questions about Lennox and knew better than to try again.

"Can I ask you something?" I said. "How do you see my problems?"

"What problems?" Mum asked.

"Learning," I said quietly, not wanting to announce to the café that I was substandard.

Mum drew in a deep breath. "You haven't talked about that in years."

"I don't like to."

"No. I know that. Do you remember what your therapist used to say to you?"

I hunkered down in my chair, recalling the smiling woman who came once a week to Belvedere and whose job it was to tell me I was doing great. "She always said there was no problem."

"That's because there isn't. Not that you can't overcome or cope with. You need more time to get used to ideas, but your intellect is sound."

"Is it, though?"

"Absolutely," Mum said, adamant. "You're as stubborn as an ox, though. It's a family trait. Getting you to believe in yourself was a whole person's job."

Even then, I hadn't accepted it. I groaned.

"Is there a reason you're asking?" Mum said.

"Not that I want to talk about right now. But thank you," I added quickly.

Mum *hmmed* me and then got down to the bones of the call. "We're a few days off the rally. Hennessey has the organisation under control, but there's a problem."

Hennessey was Mum's PA, and I'd worked with her on finalising details including those of my business launch before I'd headed to Castle McRae.

Mum continued, "Casey Warwick answered her email

on the number of cars and the facilities they needed, but she sent a follow-up to their general office and got no reply."

"Huh, I've no idea what's going on there. Casey confirmed my win." Though I'd been too wrapped up in Lennox to follow it up myself.

"He's probably sulking," Mum guessed. "Can I leave this with you to handle?"

"I'm on it," I replied, and we said our farewells.

Skye joined me, placing our orders on the table. I put the Casey problem on my mental to-do list and returned to my previous dawning realisation.

I stirred my coffee with a tiny wooden stick, and Skye raised her eyebrows at me, waiting.

"Here's the thing," I said. "For years, I've thought that Amber was the perfect match for your brother. She's beautiful, smart, and even if she's gay, she'd be right for him. Which I wouldn't."

Skye's mouth dropped open. "Amber had a nose job at sixteen. She passed maybe one of her exams. She's sweet, rather annoying in her neediness, and she's never worked a day in her life. I have no intention of being bitchy, we used to be friends, but I can happily say that I can't imagine anyone less suited to my brother than her."

My fucking brain. I groaned and banged my forehead on the table. Skye slid the coffee cups to the side.

I pointed at her phone. "What did you say to Amber about meeting up?"

"I didn't reply yet."

"Text her back and set a call. Today."

I was about to switch everything up.

*S*kye's text had prompted an immediate response from Amber, begging to speak with us both. We arranged a video chat and headed back to the hotel.

As Skye set up her tablet on the coffee table, I sent a text to Lennox.

It took a painstakingly long time for me to make connections in my brain. And an even longer time to notice that they were there. But today's headspace had worked wonders.

I cared so much about him and I'd left him angry and confused.

I'd told him I'd mess things up. It wasn't to excuse myself, but I wished I'd handled pretty much every interaction we had differently.

I miss you, I wrote.

But no reply came.

21

DARK MEN

*L*ennox

Midnight, and the single floodlight over the Glasgow car park illuminated a stark scene. Sebastian had found us a fight, and we'd driven three hours to get here.

Beside me, in my Land Rover, my friend stiffened.

"What?" I asked, watching the fight.

Two men smacked the fuck out of each other. Blood sprayed out. The crowd bayed. I couldn't spot anyone who looked like an organiser, and unease warred with my burning frustration.

"See the guy with the face tattoo?" Sebastian said, his voice hard. "That's the fucker who took me out."

I found his target. Aged maybe in his early thirties, the man watched the fight, unmoving. A lot of the time, groups attended the fights after an evening of drinking. They'd cheer on their friend and take him home with bruises as a trophy of a wild night. But lone wolves showed up, too. Dark men with no words and blinkered stares.

"Why the fuck did ye fight him?" I asked. "He might as well have gangland murderer stamped on his forehead."

Sebastian breathed through his nose. "Because I was fucking angry and I wanted to hurt."

"Well, it worked, aye?"

Seb had cracked ribs. Gordain had insisted he get X-rayed before he'd let him into a helicopter. As it was, Seb was grounded.

My annoyance grew. "You're lucky he didnae break more of your bones."

"He won't get a chance this time."

Fuck that. "Listen to me. You're not going up against him."

"Fuck off. That asshole is a dirty fighter, and he needs to go down. He only got me last time because I showed up late and hadn't seen his form. Now I know, he's mine."

"And how are your ribs holding up under a punch? How does this feel?" I smacked him in the chest with the back of my hand.

Seb winced, and a growl wrenched from his throat. "I'll survive. I have to do this. My pride is at stake."

Pride. That fucker. I knew it well.

Pride was what I felt when Isobel took my hand or kissed me in public. The same pride had been blown up when I couldn't kiss her goodbye at the airport.

What was the saying? Pride always comes before a fall? That fall wouldn't be Seb's. Adrenaline rushed through me, readying my muscles.

"I'll take him for ye," I told him.

"No."

"Aye, I will. Call it a favour. I've a fuckload of energy to burn and I'm pissed off." At his sister, but I wasn't about to say that. Just as I didn't want to know whether his anger was at Skye or himself. It was all so fucked up and complicated. "We're here for me. That arsehole is mine."

A muscle ticked at Seb's jaw. My friend's blue-green eyes —so similar to Isobel's—sparked with the need for blood. But it wouldn't be his. And it wouldn't be mine.

"I don't want you to get hurt," he finally said.

"Do ye seriously think that guy can take me?" No chance. Not in a million years.

"Fine," Seb replied. "Fucking crush him, Nox."

*T*he lights glared. The snarling crowd closed in. The motherfucker who hurt my friend watched me with dead eyes. His mouth lifted in a grin.

I didn't return his mocking smile.

We touched knuckles and took our positions, the drizzling rain and the freezing night barely touching my skin. Then it was on.

I snapped out a measured swing. It connected. A clout to the fucker's ear.

Fuck my lack of control.

Bang.

Another sweet hit.

Fuck not being able to direct my life. Not with Da, not with Isobel.

Smack. I nailed Tattoo Face in the stomach. Seb had bruises on his chest and sides, too. He'd swallowed his pride and let me and Gordain see. This asshole had been all over him.

But Seb hadn't been unlucky—he was a good fighter. Our opponent had blood in his sights.

He caught me with a slamming blow, bouncing off my

stony body. I reared back to avoid a fast follow-up then roared, showing him my teeth.

Incensed, I let my anger out. It filled my fists.

I'd been in a tank regiment, and our remit was shock action. Massive destruction of our enemies. I'd never wanted to kill anyone, not like this guy, but I'd do anything to protect those I loved.

That was my last thought before it all went to shit.

22

THE BIGGEST HIT OF THE EVENING

*I*sobel

On-screen, Amber Warwick tilted her head, her long mane of almost white-blonde hair sliding over her shoulder. "Ladies. Thank you for the call."

Previously, whenever I'd been near this woman, I'd spun around and walked the other way. I had to acknowledge why. I'd been intimidated by her. She represented everything I wanted to be. Almost the walking embodiment of my bad points made good.

Tall, blonde, elegant, and the self-declared owner of the man I wanted.

Even if she wasn't smarter than me, even if she had her own flaws. I had to get over myself. Amber was a normal human being.

Maybe sixteen-year-old-me could still hate her, but adult-me was good to rise above it all.

Amber's gaze flicked over the screen then settled on Skye. "Skye, I'm so happy we're able to talk again so soon."

"Well, you had questions about my brother. If you'd like

to know about Lennox, Isobel is better qualified to answer than me," Skye replied neatly.

I forced a neutral expression, only slightly enjoying Skye's place-putting. "Lennox is great! How's your family?"

Amber didn't smile. "Are you and he a couple?"

That wasn't a question I was about to answer to a random before I talked to Lennox, so I paused and picked over my words. But fuck it. Even if he wasn't mine, he definitely wasn't hers. "Yes," I replied, though the lie didn't sit comfortably.

"I see," Amber said. "But you have to know how that causes a problem for me."

"How so?"

To my surprise, she clutched a hand to her eyes, and her mouth crinkled in a sob. "Because he's been my boyfriend for four years!"

"Um, no he hasn't," Skye said, staring at the screen. "He pretended once but that's it. You've never dated my brother."

"Skye, please!" she said.

"What? Listen, honey. Lennox already told Isobel what happened between you. There's no point in pretending to us."

"There is! You have to help me. Isobel, listen. I need Lennox. You don't. You have no idea what it's like to be the black sheep of the family. Casey, Erika, and my mother all live on my stepfather's goodwill, and Raymond despises me. At any point, he could remove our support and leave us stranded." Her mouth twisted in an ugly snarl. "They all hate me because of what I am. You with your perfect family and perfect life, put yourself in my shoes for a minute and you'd understand."

I couldn't help my jaw from dropping. *She* envied *me*? "This is a joke, surely."

"How can you be so cruel?" Amber snapped. She hiccuped a sob.

I blinked at the dramatics. None of this really made any sense. "Why would Raymond throw you out?"

"Because he's a homophobe! He ordered me never to reveal my true self or he'd cut us all off. And he has no interest in Mum anymore. He's just waiting on an excuse to get rid of us all. Now she's ill in bed with her heart condition. It's too hard. You can help us if you just put your selfishness aside."

I exchanged a glance with Skye. With her furrowed eyebrows, she appeared as confused as I was.

"I'm sorry to hear your mum is ill," Skye said after a pause.

"Why Lennox?" I cut in, still unable to really process this. "Why don't you ask someone else?"

"Why indeed," Skye muttered. She sat back on the couch beside me and folded her arms.

"How can I trust anyone else?" Amber spluttered. "Raymond has met Lennox. He likes him."

"Okay, then why doesn't your mum just divorce Raymond and take half his money?" I pushed.

"Their prenup leaves her nothing."

An idea started to form in my head. Amber's story was too farfetched. Too desperate. It didn't stand up to logic. I neither understood nor wanted anything to do with it. "Well, Lennox is his own man," I said. "If you want him, you'll have to ask him."

Amber's face contorted to a petulant sneer. "If you want any help from my family again then you'll persuade Lennox to help me. He won't take my calls. You tell him to speak to me, and I'll tell my brother to go to your family's rally next week."

I gaped. "What's that to do with this?"

"I just made it so," she replied.

"Right," Skye cut in, her tone efficient. "I'm hanging up now. Goodbye, Amber."

"Wait!" Amber demanded, but Skye had already killed the call.

We sat back and gazed at each other.

"She's blackmailing me," I managed. "Why?"

My friend chewed her lip. "I know she and I were once friends, and this might be uncharitable of me, but I don't believe a word she says. She said she was a lesbian, and that might be true, but would her stepdad really cut off her whole family for that? You've met the guy, what's he like?"

I cast my mind back to the couple of times I'd met Raymond Warwick. "I liked him. He knew his way around a car. If I'm honest, I mostly avoided him. Probably because of the association with his stepkids." Which was why I'd dealt with Casey to organise the cars for the rally and for the endorsement.

Which I'd now lost. My stomach drew into a knot. Fuck. I'd started to rely on that in my head.

"Do you know what I think?" Skye stood and paced the hotel room. "Amber asked me and Lennox for help at the point she probably should've been going to university or getting a job. She didn't do either of those things. In fact, for four years, I'm reasonably sure all she's done is spend her family's money and enjoy a life of freedom."

I cocked my head. "All while pretending to be with Lennox? I bet you're right! In Monaco, she wanted him to fake a proposal." Then I winced. "I threw her ring into the sea. Lennox covered for me, but do you think I should have told her?"

Skye goggled at me then choked on a laugh. "No! But good going. I like your style."

I wasn't proud of it, I wasn't proud of any of my behaviour over the past couple of weeks. But I'd been true to myself which was more than Amber could say.

"I don't understand that woman," I said. "Basically, she's been living a lie, right?"

Skye's forehead furrowed deeper. "True. What if she's been playing her stepdad all this time? Pretending to be waiting on a man who's conveniently off in the military."

"And now he's out, her game is up?" I wrinkled my nose. "But what about her mum being ill, and how her family hate her?"

Stretching, Skye gave a short laugh. "I don't think any of it is true. She's lying through her teeth so she can continue her easy life. Using my brother and messing with you in the process."

I stared at the ceiling, dazed. "All this time, I've thought her this perfect person. When in fact, she's just an asshole."

God, how things changed.

"What does that mean for your rally, though? Will it impact you?" Skye asked.

"Unfortunately, yes. Let me call Casey. Maybe he'll be more reasonable." Though my hopes weren't high after Mum's request earlier.

I paced to the window, and Casey answered my call.

"Isobel," he started.

"Listen up," I jumped in. "I won that race fair and square. Why is your sister saying that you're pulling your cars?"

"How was that a fair win? I crashed out. Null and void."

"Are you kidding me?"

Casey laughed. "What happened the first time we ever

raced? You refused to acknowledge my win because your boyfriend got into your car and sent you off course. How is this any different? Besides, thanks to you, my sister is pissed off."

"That's exactly nothing to do with me. She just needs to get a job and her own life."

Casey said nothing, and I wondered if he agreed with me. Then he came back onto the line. "I'm just going on what my sister says. If you want our cars and support, make her happy. Or my life isn't worth living."

Then the rat bastard hung up the call.

I stared at my phone. The lives of others were so complicated. How the hell did people like the Warwicks get anything done when they were entrenched in bullshit all the time? I shook my head lightly, more than a little baffled.

"Casey pulled the cars," I told Skye. "Which leaves a gap in our rally programme. We've advertised it. People are going to be disappointed." Besides the loss to my own business.

But Skye had paled, her attention fixed on her phone. "I have a message from Sebastian," she said.

"What?" I leaned in to see her screen, her tone alarming me.

"Lennox has been in a fight. He's in trouble."

Lennox was hurt? No, God. Surely not.

If I'd thought the biggest hit of the evening was losing the cars, I was dead wrong.

My heart froze over and cracked into two.

I got the next flight home, the single available seat, meaning Skye couldn't come with me. But nothing could keep me back. After Sebastian's message, he'd gone dark, and we'd heard nothing more. Our families wouldn't have known about the fight, so we had nothing more to go on. No one else to ask.

Had I really thought the journey coming out a bad one? I'd take a migraine over the thought of Lennox being in pain any day of the week.

Sebastian had been hurt and thought nothing of it. I trembled to think how bad it must have been for him to tell us about Lennox.

Through the overnight journey, I gripped my fingers together and prayed that the man I cared about—fuck it, no. I was falling for him. It was more than care that had me in pieces, even if it took me a while to recognise it. My stomach dipped, and my heart swelled. I prayed the man I adored was going to be okay.

23

ROCK BOTTOM

*I*sobel

Sebastian's texts pinged onto my phone after my US flight touched down in London. I scanned them desperately, searching for my next destination.

He was in Glasgow. *Right.*

I was lucky, there was a connecting flight in an hour. With only hastily packed hand luggage, I booked straight onto the next plane and took my seat in the waiting area. Then I tried calling my brother.

He answered. "Isobel."

I jumped to my feet and paced. "I'll be in Glasgow in a couple of hours. All I need to know is that he's still alive. Okay? Just tell me that." My hoarse voice broke.

Sebastian swore. "You didn't read all of my messages. He isn't hurt. He's been arrested."

"Arrested?" I stopped at the airport lounge's windows. Outside, a grey sky held off any glimpse of the noon sun. But I was busy trying to hold back a sob.

Not hurt. Not broken.

"The fight we were at got raided. I was questioned but released. Nox is still in a cell."

"Why the fuck were you at another fight?" I jammed my fingers into my hair, gripping it in my fist and yanking hard at the roots. "After what happened to you? Did you want that to happen to Lennox, too?"

"Don't," my brother snapped. "I don't want to hear this now. Listen, I'm waiting on a call from a solicitor so I need to clear the line. Get here. Find me. Then we'll talk." He rattled off the name of a hotel and then the ass hung up on me.

"Argh!" I bit out into the half-filled lounge.

People gazed at me like I was the entertainment. I dropped back into a chair and took my first full breath since I'd left that hotel room in New York.

Lennox was okay. Sort of. But I bet I could guess why he'd needed to fight.

Idiot men with their idiot ideas. I'd been hugely unfair to my brother and, though the fight was none of my fault, part of this mess was certainly mine.

O n the short hop to Glasgow, I engaged my waste-of-space brain and tried to work out what I knew. I cared about Nox? Check. I needed to step up to life? Super-check. I wanted to somehow keep him around? Yeah, for sure.

I'd known all that before, kind of, and I'd blown it.

What about Amber and her sad story? Nah. Fuck the Warwicks. I'd tell Lennox what Amber had said, but I wouldn't ask him to help her. Not for all the supercars in the world. Not if it made my starting a new business the easiest ride going.

I had to see Lennox. I hated that he was in trouble and I had no idea how I could help. But I had to be there. To go to him.

Whatever I could do, I would.

---

*S*ebastian met me in the lobby of his hotel. His bruises had yellowed, but with his height and broad shoulders under his black jacket, he still carried a menacing air. Particularly as he bore down on me with a face like thunder.

"Any update?" I asked.

Seb scowled deeper and grabbed my arm. He hauled me through the restaurant and to a cosy corner, out of earshot of anyone. In the wide, elegant room, guests ate high tea with delicate sandwiches and cakes on tiered stands. So genteel.

Completely at odds with my brother and me.

I could only imagine what a mess I looked. I'd barely slept on the overnight flight from the States, and not eaten since... I couldn't remember.

"You had lunch?" Seb asked, reading my mind.

"News first."

He sighed and straightened, peering over his shoulder. A waiter arrived instantly, and I had to wonder if Seb had booked into the place under his viscount title. People jumped when he did that.

"Sandwiches and coffee. Don't bother with the fancy plates. Fast as you can," he requested with a warm but efficient smile.

The waiter cast a curious glance over us but dipped his head and scrammed to do my brother's bidding.

Seb came back to me. "Lennox is still being held. I haven't spoken to him, but the solicitor has just gone in."

I shut my eyes briefly and fought the urge to keep them closed. That didn't sound good. "Walk me through what happened."

"We went to a fight. It was badly organised. Nox was midway through knocking seven bells of shit out of this guy when sirens started. We were surrounded, not that we'd have run."

I sat forwards on the plush couch, my hands clenched between my knees. "He was actually fighting?"

"Yeah. It should've been me. I'm so fucked off about this."

"And the police just grabbed him?"

Sebastian rolled his shoulders. "Like I said, he was heavily into the fight. The crowd scattered and left Nox and the other man on clear display. The cops nailed them both."

"You just sat there?"

"No! I was trying to stop him, but he was in the zone."

Shit, I was being an asshole to my brother. "Sorry," I managed. "I've been so worried."

Seb's phone rang. He snatched it up then rose and stalked to the doorway, answering the call in privacy.

The waiter arrived with a wide silver tray. He set it down with a flourish.

"God, thanks," I said, my mouth instantly watering. I grabbed a sandwich and bit down and chewed.

The waiter poured two cups of coffee from a carafe then vanished. I was on the last bite of my fourth sandwich when my brother reappeared. He sat heavily.

"Now I have news. That was the solicitor. The police have until midnight to charge Nox or let him go, but so far, they're holding on to him."

In the past, Sebastian and I had talked about his fights. He maintained that they were legal, so long as everyone involved consented. But I knew that wasn't entirely true. Gambling on the bouts wasn't above board for sure. "What would they charge him with?"

"They think he's part of the organisation."

"That's bullshit!"

"I know." Seb rubbed his eyes. "He'll be released. There's no evidence against him as he's done nothing wrong."

"Are you sure?"

"The solicitor thinks they'll keep him until the last minute but more as a deterrent than anything. He'll be home tonight. I've got his Land Rover so I'll wait for his release, then we'll drive back to the castle together."

Okay. *Okay.* My mind whirred. "I'm just... I'm reeling. I thought he was hurt then I thought he'd be in trouble. But everything's going to be fine?"

"Not everything. Callum will be pissed off. He and Nox were already at odds. That's part of why he was so into the fight." Seb picked up his coffee and swigged it.

"He'd argued with his dad? What about?"

"Blayne quitting school. Apparently he wants to be a pro-snowboarder. The centre Lennox was going to build would give him a training facility."

Ah crap. I raised my gaze to the ceiling. "Then Callum refused it?"

"I don't know. Nox wasn't in the chatting mood. I figured you'd know more than I did."

My stomach sank at the realisation of what must have happened.

I'd spoken to Blayne and told him what Ally had told me all those years ago when I'd quit school. I'd happily said to Blayne that he should focus on his strengths and find ways to cope with everything else. Which the boy somehow took to mean to drop out.

Which had fucked up his dad's approval of Lennox's plans.

Ah God, Lennox hated me. He must. I'd hurt him and I'd broken his future.

"I caused all of this," I said, my heart heavy.

"I'm sure you didn't," Seb replied.

I heaved a shaky breath and dragged myself to my feet. "I did. I know I did."

"Where are you going?" my brother asked.

Now I knew Lennox was probably going to be released later in the evening, I had a chance to go ahead of him and fix what I'd broken. My body screamed at me to lie out on the comfortable sofa in the nice hotel and rest. Just for an hour. But no. I had an opportunity and I had to take it.

Even if it made no difference to how he saw me.

"When he gets out, tell him I've gone to the castle. Tell him I love him and—" My mouth dropped open.

Seb's did, too.

"Wait." I waved, flustered. "Don't tell him that." Was that true? If so, I had to tell him myself. My chin wobbled, and I grabbed the arm of the sofa to steady myself.

"Jesus, Is." Seb stood and enclosed me in a hug. "Always nought to sixty in everything you do."

For a moment, I let myself sink into my brother's warm hold. At least with Sebastian, I could mess up endlessly and I knew he still loved me.

I wanted to believe in Lennox in the same way. Maybe I could. But I had to earn that right.

"I'll see you both when you get back," I muttered. Then I pushed away and found my feet, heading for the airport once again.

*L*uck had been on my side with my previous flights in the past twenty-four hours. But there was no direct plane from Glasgow to Inverness. I slumped in the back of a taxi and stared at my phone, barely trusting myself to have performed the search right. But the driver confirmed it. It was within the same small country. I was fucking nuts.

My weary mind struggled with the alternatives.

"Get the train. It won't take long," my driver cheerfully suggested.

I agreed, and he deposited me at the railway station. Trains were plentiful, but they weren't fast. The four hours of crawling up-country, with every little station stopped at on the way, nearly drove me insane. The silver lining was a phone charging point next to my seat, so I texted Skye then swallowed my pride and called Lennox's dad to beg for a ride to the castle.

I was about to hit rock bottom soon, and I needed help. Maybe I'd finally learned to accept it.

At the tiny town of Aviemore, deep within the Cairngorms, I stumbled from the train. Night had fallen, and I shivered, hopelessly unprepared for the cold. For anything, really.

"Yo, Is!" Blayne hollered.

I raised my head to find Lennox's brother and dad the other side of the fence. Relieved beyond belief to see friendly faces, I exited the station, and Callum strode up to me and held me by the shoulders.

"What on earth has ye turning up here in a freezing evening? You were meant to be with Skye in New York, were ye not?" He peered at my eyes. "Christ, ye look exhausted. Is something the matter?"

"I came back early. Forgot my coat at the hotel. Need to talk to you both," I mumbled.

"All right, lass. First things first." He drew a big arm around my shoulders and guided me through the car park and into his car.

Blayne gave me a confused but happy smile and took the seat next to me in the back. As if he knew I needed bolstering.

The warmth and the safety had my eyelids drooping.

Next thing I knew, Lennox's brother was shaking my arm. I sat up and gazed around. We were at the castle.

"Did I sleep the whole journey?" I asked.

"Aye, and ye snored on my shoulder. I tried to talk to ye, but ye were dead to the world."

"Whoa. Sorry about that." I undid my seat belt and hopped out. The catnap had done away with the raw edge of my fatigue, and I stared up at the huge stone castle, ready to do battle.

"Ma's got dinner ready for ye. Come on." Blayne led me into the great hall and straight through to the dining room.

Lennox's mother entered from the kitchen door with a bowl of food. She placed it on the scarred oak table and pointed at the chair in front of it. "We've all eaten, so go ahead and get this into your system."

Callum strode in and exchanged a glance with his wife. The three McRaes stood in a row, staring at me.

I took a forkful of the richly scented casserole and nearly died from the pleasure. "This is delicious," I said as soon as my mouth was clear.

"Are you and Lennox dating?" Blayne blurted out. "Seriously, I mean."

"Blayne!" Mathilda scolded. "That's none of our business. But it would be nice to know where Lennox is. He went out yesterday evening and hasn't been seen since."

"He and Sebastian are...in Glasgow. They'll be back tonight. Probably in the early hours." Huh, look at that. I'd learned discretion after all.

Then my mouth ran away with itself after all. "I love him, but I don't think we're dating. It's complicated, and I made everything go wrong."

In unison, Lennox's family members gawped.

Ah hell. I drew a deep breath and tried again. "What I mean is, he might like me better if I clear a few things up. Blayne, I need to start with you. Can we talk?"

24

NO ROOM FOR NEGOTIATIONS

*L*ennox

Home lay across the loch, a single light illuminating the castle entrance and reflecting on the water. A beacon for late travellers. Sebastian and I fitted neatly into that category as it was past four AM. He sat in the passenger seat, his dark, brooding presence matching my mood.

At least now, after a night and a day locked in a police cell, I'd burned up my anger.

Still, I sped the remaining distance. I needed my bed. I needed to know what had happened with Isobel. If she was here or if she had gone. All Seb knew was that she'd flown in from the US in a state of shock, thinking me hurt, then fled north to my home after she'd found I was fit and well.

Outside Castle McRae, I idled the Land Rover's engine and hopped out. Seb took my place in the driver's seat and leaned, punching me once in the arm. I slammed the door closed on him, and he drove off, heading to Braithar. We'd already agreed that he'd borrow my car and return it tomorrow.

I could've just dropped him there, or he could've slept in his usual bed here, but we needed our space. As quickly as possible.

The fight had gone spectacularly badly. Neither of us wanted to choke over the details, at least for a few days.

With his taillights disappearing around the bend, I jogged over the gravel. But then I changed direction. Some strange intuition had me entering the castle by the main front door, rather than the tower entrance that led straight to my apartment. I closed the heavy door behind me and stepped into the darkened great hall.

In front of the fire, slumped in a chair, was Da.

His head rose an inch, and he focused on me then clambered to his feet.

As a teenager, I'd never been one to sneak home, hoping my parents wouldn't notice the late hour, or that I stank of booze. Da had always trusted me. If I'd come home drunk, which had been a rarity, he'd shake his head in humour while I stumbled to my room.

But now, I'd blown up and scattered any trust he had in me. On heavy feet, I crossed the floor. He met me with open arms. Da hugged me, just like he would've done when I was wee.

"Are ye okay, lad?" Da asked against my shoulder, his deep voice thick with sleep.

Ah God. Emotion rolled through me.

I wasn't okay. I'd fucked up everything. "No," I managed.

"Are ye hurt?"

"Naw." Not much, anyway. He'd asked me the same question years ago when Isobel and I had wrecked the Tesla. This was very different to that.

A complete role reversal.

I sucked in a breath then stepped away. "I was arrested after an organised fight."

Da stiffened then focused on my eyes. Firelight played over his serious expression, and I could only guess what he was thinking. His eldest born, his solid, serious, law-abiding son had been taken in by the police. I half expected him to ream me out. But he only nodded. "Are they pressing charges?"

"No." Thank fuck. I'd been released when they finally accepted the lack of evidence against me. I had no wad of cash, no underworld links, and it had only been the fact that I was fighting a known criminal that had me busted in the first place.

My father palmed my shoulder. "Do ye need anything?"

"Sleep." I didn't want to talk this out. Not now, or ever.

"Aye. Go on up. I need my bed, too."

I lifted my chin, unwilling to play the child. The hug had been enough, and I didn't need permission to rest. Da and I had to meet as men now. "Thanks for waiting up for me. Ye didnae have to."

One side of his mouth moved in a smile. "Aye, I did. When ye have bairns of your own, no matter how big they get, you'll understand. By the way, your lass waited up, too, but I sent her to bed an hour ago."

"Isobel?" I stared at him.

"Unless ye have another I don't know about?"

I gave a short laugh. "No. Just the one."

He raised a hand, waving me off. "Good to know. Night, lad."

I was already halfway across the hall. Renewed energy had me bounding up the tower's spiral staircase. Past the gym, and to the last storey to my apartment. I fell through the door, locked it securely behind me, and entered my bedroom.

A small form curled under my blankets, barely visible in the dark.

My fucking heart melted.

Unhurried, now I knew she was here, now I knew she was mine, I toed off my boots and shucked off my clothes, discarding them to a chair. Then, bare-arsed naked, I shut the world away and crawled into my bed, sliding in behind Isobel. I pulled the blankets up and wrapped myself around a very nude lass.

She stirred in my arms.

"Lennox," she mumbled. "Thank God."

My chest ached, and I buried my face in Isobel's hair, snaking my arms around her so I could hold her close, her back to my front. She took my hands and held them, then intertwined her smooth legs with my rough ones.

We relaxed into the hold. Neither of us said another word. I took deep inhales of her scent, steadying myself after days of being at sea.

This. Fucking this.

Isobel's warmth sank deep into me, and all that had been bitterly wrong, righted. How had I doubted what I knew? I'd been lying to myself. This dangerous feeling of contentment was everything.

She belonged to me.

"Yours," Isobel suddenly said, her voice clearer now. She pressed our joined hands to her chest, above her breasts.

My hard cock throbbed against her ass. I'd been trying to ignore it, but that was a challenge too far.

Then Isobel twisted in my arms, and suddenly we were face to face. She placed her palm to my chest. "Mine," she said.

It could almost be a question, her second word. But I knew how to answer it.

Hell yes, I was.

I found her mouth, and our lips met in perfect kiss. Isobel opened for me, and my soft kisses turned to hungry, insistent pulls.

For a long while, in the dark, private cocoon of my bedroom, we just kissed, hands caressing, bodies close-fitted and warmth gathering.

Then somehow, my dick was between her legs, gliding over her wet, slick pussy.

Isobel adjusted her position, and I was at her entrance. I stalled, locking my muscles, though every cell in me screamed to keep moving, to push an inch, and another, and to keep going. But I needed to get up and find the condom box.

I rose on my elbow, struggling with myself. Isobel took hold of my neck and brought me back down. She hooked her leg around my backside, and my dick was right back in the zone.

I flared my nostrils, opening my mouth to speak.

Then she rolled her hips, taking me inside. Bare.

I grunted with surprise, and Isobel stole another kiss, the invitation clear. Fixated, I took over and slid deeper, my attention never more focused than at this moment.

The sensitivity blinded me, and I was a slave to the little sounds Isobel made.

I'd never had sex without a condom before, nor even considered it. But this wasn't sex. This was love-making, fucking hot and all-consuming.

The position, on our sides, gave us both control. In a never-ending kiss, we moved together, a slow grind that had my temperature spiking.

Yours, I told her with every hit. *Mine,* she agreed.

Pretty soon, Isobel arched into me, panting, before moaning and pulsing around me. The wild, fucking gorgeous feeling caught me, and I was a goner. I rolled Isobel to her back and drove into her, my forehead to the mattress over her shoulder and her breasts in my hands.

I came with a shout, spilling deep inside her. Isobel's pulsing kept my orgasm going, and I collapsed on her, my groan low, my head spinning.

Fuck. Me.

There was no going back, not after this.

I was an alpha male, and she was my mate. I wasn't the type to be profound, but everything had changed. Moved on. Stepped up. I didn't care what had brought her here, or anything that had happened in the past couple of days, so long as she was mine.

Still dizzy, my erection undiminished, I dug my fingers into Isobel's hair and tugged her head up, exposing her neck. I laid rough kisses on her throat, letting my teeth graze her skin.

My weight held my woman in place, and I pinned her down while I loved on her. She let me. Held me. Stroked circles into my sides and over my spine.

Tiredness, contentedness, eventually crept in, and my eyelids became weighted.

Isobel wriggled. "Bed's a mess. I am, too," she said. "No sleep until clean-up's done."

I pushed upright and got what she meant. No condom meant damp sheets. That was new, too.

"Get in the shower," I said, gruff and direct. "I'll strip the bed then I'll join ye."

She did as I told her, and I changed the sheets then followed her into the bathroom. After the police had released me, I'd gone to Sebastian's hotel and showered. He'd had my clothes so I'd been able to bin the jumpsuit the police had given me. I still felt dirty, though. Tainted by the events. Isobel drew me under the water and drove the feeling away.

We washed then dried each other and got back into the clean bed.

There was so much to be said. But Isobel came willingly into my arms, and that was all I needed to know.

When we slept, it was deep, and utterly entwined. Everything else could wait.

———

$\mathcal{M}$y apartment door thudded, and I jumped upright, awake. Isobel appeared in my bedroom doorframe, tousle-haired and grinning.

"Where did ye go?" I asked.

I guessed the answer with a glance at her hands. She carried two steaming mugs in her petite fist and a plate in the other.

"Coffee and a bacon sandwich," she announced. Then she dropped my eye contact and added, "Birthday breakfast of champions."

I took the mugs and the plate from her and placed them on my bedside table. Then I pulled her onto the bed next to me, my smirk spreading. "Happy twenty-first."

"Thank you." Isobel eyed my bare torso. I had a couple of bruises forming, and she stooped to kiss them.

Last night, I hadn't wanted my father's comfort. Isobel's, though, sent me into a spin. I fucking loved her gentle touch.

"How long do I have ye?" I asked.

"Not long enough. I need to go home this morning. It's the rally tomorrow, and I have to prepare. Plus my parents want to see me. Seb's coming with me."

I almost asked to go, too, but I had issues to fix here.

Isobel bent over me and collected the plate. "Eat. I already had mine while I brewed the coffee and chatted with your mum."

Hunger had me demolishing the sandwich and draining half my coffee in a minute. Isobel sipped from her mug and tucked her knees under her chin. She'd found my t-shirt and hoodie to wear downstairs, and now removed the top layer. I let myself openly stare at the shape of her tits through the thin material.

"I need to tell you some stuff before I go," Isobel said. She tracked my gaze, and a smile ghosted over her lips. "Skye and I talked with Amber in New York."

My leering stopped. "Way to kill my erection," I deadpanned.

Isobel chuckled. "Sorry. I bet I can get it back. But you need to hear this first."

She informed me how Amber had been using me as a fake boyfriend for years, and why she'd done it. According to Amber, her sick ma needed support and had no other way to secure it.

"Skye doesn't believe her. She thinks she's lazy." Isobel set aside her coffee and brought her gaze back to me. "Amber offered a deal. She wants you to continue the ruse so they aren't thrown out by the stepdad."

"Fuck 'em." I discarded my own cup and leaned in to kiss my lass. "Why would I be part of their make-believe?"

She sighed. "I agree. I don't like lies. None of it sits well with me."

A sense came over me of there being more to this story,

but it wasn't my problem, and right now, I needed more of my lass.

"Come here," I commanded.

Isobel slid onto my lap, sitting astride me.

"I'm sorry if ye were scared about me. Your brother told me about ye flying back, and I hate the thought of ye panicked on my behalf. So there's something I've decided."

"Oh?"

"You're my girlfriend. There's no room for negotiations. It's a fact."

"Okay," she said quickly.

I grinned, taking her waist under the t-shirt. "Ye agreed to that far more easily than I expected."

"Want to fight me over it? That could be fun." Her eyes flared, and heat rose in me once more. I'd better get used to living in a permanent state of arousal every time Isobel was around.

I eased my hands north, taking two lush handfuls of her tits. "Ye have no idea what you're letting yourself in for. I'm going to be a badass boyfriend."

"Oh, I know." She squeezed my hand on her breast. "Brawler." Then she kissed my jaw. "Jailbird."

I slid my other hand to her arse, finding lacy underwear in the way of where I wanted to be. "Does that turn ye on? Me fighting?"

"God, yes." Her brow furrowed. "Except it would piss me off if you were arrested again."

"How about I join a boxing club?" Seb and I had discussed it before, but it hadn't happened since we'd quit our military jobs. It was time.

"So long as I can watch, tough guy, I'm there."

I inhaled, pleased, my contentment growing by the hour. "What about my racing? Does that bother you?"

It did, but I didn't want her to stop something she loved. "I was scared out of my mind when I thought you were hurt in Monaco," I admitted.

Isobel twisted her lips to the side, her expression thoughtful. "I've been thinking about that. The MGB was a bad car to race as the safety features are low rent compared with modern standards. But the reason Casey crashed is because he took risks in order to beat me. How about, in the spirit of reciprocation, I don't race unsafe cars anymore. Or Casey Warwick."

I took her mouth with a savage kiss. "That would suit me fine. I fucking hate that guy. And his whole family. Even more now I know he put you at risk."

Isobel's eyes glinted. "I love it when you get mean. Now, how about we help each other forget our mistakes and make some better memories?"

She ran her hand down to my groin and found my hard cock then fisted me through the sheet.

Hell yeah. Very eager to take up her offer, I rolled Isobel to her back and whipped her underwear down her legs, kicking the blankets away. Ready to go, I lined up and sank into her tight heat once again.

We lost another hour of the morning to celebrating our new status.

Eventually, we had to face the world, and we dressed and got Isobel's things ready for her to leave again. Sebastian was already downstairs, and Skye had returned. She and Isobel caught up briefly then the Fitzroys needed to leave. I took them to the airport once more and this time had no bones about kissing Isobel firmly on the mouth.

"Call me later," I ordered. "I'm not asking. I'm commanding ye to."

She patted my cheek and beamed at me. "It's so weird

how I like this bossiness in you now. Tell me what to do. I love it."

I loved her.

I stilled, and my smile diminished. I pressed my forehead to hers, blocking out the airport chatter, plus the fact that her brother, my closest friend, was six feet away. Now wasn't the time for any kind of big declaration. Even if I wanted to yell my love to the roof.

This time, I didn't think she'd mind so much.

"I want to see you very soon," she said.

"Then ye will." I kissed her, then that was that. They needed to go.

I returned to the castle, a man on a mission. A brother to set right and a father to bring around.

25

IN FOR A PENNY

*L*ennox

Blayne was first on my hit list when I got home. But my twin waited at the door and kept pace with me as I walked through the great hall. Like Isobel, Skye had come home earlier than planned, getting the overnight flight instead of one later in the day. She'd already given me the same once-over she'd given Seb when he'd been in this situation and was reassured I wasn't injured.

"About Amber Warwick," Skye said. "I just need to tell you this: I'm so sorry I put you into a difficult position with her. I know better now. I can safely say I've taken her off of my Christmas card list."

"Good to know. Isobel talked to me about her, so don't stress it." I gave my sister a swift hug and changed the subject. "How did your intern research trip go?"

"It was good. Working there will be a challenge, but it's the best way to get my foot in the door of the industry."

Skye produced a smile, but I was her twin. Though we weren't as close as we could be, I knew when she was masking her emotions. I'd worried about her after whatever had happened with Sebastian. I worried about him, too, not that I could help him.

"I wish ye didnae have to leave," I said, bumping her shoulder with mine. "I always hoped that after university, you'd settle here."

"It's better if I go. I need the space. Maybe one day I'll be able to run my own company from here. From my own place, I mean." Her gaze distanced.

As the first-born twin, I was the one to inherit Da's position plus the estate and Castle McRae. It wasn't a responsibility I took lightly, and I felt for my sister. We had the same drive but she had no constraints. Standing in the great hall, where countless ancestors had stood before us, I liked the binds I had. Relied on them to keep me steady.

I could only imagine how adrift Skye felt.

"You're braver than I am," I said. "If ye ever want a place built, with a studio to work in, a store for your materials, whatever ye need, consider it done."

Skye gave me thanks and a swift hug, visibly shaking off her thoughts. "How did you like the photo I sent you?"

My heart gave a hefty thump. Skye had only sent me one picture, of Isobel in a wedding dress. "I liked it a lot," I said, trying to stop my lips from curving.

A genuine smile appeared in the place of her forced one. "Can I ask questions?" Skye said. "Are you two serious?"

Blayne appeared at the dining room entrance, a book in his hands. "They're in love," he answered for me.

"Hush your mouth," I told him.

"Fine, then she's in love, and he's playing it cool." My brother grinned. "She told us all last night, so we know it's true."

Now, I stared.

Ma appeared behind him and ruffled his hair. "Blayne, mind your own business."

"What do ye mean she told ye?" I questioned.

"Isobel said, out loud, that she was in love with ye. It's the power of the kilt, aye?" Blayne sniffed.

"Whatever she said, it isn't for you to gossip about," Ma scolded.

Ah fuck. My heart panged. She did that? What an utterly Isobel type thing to do. I should've told her the same when I had the chance.

I opened and closed my mouth then forced myself back on track, needing to divert myself before I said something stupid in front of my family.

"What the fuck are ye thinking deciding to quit school?" I blurted to my brother.

"Oh, that." He waved his book. "Isobel told me not to so I'm staying on."

"Ye changed your mind just like that?" I said, strained.

"Aye, well, she made the point about Uncle Ally's modelling career not working out and how she doesn't have a job. I heard her argument. I still want to snowboard as a pro but I'll wait until I'm eighteen at least."

"Good to know," I managed.

My brother shrugged. "We had a good chat. She makes a lot of sense. Hey, isn't it a pity that her rally is going to be ruined? She was really pissed off that the supercars pulled out."

"The Warwicks' cars?" I said.

Skye folded her arms, her gaze darkening. "Those arse-holes. Amber held that over Isobel in New York. She was desperate to get you to continue your role as her beard. She tried to blackmail Is."

"Isobel told me part of that, but she didnae ask me to do it," I replied.

"Of course not. Would you have?"

I'd made it clear that I wouldn't. Which cost Isobel her cars. I rubbed the back of my neck, suddenly seeing a bigger picture.

"Lennox?" Da called across the hall. "Got a minute?"

I switched my gaze to my father then joined him, Ma escorting me. We entered the den, and Ma closed the door.

"I owe ye an apology," Da said.

Ma gestured for us all to sit, and we did, them on one of the new cream couches they'd bought and me on another.

"I was too hasty when we spoke before about your business plan. I brushed over it. I shouldnae have," Da continued. He placed his hands in his lap. "If that's what ye want, I willnae stand in your way."

I gave a huff of a laugh. "Da!"

"All I want is my family thriving alongside me. That's always been my dream. My own father was such a terrible presence in my life and your uncles', so you'll have to excuse us if we're all focused on making everything perfect. I called it wrong. I can admit that. You will inherit this land one day, and it's your right to start living on it in the way you see fit. In fact, if ye want my help, I'll work with ye."

"I do. Thank ye," I said, fast.

We hugged it out. Both my problems with my family had vanished in a flash. My project was back on. Da had come around.

"Isobel gave me a talking to," Da said with a grin. "She informed me in no uncertain terms that I had to stop trying to be the boss of ye."

Ma pressed her lips together. "That's her job now, we take it?"

I rolled my eyes. "I thought ye were all going to mind your own business?"

"Not likely." Ma stood and retrieved a folder from the side table. It was my project breakdown. "For now, I'll spare you the third degree, but I am going to walk through your finances with you. I've made a few notes."

This was Ma's area of expertise, and I'd asked her to give it the once-over. I hoped she wasn't about to tear it to shreds. I'd purposefully described how I'd make it work, building in stages if I couldn't get the investment in one go. That was a problem for another time.

"This is good," she said, her brown eyes kind. "Well done, Lennox. We're both so proud of you."

"I want to build my own house, too," I said. In for a penny, in for a pound. I held eye contact with each of my parents in turn. "I have a family home in mind. My own space." Then I added with a thrill in my belly, "And maybe one day with a garage to the side where a lass can fix cars to her heart's content."

They shared a warm look, and sharp relief filled me.

The past few weeks had turned my life upside down. From the expected jolt of leaving the military to the whirlwind that was Isobel Fitzroy. Finally, I had a path to follow. A business to develop, a home to build, a lass to make mine. All was right with the world.

I spent an hour talking numbers with Ma then left the den and stood in the centre of the great hall. Alone, for once.

One day, this castle would be mine, the land it stood on, too. I had my own life to live until then, and I'd found a way to make it work.

No move to London. No need to look elsewhere for my occupation.

Then Isobel's problem returned to my mind. Blayne had said that Isobel's rally was ruined because the Warwicks weren't going to show. She had been relying on them, and now there would be a gap of missing cars. My chest ached when I thought of her unhappy, and of her disappointment in not getting what she'd worked to achieve.

Maybe there was something I could do to help.

I found my phone and brought up the number of my old army unit's base.

I had just the idea of how to try.

26

SHOW 'EM YOU MEAN BUSINESS

*I*sobel

Seb and I boarded the plane, and I hunkered down in my seat, my head in a spin. I'd had so much to say to Lennox, but we'd covered the basics. We were dating, and this time, I wasn't going to fuck it up.

He was mine.

That little fact put a smile back on my face, and I toyed with my phone and quickly sent Lennox a cute message before I had to switch it off for the flight.

Me, being cute. What a turnaround.

My text tone pinged, and I focused on the screen. I had a message from Casey Warwick.

Did Nox agree?

Ha!

Nope, I replied. *And I'm not asking.*

Then I switched off the device and started a conversation with my brother instead. I had the distinct feeling that this, us going home together to a place we both lived, wouldn't be a common occurrence. Even with my brother out of the military now, life would change in some way soon.

So we talked. We steered clear of tricky subjects, but it was nice.

We touched down in Manchester, and Mum and Dad picked us up, big hugs and birthday wishes for me, and kind smiles for both of us.

Mum drove us home into the Peak District and, at Belvedere, rally fever filled the air. All manner of vehicles took their places on the grassy park, and their owners readied pitches ahead of the main events tomorrow. Stewards made walkways, and food vans were set up like at a festival.

A large, central area stood empty. The place where Warwick Supercars would've had their crowd-pleasing motors.

Their absence would be noticed.

We could still do time trials with other cars, and just take the big-ticket numbers off the roster.

It was a shame, but not the end of the world. If the public were disappointed, there wasn't much we could do about that. I explained the problem to Mum, and she grimaced, cursing the Warwick name. I hated being part of her dissatisfaction, but there was nothing else we could do.

We continued on through the wide fields in the expansive park below the house, checking out the rally preparations.

"Now, I know you said you didn't want a birthday fuss," Mum said, peering at me in her rearview mirror. "And we're not, but we are going to have a family meal. Your grandmother is here, plus your Aunt Ella is coming with Gordain and Viola."

"We wanted to invite the whole family," Dad added. "But we know your limits."

My cheeks warmed. Before, I wouldn't have thought

myself worthy of the fuss, but it was high time I accepted myself for who I was. "Thank you. Actually, I love the idea."

My parents both glanced back at me, eyes wide.

"I wish we had invited everyone now," Dad said with a laugh. "That way, you'd have Lennox here, too."

"Another time," I murmured and pressed my fingers to the ache in my chest. I'd barely left him two hours ago, and I missed him so much it hurt.

We passed a grand display for Parker's Restorers—a classic car repair company I'd worked with last year. I waved, and Edie Parker waved back. They were local, and therefore the competition, but our rivalry would be of the fun kind. I looked forward to swapping ideas and seeing who'd won jobs.

My brother raised his chin at me. "Are you going to do something like that? Have a stall? Show 'em you mean business? This is your home turf, you have the advantage, right?"

I'd already chosen my own stall in a prime spot near to the house, arranging the details with Mum's PA.

Including how I'd wanted to represent the Warwick endorsement.

I leaned forwards. "Mum, can you stop a minute? I want to show Sebastian something. We'll walk back later."

Mum did, and my brother and I climbed out of the car. Our parents continued on, and I led my brother across the field. Hennessey, Mum's PA, strode out from between two vans, a clipboard in one hand and a tablet in the other. I hollered her name, and she stopped.

"Can't chat," she said and waved the clipboard. "It's one disaster after another. Some idiot leaked oil all over the road, and there are disputes over boundaries. I'm in utter turmoil."

I grinned, as Hennessey always claimed everything was going wrong, even when it was perfect.

"We won't get in your way," I replied. "Let me know if I can help."

"No need, I've got it. If you want to see your pitch, it's set up and ready to go." She turned to answer a question from the collection of people swarming her, and Seb and I moved on and found my space.

My work-in-progress Jaguar had already been brought over and the signs and banners put up. I had a small marquee providing shelter from any rain that dared come, and it looked amazing, the afternoon sun casting a spotlight over my business launchpad.

"Warwick's sponsoring you?" my brother asked, shielding his eyes as we approached.

I sighed. "Not anymore. They were, but Casey pulled it when I wouldn't persuade Lennox to fake date his sister."

Sebastian stopped. I glanced at him to witness utter confusion spread over his face.

He pushed his hair out of his eyes. "He did what? That little shit."

I sighed and strode to the nearest sign. It rippled in the light breeze, my business name 'Fitzroy's Classics' standing out in a glossy dark green. None of this was usable now, and I had to start from scratch. But if it was a choice between defending Lennox or having an easy ride into the world of car repair, there was no comparison. My name was the most important thing on the canvas. I was good at what I did, and so what if it took me longer to build up my reputation?

"It doesn't matter," I told my brother. God, when had I become so reasonable? "I think I was hiding behind the idea of a big launch, then hiding behind having a sponsor. The only problem is that I'm stuck with this now. Hennessey took a week to get the signs printed. The rally is tomorrow. What do I do?"

Sebastian ran his gaze over the display. "Nothing."

"What? I can't advertise that Warwicks are backing me if they're not."

"Why not?" He slapped the sign with the back of his hand. "You agreed with them to sponsor your launch. The launch is tomorrow, and it's going ahead whether they choose to be here or not. You can tell anyone who asks that they reneged on the deal but otherwise, style it out. Get your name in people's heads. Get their contact details and start as you mean to go on." He rolled his shoulders and cast a look over the field. "I'll help."

My grin crept back. Seb always hated the rally and, even before his military job took him away, he'd usually find an excuse to be absent. My confident, strong elder brother was not one for crowds.

"Thanks. That means the world to me." I shoulder barged him.

His mouth lifted in a smile. "No problem. Don't forget, Nox and I are going to build your workshop."

That was another thing I'd had on my list of can't-start-withouts. "Actually, there's no rush. I can work from Mum's garage for a while. It's not like I'm going to be inundated with orders right away."

A man ambled past. He paused and eyed the Jaguar then my signs. "This your work?" he asked, gesturing to the car.

"It is!" I exchanged a happy smile with my brother then strode over.

"Nice welding work. I've got an Austin Healey with the same rust patch here." He pointed out the wing repair I'd done and explained his problem.

I got caught up in the detail, and it wasn't until a while

later I noticed my brother snapping pictures. The Austin Healey owner left with my contact details saved on his phone, as I'd yet to collect my business cards from the house, and I suppressed my screech of excitement until he was out of earshot.

"Was that your first customer?" Seb asked.

"Maybe. All I know is that was easy. I could do that work in my sleep. I have no idea why I was so worried."

"Here." He held up his screen. "I took this to remind you of where it all started. I'm so proud of you."

My big brother pulled me under his arm, and we set off for the house. I'd come full circle with my problems and, in no small way, felt invincible. I had Seb forward me the shot then I went to my rooms and plonked down on my couch.

I sent it on to Lennox then called him.

He answered, then swearing came from his end of the line. Other male voices yelled in the background. "Hang on a second, sweetheart," he said.

Engines roared. The sound diminished, then a door slammed. Lennox came back onto the line. "How's my favourite lass?"

"Thinking about her favourite man. Did I call at a bad time?" I asked.

"Never. Your calls are always going to be top of my list."

I grinned at his sweetness. "Ditto. Did you see the picture I sent?"

"No. Wait." There was a pause, then he came back. "Ah, woman. You're all set up!"

"I am! And I had a customer and everything." I couldn't stop my grin and I laid out on the couch.

"You're stuck with the Warwick name, aye?"

"Yeah. Too late to change it now. I'll use it for the draw, but after that, they're dead to me."

He grumbled acknowledgement, then he paused. "I have to ask ye something."

"What is it?"

"Can I see ye?"

My heart swelled, and just like that, my happiness was complete. "Whenever you like. Always."

Fuck, and I meant that. We'd been thrown together and flying from place to place. I wanted a pause point with Lennox. A very long break where we did nothing but talk and share stuff. And not only naked. I wanted all of him.

Then maybe after, I wouldn't want to go back.

"Tonight?" Lennox asked, caution in his voice.

"Are you kidding? Yes! Will you make it in time for dinner?"

"Probably not, but I'll be there as early as I can." He gave a short laugh. "I have a surprise for ye. Ye might regret the invite."

My pulse quickened. "What are you doing?"

"Wait and find out, love." With that sneaky little *love* added in, he hung up.

27

HUNTING GROUND

*I*sobel

In the interval between dinner and dessert, I slipped out of the dining room into the hall and grabbed my phone from my dress pocket. I might be a brat but I didn't want to disrespect my parents by checking my messages every five minutes. Growing up, we'd had a no-phones-at-mealtimes rule, and it had stuck.

But I'd felt the buzz of Lennox's text, and a thrill had gripped me ever since.

I took a seat at the bottom of the grand staircase and scanned the screen. My heart sank. The text was from Casey.

You're still running my company's name. What the fuck?

How the hell did he know that? Spies in the camp, I guessed. I tapped an irritable reply. *You bailed on our deal, not me.*

Then my phone rang with him calling. Seriously? Fuck this guy.

"What do you want?" I snapped down the line. "I'm not taking the banners down. In fact, you're lucky that I'm not bad-mouthing Warwick Supercars to everyone who comes here."

"You're threatening us?" He laughed. "Thanks to you, my sister has been cut off, my family are in turmoil, and everyone is arguing. You caused that."

"The fuck I did, and besides, maybe it'll do her good. Either way, I don't give a tiny damn. After tomorrow is over, I'll shred those banners, and my association with your family will be done."

Casey snarled. "How about if I tell every car club that you fucked over work you did for us. Not only are we publicly boycotting your rally, but you'll be seen as a liar, too. Kiss your career goodbye."

I dragged in a sharp breath. If he did that, I'd never work again. Anger shook my hand, and I gritted my teeth, standing as my muscles refused to remain still. I wouldn't be baited. Not again. "Whatever, Casey," I said. "It wasn't fun knowing you. Gotta go." I drew the phone from my ear.

"Wait!" Casey shouted down the line. "You and me. One last race on Belvedere's track. Tonight."

"What? No! No deals. I told you, I'm through."

"I'm not offering a deal," he replied. "You're right. Amber can get a job like the rest of us. I'm talking about us. Who's the better driver."

"Why the hell do you think I'd—"

"I'll bring the Bugatti Chiron," he said, cool as you like.

I stopped talking.

To my right, the dining room door opened, and Viola emerged, Sebastian following. Both gave me a quizzical look, and I raised a finger to pause them.

"You're prepared to race your Chiron? Here?"

Casey sucked in a breath. "Nah. You can drive it. I'll take my pick from your garage, you take the Chiron. I know you've always wanted to drive that car. It's your dream motor, right?"

Oh my fucking life.

The Bugatti Chiron was sex on wheels. A curvy, gorgeous beast that had a top speed of over two hundred and sixty miles per hour and a whopper of an engine that produced fifteen-hundred horsepower. Compare that to the MGB's one-fifty-five horsepower, and my tongue was out and I was panting.

I'd never driven anything that fast.

On Belvedere's track that looped from the garage, out around the rally's central field to the lake and back, I wouldn't get near that but I'd surely beat Casey in anything we owned.

Was the Chiron my dream? I'd coveted it from afar, though I'd never been sure why. I liked the speed and efficiency of modern cars but preferred classics.

But Casey was pressing that competitive button, the one I never could ignore. He hadn't offered a deal. Nothing but a straightforward car-on-car brawl. That was my hunting ground.

I knew the mature answer, and I knew the alternative.

And I knew how to get the Warwicks off my case permanently.

"Whatever, Casey. Midnight. Be here," I said then hung up the call.

"What the hell was that about?" my brother asked.

At his side, our young cousin's eyebrows were in her hairline. "You're racing tonight?"

I turned on my heel and darted up the stairs. "I need your help. Both of you. We've got a stunt to organise."

28

TO IMPRESS A LASS

*L*ennox

    Vibrations filled the air around me, the deafening clatter of heavy machinery jarring, unless you were used to it, which I'd become over four years. Blayne, my co-pilot on this mission, whooped from his position in the turret, his excitement driving up my own fever.

Cars gave us a wide berth, and people gaped as their headlights picked out our ride. At twenty or thirty tonnes of hulking metal, the massive, armoured, road-legal tank thundered down the Peak District road on a cool, crisp night.

We were closing in on midnight and Belvedere. And on Isobel.

Ah Christ, I hoped the lass would like what I'd done.

"Your phone's ringing," my brother yelled. He had an arm slung over the gun and a broad grin on his face.

"Aye, gunner, answer it. It's probably Ma wanting to know how we're getting on," I replied.

My whole family had got behind the idea as I'd called up my old military contacts and secured my vehicle of choice. Blayne had insisted on accompanying me, and I was glad for it because, for once in my life, I was nervous. Skye had been packing to go on another trip, and she'd demanded that Blayne take videos so she could watch the fun later.

Aye, fun.

What lad had ever commandeered a tank to impress a lass?

Then it had been a mad dash down into England to get this show on the road.

I focused on staying in my lane and fought my grin at the reception I'd receive. Isobel was going to go nuts.

"Uh, Lennox? Sorry, it's some woman. She's blathering on. I can hardly hear her," my brother called.

I glanced back from my seat in the front hull and took my phone. There was no name on the screen, but I recognised the number. Fucking Amber Warwick.

Fine. I hadn't tackled her, not properly, and now I was finally going to get her off my back.

I put it to my ear. "What do ye want now?"

A string of garbled yelling followed. I saw what Blayne meant. Amber was incoherent with rage. I managed to pick out, "I've been cut off!" before a laugh rumbled out of me.

"Listen up, Amber, I'm sorry your life sucks, but the only person who can change that is you. Not me, not Isobel, and not your family. We're all making our own happiness, and so should ye. Leave us be, aye?"

"You deserve each other!" she hissed, her voice now clear above the engine. "I hope Isobel destroys that fucking Bugatti tonight and Casey puts her in her place and wins."

My laughter stopped. "What did ye say?"

No answer came, and I checked my screen. Amber had dropped that bomb and hung up on me. Isobel was racing Casey?

She'd promised she wouldn't.

Last time they'd raced, he'd crashed.

No, no way. That wouldn't be her.

"Right turn ahead!" Blayne shouted. "Slow up, driver."

I broke my stunned state and slowed the tank, taking the tree-lined road that led to Belvedere. Even at this late hour, cars were arriving for the rally. All manner of classics and sports cars, plus support vans and trucks.

We cleared the turning, and I stepped on the accelerator. If there was a race about to start, I needed to get there fast.

29

ALREADY WON

*I*sobel
 In a scene that took me back four years, I waited, poised in the hot seat of the Bugatti Chiron, about to do something reckless. In the next car over, Casey preened and checked his reflection in the rearview mirror, waiting on my move.

Oh, it's coming, you jerk.

A crowd had gathered, and people elbowed their neighbours, commentating on the spectacle before them. Headlights and a bright moon lit the night. There were car clubs and rallies up and down the country, but at the core of it was a tight unit of families. We all knew each other. It was a gossip-worthy event that Isobel Fitzroy and Casey Warwick were going head-to-head at midnight.

My mother was lapping it up, but her focus was firmly on me. Every time I glanced her way, her expression held a warning.

I drummed my fingers on the Chiron's steering wheel. Temptation held me in its thrall. The power of this gorgeous car was almost mine for the taking, and all I had to do was turn on the engine.

Such a pity that I'd never get the chance.

"Come on then! What are you waiting for, a parade?" Casey taunted. Pointedly, he picked up his helmet and yanked it over his head. He hit the ignition on the long-repaired Tesla Model S—used with Mum's permission, this time—and got comfortable in his seat, his eyes gleaming.

Between the two cars, there was no difference in the nought-to-sixty. Both would blaze off the starting line at a lightning pace. I'd immediately have to angle to get into the lead, there wasn't enough road for more. I'd need to brake sharply to take the corner and follow the track up to the lake, around its length, and back. The road wasn't designed for a full-on race. There was oil spilled somewhere, Hennessey had mentioned, and too many people flittered around. Anything could leap into my path and cause a crash.

Even if I'd intended to race, I would've called it off.

Panic struck me. I eyed the road that led to Belvedere's main entrance, the gates themselves out of sight from my seated position.

"Come on!" I muttered to myself. My knee jiggled.

I was almost out of time.

A buzz came over the crowd, along with a low, rumbling sound.

People shifted, all attention on what was happening over the rise. A fresh excitement rippled through the throng.

"Oh my God!" someone gasped.

"Holy fuck," came my brother's voice. His dark laugh filled the night. "Is that a tank?"

Agog, I clambered out of the Chiron and stared. Coming

down Belvedere's circular road was an enormous armoured vehicle.

But that wasn't the only thing that had me staring. The tank closed in, Blayne McRae sat proud on top, waving, and —oh God—Lennox was at the helm.

I clapped my hands to my mouth and gaped.

The military vehicle stormed down the road, blocking our path. The weight of it shook the concrete under my feet. The gun pointed right at us. No, at the Tesla containing Casey.

"Isobel!" Lennox called.

"Lennox!" I yelled back.

"You have got to be kidding me!" Casey spluttered.

My Highlander brought his ride to a halt and lifted himself out of the driver's hole. He landed on the ground with a heavy *thud*. Then he stomped to me, his face a picture of longing and anger, and my heart swelled with the utter fucking romance of it all.

I ran the last few steps to meet him at the front of the car.

"What did you do?" I snickered and looped my arms around his neck, pressing up on my toes to bring my face to his.

Lennox's stare bored into me. "I told ye I'd see ye tonight."

"In a tank?" Happiness overspilled my heart.

"There's a story behind that. But first..." He paused and tipped his head at the car, a question warring with the worry in his eyes. He wanted to go all alpha on me, that was plain.

I'd told him I would never race Casey again and yet here I was, apparently doing exactly that.

My smile hurt my cheeks. "Oh that? Do you trust me?"

Lennox dipped his head, though his concern didn't shift. "Aye."

"Give me a minute and all will become clear."

We gazed at each other.

"McRae, your slow-assed ride is blocking the road," Casey complained.

Lennox's expression darkened. He released me and, like rolling thunder, stalked to Casey. He got in his face. "Say one more word, Warwick. Just one. I dare ye."

Casey shut his mouth.

Another engine roared. A black Mercedes dodged Lennox's tank and approached at speed. Recognition spread over the crowd because this man was as well known as anyone here.

Raymond Warwick halted his Mercedes and climbed out. With his features held tight, he approached his stepson. "Casey, a word," he said.

Casey sent a baleful look my way. "You called my dad on me?"

I let out a huff of breath, and at last, my self-righteous blast could land. "You came steaming in here all geared up for a fight, but do you know what? You need to grow the fuck up. What you proposed was just plain dangerous, and we aren't teenagers anymore. You know there was no chance in hell that Raymond was going to let you race that car. Or me, for that matter. So yeah, I called you in. Maybe next time, you'll think twice about what you're doing."

Applause and whistles came from my little family group, all of them in on my plan. I knew for sure I'd disappointed our audience who would've loved to see the clash, but they'd got a spectacle all the same.

Raymond and Casey commenced a low argument, but my attention for them was long over.

Lennox ducked his head and gave me a kiss that knocked my socks off. I matched his passion. He'd come here for me, ready to do battle.

I was about to show him he'd already won.

*L*ennox

    In a move that felt well-rehearsed, I picked Isobel up, bringing the tiny and mighty woman as close as I could get her—with our clothes on—and kissed the hell out of her mouth.

This lass would never cease to amaze me.

She smiled against my lips, and triumph lit her up.

"Admit something to me," she said, her breathing coming heavily.

"Anything."

"Did you think I was about to do it? Go through with the race?"

I paused, unwilling to say the truth. But I never wanted to lie to Isobel. "Aye, for a moment."

Heat flickered in her gaze. "I wanted to. But I don't give a flying fuck about Casey or beating him. Don't you go thinking that I'm hot over another guy. I just wanted to have a go at that Chiron."

I followed her gesture to the fancy car. It was obviously

pricey, with highly polished bodywork and silver curves around the doors. "Not your style," I observed.

"No, it really isn't. But it's fast, and I wanted to tick it off my list." She gave a sigh, but it wasn't an unhappy one. "You know what else is on my list?" she added.

I raised an eyebrow. "A tank?"

Isobel hopped in my arms. "Yes!"

A man approached us—the Warwick stepfather, I recognised.

Isobel slid down my body but kept close. She shook the man's hand. "Hi, Raymond. I think you already know Lennox McRae? My boyfriend," she said, proud as punch.

Raymond offered his hand for me to shake then looked me over. I did the same, taking his measure. I'd bet his children had given him the deeply lined forehead and dusting of silver at his temples.

He drew a heavy breath. "On behalf of my kids, I owe both of you an apology."

Isobel shrugged. "For Lennox, maybe. I'm on a par with them for shenanigans."

"I doubt that," Raymond continued. "My wife and I spend half our time despairing over Amber's lack of responsibility, Erika's mean temper, and Casey's competitiveness. We hope they'll grow out of it before we retire."

"Retire? Your wife still works?" Isobel asked. "She's not ill?"

"Ill? No, she's very well. She'll be joining us here tomorrow. She's excited about coming, as a matter of fact. We don't like to spend time apart, so she'll be early."

We exchanged a look. So Amber lied about that, too.

"Is Amber gay?" Isobel said, fast.

Raymond opened then closed his mouth. "I don't think so. She kept saying she was waiting to marry but..." He threw a glance at me but cleared his throat and moved on. He grasped his hands together. "Isobel, your call earlier this evening was the first I'd heard about Warwick Supercars being here. I've been so busy, and Casey has been handling more and more of the business. I can only apologise for letting you down. I've already said the same to your mother. She's been gracious enough to let us stay over, and Sandra, my wife, will bring a few of our vehicles in the morning. But those plus the Chiron is the best that we can do."

"Thank you, I'm glad you can make it at all," Isobel said nicely.

"What about Isobel's sponsorship?" I asked.

"Warwick Supercars is giving its full backing to Fitzroy's Classics. I've been aware of your work and admire you immensely as a driver," Raymond said to Isobel.

"Sweet! I appreciate that." She rubbed her hands together. "I just have one question. The Chiron is staying?"

Raymond glanced over to no doubt the most expensive car in his, or anyone's, fleet. "She sure is. Do you want to take her out for a spin?"

———

*T*wenty minutes later, and Isobel was gunning the engine of the powerful car.

"Aw, yeah!" she howled. "Go, go, go!"

We punched forwards, the open, well-lit road ahead of us.

"What do you think? Does this car do it for you?" Isobel asked, relaxing back though her body was tense with energy.

I got the appeal—the Chiron was unlike any vehicle I'd ever been in. Every surface was designed within an inch of its life and, though a two-seater, it was roomy enough for my six-five height. Fuck driving something like this, though. I had far better plans in mind.

"You do it for me. Pull over and I'll show ye," I said.

A wicked grin crept over Isobel's face. She sucked in a breath, gaze firmly ahead. "I've dreamed about driving this baby for a long time. If you want me to stop, you better get persuading."

I barked a laugh. "Ye want me to dirty talk ye into submission?"

"Got it in one." She wriggled in her seat.

"Fine." I reclined, getting comfortable. But I'd come here with a message for her, and that was forefront in my mind. I'd fallen for her, in every way, and she needed to know.

Though fucking her in this overpriced toy was pretty appealing, too.

I warred with myself, split between tender words and filthy ones.

My silence went on too long, and Isobel took the initiative. "Ask me what I'm wearing under my race suit."

My groan came unbidden.

She continued, "Earlier, I swapped the dress I'd worn to dinner and got ready to race. But my lingerie is all for you. I've been dying for you to get here. I wished I'd let my folks arrange a birthday party so you could've been invited. I would've snuck away with you and hidden us in some darkened room."

I adjusted my junk, hardening. We'd swapped roles, and I didn't care. "What did ye want to do to me?"

"Everything. I'd tear your clothes off, and you'd shred mine. We'd be too rushed for niceties, so you'd have me against the wall, naked." She changed lanes to overtake a slower car, her cheeks flushing red. "You'd slide inside me and fuck me, pinning me in place. I'd just have to take it."

"Ye like it when I'm in control," I observed.

"Oh yes."

"Isobel?" I twisted in my seat.

"Yeah?"

"Pull over."

Her smile returned, and she shook her head, once, then floored the accelerator. "Try harder," she said on a breath.

"How about I pin ye to this car. How about I make ye come, screaming my name into the night?"

"Ooh, better. I love that," she said.

"And I love ye."

Silence hit.

Isobel dragged in a shocked gasp. "What?"

"Ye heard me. Get your arse out of that seat and come here."

"Fuck," she whispered. Then she checked her rearview, indicated, and pulled into a lay-by. She killed the engine.

Though the road was well lit, this part wasn't, and the countryside darkness fell over us. I welcomed it, the exposure of my heart painful, though I couldn't, and wouldn't, hide how I felt.

She liked me well enough. Loved me, I hoped.

Isobel unclipped her seat belt and reached out to take my hand.

"Say what you just said again," she ordered.

I gazed at her, at her pert mouth and pretty eyes. So gorgeous. So mine.

"I'm in love with ye. I know it's fast and I don't want to scare ye, but it's real. I can't help how I feel and I won't hide it. I know how much ye hate lies—"

"I love you, too," she interrupted, hushed and reverent.

"Totally scared of that, but you know me, I've fallen so hard I'm seeing stars. If you hadn't had said it then, I doubt I could've kept quiet."

"Come here," I repeated, my head swimming with fucking joy.

Isobel climbed onto my lap, removing my seat belt as she went.

Our lips met naturally, but the urgency had evolved into something fiercer, warmer. I speared my fingers into her hair and held her head.

"Tell me again," I demanded.

Isobel placed her hands on either side of my face. "I'm yours and you are mine. That's what you were trying to tell me, that we were falling in love. Sorry that it took me a while to realise."

It had taken no time at all. But in that, I was just like my lass: nought to sixty for feelings.

She laid a kiss to the side of my mouth. "I love this mouth." Another landed on my cheek, then she turned my face, kissing under my ear. "And this bit is one of my favourites."

"Aye?"

"But do you know what I love the most?"

I jerked my hips, and Isobel laughed.

"I was going to say your big heart, but that, too."

Our next kiss came harder, and I found the zip of Isobel's race suit and dragged it down an inch.

Headlights flooded the car, and vibrations shook us. A horn blasted.

"What the ever-loving fuck?" I grasped Isobel and lifted her, placing her back in her seat, then I peered behind. A lorry had pulled over, the driver leering down at our car.

"For fuck's sake." Isobel snickered. "Let's go home."

"Ye don't want to keep on driving?" I strapped my seat belt back in, my frustration rising.

"No. I want you. Under me. In my bed. Behind a locked door." She pressed the engine start button and sped us out of the lay-by and back onto the road.

The countryside fled by, and neither of us said a word. Speed limits were eclipsed. At Belvedere, Isobel steered around my tank, which still blocked the road, and stopped at the garage. She used her phone to open the end overhead door then stowed the expensive car.

Then we were out and sprinting for the house.

Inside, I ignored a passing Blayne's dirty laugh and took the stairs two at a time, dragging Isobel behind me. In her rooms, we fell on each other. Her racing suit zip parted to give me a stunning sight of her breasts. The sexy maroon lingerie got a token nod, but I was yanking down the cups and exposing her to my mouth.

Isobel stumbled and fell on her arse on the polished floor, then struggled to pull her trousers down. I helped with one hard yank. Ah, that was better. My mostly naked lass, ready for me.

"Strip. Now," she said.

My shirt, jeans, and boxers followed the race suit, strewn across the room. Then I picked up Isobel and carried her to the nearest flat wall.

"Is this how ye pictured it?" I asked and lined us up nicely. My knee hit the plaster, and I held Isobel at exactly the right height.

Except her sexy knickers had to go.

I snapped the lace side, and Isobel gasped then laughed.

"I love it when you do that, fucking caveman."

I fitted my dick to her heat and pushed home. "And I love you," I said.

We both groaned. I withdrew and thrust again, working myself in as deep as I could into Isobel's slick, tight pussy. My dick hardened more, and the pleasure spread through me.

Isobel grasped my hair and tugged until our mouths met again. Her tongue slid over mine as my dick filled her. As always, already turned on beyond belief. The journey here, the sight of her ready to race, the fact that she loved me...

"Tell me." I broke our kiss. "Now."

"I love you," she said sweetly. "I'm madly in love with you, Lennox."

Rocket-charged, I pounded into her. Slow and easy could come later, I was making a claim. Isobel was mine. Every hard hit, she absorbed. Every groan that ripped from me, she amplified. She took every one of my demands and fed back her own hunger.

If she liked to race, I did, too. But my race was in getting her off.

"Harder," she commanded. "Everything! Lennox!"

"You're mine," I uttered, obsessed, and my breathing hard.

My hips snapped to a rhythm. I loved this, the raw, animalist banging. I fucking adored it when she surrendered to me.

Isobel clung on, tension through her body. She clamped down on my dick and dropped her head to my neck. "Keep doing that. Hitting me right there. I'm going to come!"

I kept going, hopelessly turned on. Nothing could drag me away now. My world was here in my arms. I tucked my head against hers and kept going at my unrepentant pace. She needed this as much as I did.

Her body gripped mine, her moan growing louder.

If I gave a shite, I'd worry that we'd be heard down

Belvedere's echoing halls. But naw. I was so proud of this, of having her. Of her loving me.

Isobel dug her nails into my shoulder blades and howled, coming. Inside, tremors constricted me. Impossibly, I got harder. Thicker.

Ah fuck. I was a goner. My orgasm crashed into me, and I followed Isobel over the edge. Powerful waves broke in my head. My dick pulsed, and I spilled inside her. Emptying my balls. So right.

I sank to my knees, holding her close.

Isobel trembled in my arms. I expected a smart remark, but when I raised my gaze to hers, I only saw deep emotion.

"So fucking in love with you," she whispered. "I never expected this. Never saw you coming."

She paused, then we both burst out laughing at the same time.

"Keep your eyes open next time and you'll see me coming as often as ye want," I joked. "And I love ye, too."

Isobel giggled and wrapped her arms around me. I still had one more surprise for her. Well, one more for today, anyway.

We linked gazes, and my fears and worries vanished. I was a man deeply in love, and Isobel was my everything.

---

*A*fter a shower, with a lot of kissing and soaping up, we dried off, and I padded over the cool floorboards to Isobel's bed, holding her close.

I hadn't noticed anything of her rooms when we'd entered, being so hung up on her. A lamp had been left on in the corner, and I took in the comfortable couches and family pictures on the wall. It was nice, but not what I'd expected. Too neat and neutral, maybe. As if she'd never left her stamp on the place.

I lay Isobel out on the sheets but stayed standing.

"Lie down. Snuggles. More sex," she ordered.

"I need to go move my tank," I muttered.

"Leave it. We'll make it a feature for the rally. People love military vehicles."

I grinned and sat beside her. "About that…"

Isobel pushed up on her elbows, peering at me.

Though she'd tried to keep her curls from getting wet in the shower, they had all the same, and now were drying fluffy and five times their size. And the light in her blue-green eyes was a gentle one, no punchy antagonism here now. I adored seeing her like this. Without armour. She was always wild but on her own terms.

Now, those terms included me.

"You're so fucking beautiful," I said, lost for a minute in her.

"What did you mean by 'about that?' I scent a story," she said, ignoring my quiet reverie. "How can it be any bigger than storming my home in a tank?"

"Fine. I did a thing."

"What kind of thing?"

I blew out a breath. "Can ye wait until the morning and I'll show ye?"

"No way."

Still nude, I leapt up and strode back to the lounge, snatching up my jeans to collect my phone. I returned to Isobel and held up a picture. It was of me at an event a couple of years ago, standing in front of a gathering of armoured vehicles. I'd not only trained in driving tanks but in fixing them, too.

And when I'd asked for a favour, it had been granted.

Isobel gazed at the screen. "You are so hot in a uniform. I want that picture."

I snorted a laugh and took a seat next to her again on the bed. "Look at what's behind me. That fleet will be arriving early in the morning. They'll take up the space left by Warwicks."

Isobel's jaw dropped, and I continued.

"I couldnae bear to think of ye disappointed. I know these aren't fast cars that ye can race, but they make a hell of a spectacle when they're lined up. It's a draw, aye? The huge tanks, the guns. It's impressive. Plus ye told me not to buy ye a birthday present. I had to do something, so this is it. Wrapped in metal and gifted to ye."

She didn't say a word, and uncertainty crept into my head. I cast my mind to what I'd seen outside. The lines of classic cars. The crowds of people who... Who weren't military.

Ah fuck. I'd misjudged this.

"This seemed like such a good idea. If ye don't want it, I can cancel—"

Isobel pounced on me. Her mouth landed on mine, and I brought her into my arms, clutching her as I rolled onto the bed.

Her kisses rained down, and I absorbed her enthusiasm, my doubt lifting.

"You are the best man I've ever known. You did that for me? I can't believe it. Except I can, because you're fucking amazing." She kissed me again.

My heart ached. "Ye like the idea?"

"Like it? It's perfect. You're perfect. Oh man, Mum and Dad are going to go nuts." Delight lit Isobel up, and she banded around me, getting as close as she could. "Thank you. For that, and for everything. In case you didn't know, I am madly in love with you."

I did know. It had sunk in. We got under the covers and set about showing each other the strength of our emotions. I never knew it could be like this. Never understood what it meant to be head over heels. But Isobel Fitzroy had stolen my heart, and I'd gladly let her.

From now on, we were *yours* and *mine* and we both knew it.

31

CLASSIC ISOBEL

*I*sobel

Morning found me wrapped up in a very hot Lennox. Our kiss led to the best wake-up call I'd had ever but, eventually, duty summoned.

Today, I launched Fitzroy's Classics.

In the past, the rallies had always been huge, with a holiday atmosphere and something new to surprise us. Never before had we been invaded by an armed military unit. After an ultra-quick breakfast, Lennox gave me the nod, and I led my parents and a few other family members outside. I'd already sent a string of late-night texts to Hennessey to avoid giving the woman a heart attack, but my parents were clueless.

Watching them would almost be as much fun as seeing it for myself.

The first rumbling had the already active crowd on their toes. Lennox's tank sat proudly in the road and, behind, heavy, substantial vehicles loomed.

Mum frowned and stared at the gate. "What the actual flipping heck is that? Not another tank?"

"Not a tank, Mum," I said very happily. "A whole army of them. Here to fill the gap that Warwicks left."

Mum pressed her fingers to her mouth, and she and my dad stared at us.

Dad snorted. "Lennox, that is one hell of a romantic gesture."

My Scot's chest expanded, and he twisted his lips to hold back a grin. I pushed up on my toes and kissed his cheek.

I knew he missed his military life, no matter how right it was for him to start over as a civilian. One last blast never hurt anyone. "Go, join them if you want."

He glanced down at me. "Ye sure?"

At my grin, he laid a hard kiss on my mouth then was away.

I moved to stand between my parents, slipping an arm around each of them. Behind us, Sebastian, Viola, and Blayne took positions on the steps, staring. Then Raymond and Casey Warwick appeared, too.

"Bloody hell," Casey muttered.

I smirked at him, and he rolled his eyes but then summoned a smile. Casey might've behaved like a brat, but I wouldn't hold it against him. I'd done worse myself.

Lennox sprinted to his tank and clambered in. He started it up with a snarl and waited for a beat until his convoy caught up with him. Then he punched the air, yelled something that they all echoed with booming masculine voices, and drove on.

They bore down on us, engines roaring, horns blaring, shaking the ground. The gobsmacked car owners stared at the spectacle. At the bottom of Belvedere's steps, Hennessey banged her head on her clipboard.

As they passed, Lennox blew me a kiss, and it was so ridiculous, so wonderful, I couldn't help myself.

"I love you!" I yelled at him.

The soldiers hollered and saluted, the crowd cheered and gave us a round of applause. Held up by my parents, I laughed until my sides hurt.

"Only my sister could hate someone then fall in love with them a heartbeat later," Sebastian observed.

"Classic Isobel," Mum pointed out. "She wouldn't settle for less. Besides, I think this was on the cards for years, no?"

It was true. Lennox was everything I wanted, I just didn't know it until now.

The military fleet continued on, taking positions at the top of the field.

Three sports cars made up the rear guard, and Raymond Warwick waved to the woman in the first car. His wife, I guessed. She waved madly back, beaming at him, long-held devotion clear in both their expressions.

In the car to her left, Erika raised a tentative hand. I grinned back, full of forgiveness today. In the car to her right, Amber glowered, not making eye contact.

"Amber's going to be working in my office, starting Monday," Raymond said. "She'll start at the bottom of the pecking order. Her mother and I feel it will do her good." Then he winked and went back to waving at his wife.

People followed, and the rally was officially open.

"I need to get to work," I said to my parents. I had a stall to run, car owners to chat up, and jobs to earn. "But there's something I need to talk to you about later. It involves Lennox, too."

"Find us when you're ready," Mum said.

I had my own surprise for my man. Lennox had given me so much, changed my whole way of thinking, and it was about time I gave something back. I was going to blow his socks off, so long as he said yes.

*T*he day went spectacularly. For once, the March weather didn't soak us, and a crisp, clear day saw out the events. Sandra Warwick showed up with two friends and three very nice cars between them. We ran time trials—which Casey helped with, his sulk over—and people lined up to take pictures with the sports cars.

But, by far, the military fleet drew the most attention. As often as I could, I took a jaunt up the field to visit with Lennox and his friends. Each time, Lennox was thoroughly roasted for his grand romantic gesture, but he let them at it with a grin and a promise in his eyes just for me.

By the time night fell, and the throng dispersed, I had examined more cars and handed out more business cards than I could remember. I'd also already taken a down payment to work on a Rolls Royce Phantom and had two more bookings lined up.

I was officially in business.

With so much going on, I didn't get time to talk to my parents, and Lennox and I took to our bed late and exhausted. Not that it stopped our passion. I really liked having ready access to him, and that thought formed a big part of my surprise.

The next morning, after breakfast, I summoned my parents to one of Belvedere's formal living rooms. Though this wing of the house was ours, we still had many rooms left stuffed with antiques and decorations, most from well over a century ago.

Maybe because I would never inherit the mansion, I'd never developed a deep love for the history of the place. It was home, but even then, I knew that was a temporary thing.

Sunlight filled the room, and Lennox held my hand as we sat. Warmth filled my heart.

Across from us, a huge oil painting of an ancestor stared down at us. I wondered if she'd approve of what I was about to say.

"What's going down?" Mum asked. She landed on a gold, overstuffed sofa, and my dad took the seat next to her.

They had twin expectant expressions.

"For years, you've tried to get me to choose a path in life," I said, keeping my hold on Lennox's hand but eyeing my parents, each in turn. "I've started this amazing business, and I'm so grateful for your support in that. Yesterday, I turned twenty-one, and you both carefully didn't mention the big change that that number brought about."

They both nodded but didn't interrupt.

Lennox gave me a curious look, so I addressed my next words to him.

"My twenty-first birthday unlocked a trust fund that Mum and Dad set up for me. Unlike Sebastian's inheritance, I can do what I like with it, except I've never wanted to. I never felt worthy of having such a wonderful family, let alone a huge sum of money."

Mum's gaze softened. "Oh, honey."

Dad blinked hard.

"That's all on me. I've had a long time to get over myself, but in my usual way, it's been all or nothing. Now, I'm done feeling sorry for myself. I want to thrive. I don't need to invest a big amount in my business because it'll fly on its own."

I switched my gaze to the man I loved. "But there is another business that I want to invest in. I want to help build the winter sports centre on Mhic Raith. I want to own it alongside you, Lennox. I want it to be ours and I want you to build it all in one go and not have to wait for the money to roll in. You're good to start it soon, right?"

Lennox's jaw dropped, then he blinked. "Aye, but we haven't even talked about that. How did ye know?"

"I spoke to a couple of your army friends yesterday. One said you'd told him your dad had approved the project and that you wanted to go ahead with it soon. But in stages, as and when you could raise the money." Excitement had me jiggling. "Let's build an amazing place. Somewhere that we can be proud of. You and me." Then I added my killer line. "We'll make it yours and mine."

Lennox closed his eyes for a long second. When he opened them again, heat and devotion burned in them. "Are ye sure this is what ye want?"

"Utterly and completely." I threw a glance at my gooey-eyed parents. "If I've read the rules right?"

"You have," Dad said. "You can do what you please. All we want is for you to be happy."

I turned back to Lennox. "Then this is what pleases me. But I have one condition," I added.

"Anything."

"I still want you to build me that workshop." I didn't say where. We were still so new, and I didn't want to jump the gun. But Lennox wanted to build a house in the Highlands. I wanted to live in that house with him and I wanted my workshop nearby, embedded in that Scottish ground.

We had all the time in the world to get there.

"Deal," Lennox said simply.

And that was that.

32

BIG TITLE

Isobel - late summer

The engine turned over on my first try, and the Morris Minor purred into life. I whooped into the interior of the garage. Dougal, Mr Campbell's Scottie dog, yapped and howled along with me, then Mr Campbell himself appeared.

"She runs!" I exclaimed.

"Ah, lass, I never doubted ye," the old man said. He circled the vehicle, taking in the areas where rust had eaten the metal, and patting the good-as-new patches. "Or my car. She's been a good 'un for a long while. Ye can keep her going for another forty years now."

I talked him through my repairs, which I'd done for free, calling it experience for the sake of his pride, then hurried to scrub the grease from my hands.

I had somewhere to be this sunny afternoon.

I'd been living in the Highlands, at Castle McRae, for the best part of two months. Lennox grumbled and complained if we were separated for more than a couple of days, and I wasn't much better so, once my new clients had been catered for in England, I'd upped sticks and taken my business north into Scotland.

Best decision of my life.

For most people, living with their boyfriend's parents wouldn't be ideal, but I loved the McRaes. I'd always adored Mathilda and Callum, and being around the cousins was never-ending fun. On the downside, a short while ago, Skye had left for New York and her placement as wedding dress designer. Her start date had been delayed, so I'd got to spend months with her, and now, I missed her hugely.

But I couldn't complain about life. I had Lennox. All the time.

Happy didn't even describe my existence.

Outside Mr Campbell's, I hopped into my ride and sped away to the mountain. Everything had me smiling nowadays, but this took the biscuit. Lennox had taken me to task about owning a car. He drove me to dealerships all over Scotland, but nothing suited. No classics we found met the conditions it would need to face in the harsh Highlands winters, and no modern car got me in the gut.

Then, one day, he'd taken me out on a mission. A friend of his was selling her car, and Lennox thought it would suit me. But he was cagey about it and, when we got there, I realised why. It was an MG LE50—a modern version of the MGB in which we'd driven to France.

But this car had heating. And comfortable seats. It was fast, but not insanely so, and had safety features that would ensure I wouldn't slide off the road in the first frost.

I bought it there and then. It made so much sense, and I loved how it reminded me of the time we'd begun to fall for each other.

My drive today through the McRae estate had me hopping in my seat for another reason. For Lennox's other triumph. All spring and summer, he'd been working on the mountain. Troops of army personnel came and went. The groundwork went in as soon as the weather allowed, and slowly, the building had emerged from the ground.

The MG climbed smoothly, and I palmed the steering wheel and took the corner of the mountain road. There, ahead of me and lit by glorious sunlight, the Fitzroy-McRae Snowboarding Centre shone.

I gave a yip of joy and parked up then set off on foot over the last stretch, shading my eyes to see what they'd done. The last panels of the roof had gone on, and now the insides could be installed. Electrics, plumbing, interior design—all had been waiting for this final push. They were dead on target for opening the centre for autumn hikers and then the slew of winter visitors once the snows started.

Viola and Blayne were beside themselves. I was going to learn to snowboard if it killed me.

Lennox braced himself on the roof and raised a hand at me. "Up here, sweetheart."

Like I couldn't spot him a mile off. "You did it!"

"Aye. Get your backside moving and take a peek."

I scampered up the ladder. Farther down the structure, Sebastian lifted his chin before returning his attention to whatever he was doing. A few other people laboured at various points, adding finishing touches.

I carefully stepped onto the roof. It had a clever design with a gentle slope, developed by Lennox's friend, Artair, so it didn't get either battered by the wind or collect too much snow. On a day like today, it was hard to imagine what the winter would bring.

On cautious feet, I moved over the panels to Lennox. My man folded me into his arms and held me close.

"Done," he said.

"I'm so proud of you," I uttered into his chest.

"That makes me the happiest man alive," he replied, his beautiful Scottish brogue soft and his satisfaction plain. "I needed ye here today. Look around us, what do ye see?"

I spared a glance for the view, of the mountainside around us, the deep valleys, high hills, the blue loch.

"Fresh air. Beauty. Home," I said, trying to work out how this was connected to him finishing this stage of the build.

He stared right at me. "Home. Aye. That's what I wanted ye to say. I know the past few months have been crazy. We don't have our own place to live yet and we've both been flying around, getting our businesses underway. But I want to make it official. Your move here, I mean."

I snorted a laugh. "Sounds like you're about to propose."

We'd discussed this, once, in bed and wrapped up in each other. Lennox was content to wait until we'd been a couple for longer, besides the fact that the whole idea freaked me out, but I knew him. He wanted me to wear his ring. Or stamp 'Property of Lennox' on my forehead.

"I will. When it's time," he said, cutting to the chase. "And you'll say yes and cry over the ring I've bought ye."

My breath hitched. "You've already bought me one?"

His eyes gleamed, and all manner of fireworks exploded in my belly. "You'll have to wait and see. I hadnae planned to admit that right now, but now I'm thinking I made a mistake."

A grin stole over my face. "No. We have all the time in the world. Choose a day when my brother isn't watching. Just don't feel like you need to top your tank invasion."

Lennox bent to kiss me.

I met his lips, hungrily, and happily ignored Sebastian's gagging noises.

An engine roared up the mountain track, then a door slammed.

"Nox!" came a yell.

"Up the ladder, man," Lennox called back. His gaze sought mine. "Artair helped me out with a new set of plans. For our house and for your workshop. Nothing is finalised, and every inch needs your stamp of approval. I asked him here to show it to ye. Then, next week, my team starts on that build."

I gaped at him then rose on my toes and kissed him again. He'd said nothing about this, letting me think the winter sports centre had been dominating all his time. "You secretive thing."

"I wanted to do this for ye. Just like one day, I want to be your husband. And you'll be mine. My wife."

"Wife? Oh, jeez." I spluttered a laugh. "That's a big title. Bigger than my other one."

"But better, aye?"

Sebastian's angry voice rang out to the side of us. "What the fuck business is that of yours?"

Lennox and I broke eye contact to take in Sebastian who was squaring up to Artair. Head to head, glossy black to scruffy, dark-brown hair, they glared at each other.

"It was a simple question." Artair raised his eyebrows. "Why are ye acting like I cannae ask?"

"Because Skye is none of your concern," Seb retorted. "I don't like her name coming from your lips."

"And you're the authority on what Skye wants?" Artair replied.

"Oh hell." Lennox rolled his eyes.

"They're fighting over Skye?" I gawped at the two men.

Once upon a time, I thought Seb was perfect for Skye, but now I knew that wasn't true. He was dark and possessive, thought with his fists, and was moody ninety percent of the time. Not right for her at all.

I'd thought about her a lot after our talk in New York. Skye was such a giver, she would've hated herself for not being what Sebastian wanted. She'd even said she felt responsibility for their lack of a relationship, which sucked as it wasn't her fault.

Why should she carry that guilt?

The other thing she'd confided had stuck in my head. I'd wanted to ask if she'd relented and gone ahead with my brother's indecent proposal.

Either that or met up with Artair again to explore that chemistry they had.

Artair had been here often during the course of the build, but I hadn't seen him and Skye together. He, in comparison to Sebastian, was friendly and light, action-focused and driven. He had an awful home life that made me pity him as much as I liked him. He handled it all and didn't descend into moods, finding other ways to manage his stress.

Sort of the anti-Sebastian, in a way.

"Artair," Lennox called, breaking up the verbal sparring and death glares. "Get over here. Seb, eyes on your task, aye?"

Before his friend joined us, Lennox settled his gaze on mine, such love and devotion shining through. "Where were we? Ah, wife. That big title... Still want it?"

"Maybe I do."

He chuckled then kissed me. Once and hard. "I do? Sounds like ye know your vows already. Good to know you're practicing, but save that for our wedding, aye?"

Who would've thought, Hard Nox had a soft heart, and it was all mine.

EPILOGUE

S kye

    I stumbled in the door of my tiny, shared apartment and slammed it tight closed behind me, ending my race home through the blustery autumn Manhattan night. My evening impressing a potential new client was a bust, thanks to me being unable to sit at the table for ten minutes straight, let alone work through dress designs or chat over cocktails.

Ugh, the mere thought of fruity, sweet-smelling alcohol...

My head swam and my stomach lurched again, and I pressed off the door and flew to the bathroom, making it just in time for another round of throwing up. Sweat dotted my forehead, and I slumped against the shower cubicle, knees under my chin, and tears threatening. My sparkling dress pooled around me, and water collected in my eyes.

I had to face facts.

Life in the States, working endless hours at my internship, wasn't the cause of my illness. And God knew, I put in enough time to send anyone's health spiralling. The industry was fierce, with extreme competition for work and to get your face seen and known.

I'd had an in this evening. A once-in-a-million chance to shine in front of one of the most sought-after celebrities to ever announce her engagement. But I'd blown it.

More, my situation had blown it.

But how was I to guess? I hadn't just been retching in the mornings. No, this was an all-day, eat-nothing kind of sickness that hadn't gone away for over two months, no matter how much I ignored it.

Everything turned my stomach. Even the salty crackers that I'd tucked in my handbag, desperate to claw my energy back as I flew in taxis between fittings and consultations.

I placed my fingers over my belly.

Then there was that night... A passionate, unexpected, and unforgettably hot one-night stand with a guy whose name I refused to bring to mind and who I hadn't seen since.

Unforgettable was the right word.

With increasing certainty, I admitted the truth.

I, Skye Storm-McRae, was pregnant.

The End.

***

Thank you for reading Isobel and Lennox's story! Click here to order Skye's beautiful romance, Perfect Storm (Wild Scots, #2).

Did you know the parents of the Wild Scots have their own series? Read how alpha laird Callum McRae fights for the lass he can't have and start the Marry the Scot series today. Download Storm the Castle (Marry the Scot, #1) or read on to get a sneak peek at the first chapter.

ALSO BY JOLIE VINES

Wild Scots series

1) Hard Nox

2) Perfect Storm

3) Wild Scots, #3

Marry the Scot series

1) Storm the Castle

2) Love Most, Say Least

3) Hero

4) Picture This

5) Oh Baby

Standalones

Race You: An Office-Based Enemies-to-Lovers Romance

Fight For Us: a Second-Chance Military Romantic Suspense

Visit and follow my Amazon page for all new releases amazon.
com/author/jolievines

Add yourself to my insider list to make sure you don't miss my
publishing news https://www.jolievines.com/newsletter

ACKNOWLEDGMENTS

Dear reader,

Here we are with a brand new series! When I came to the end of the *Marry the Scot* books, with all the men of Castle McRae having found their lasses, I polled my reader group and asked what they wanted to read next. The *Wild Scots* are the result. This fascinating pack, raised in castles or palaces, won by a landslide.

As you can no doubt tell, there are several more McRae cousins with stories to tell. Who are you most interested in reading?

Now for the acknowledgements. I'm endlessly thankful that you, my lovely reader, have picked up my work. You've helped me build an author career and I intend to honour that with delivering the stories you want to read.

Do you get my newsletter? If you have a thought or idea

you'd like to share with me, hit reply to one of my emails and tell me!

https://www.jolievines.com/newsletter

The beautiful cover was made by the talented Elle Thorpe at Image for Authors, copy editing by the eagle-eyed Emmy at Studio ENP, proofreading by the fabulous Zoe Ashwood. Elle, Shellie, and Katie, your early reviews made this story a good deal better and I adored your comments.

I'm so grateful to my ARC team and bloggers for every review, post, and share.

I want to give an extra special shout out to Linda (clary_linda_starfall_ on Instagram) who loves the Scots so much, she had a book sleeve made with the covers and teaser graphics. I treasure that gift.

Also, to Ally (Ally.always.reads), I'm sorry your alternate cover idea didn't make the cut. It was a tough choice but the hot guy won out in the end.

Love, Jolie x

SNEAK PEEK - STORM THE CASTLE (MARRY THE SCOT, #1)

*C*hapter One – A Wall of Man

*M*athilda

As a little girl, I'd dreamt of hearing the words 'Marry me'. Soft music playing in the background and a ring offered from my lover's eager hands. This, of course, was before my closest example of marriage became a warning rather than an inspiration.

My childish, rose-tinted vision had never involved me standing in the corner of a glittering conference, freaking out over the proposal I'd just received.

Dominic Hanswick, my father's business partner, had watched Dad leave then taken me to one side. He'd been polite and concise as he'd laid out his terms. "Marry me, Mathilda. Save my reputation. Save your sister in the process. Think about it. I'm sure you'll find it a reasonable idea." He'd offered it so easily then he'd smiled and moved away through the tables, murmuring pleasantries to colleagues.

A business deal, he'd called it.

Who said things like that?

My head already ached like I'd been in a hit-and-run, the dreadful lunch I'd had at my parents' home still forefront in my mind. Scarlet's behaviour was the only reason I wasn't laughing this off.

Shocked, I'd barely asked Dominic any questions, but now dozens came to mind. God, he wouldn't expect me to sleep with him, would he?

I needed answers, and standing around in my flat sandals wasn't getting me anywhere. My job for the evening was done—I was only at the event as a favour to Dad, meaning I could leave and return to my hotel, but this had thrown me for a loop. With a calming breath, I left the safety of my alcove and crossed the hall.

"Mr Hanswick?" I tapped the shoulder of his smart suit, and the man turned. My would-be fiancé was a businessman, a senior partner with Storm Enterprises, the conglomerate my father ran. He was smart, had the stout figure of a man used to finer things, and at forty-two, seventeen years my senior.

Overall, Dominic was not what I had in mind when I'd envisaged my groom.

"If you have a moment, I need to ask a quick question." A vast understatement. I backed away from the group, smiling at people important to my dad. The model of a dutiful daughter.

Dominic excused himself and followed. His brow crinkled. "You have my business card. Set up a meeting, and we can talk through the finer details."

Right. And yet, "You said you wanted a marriage of convenience. In name only."

He glanced around, presumably to make sure we were out of earshot. "Naturally."

"What happens if I want to date someone?" Why was that so important? I hadn't dated anyone in months.

He sighed. "The point of selecting you, Mathilda, is that you're young, single, and practical. My home is big enough for us to live separate lives: you with your sister on one side, me on the other. This arrangement works for all involved. As for other...needs you might have, sleep with whomever you choose, but I'd recommend you stick to one-night stands. At least until we near the end of the five years. And for Heaven's sake, be discreet. I've had enough scandal to last a lifetime, and a cheating wife would set me back to square one."

"I see." I nodded along like this was anything other than insane. I knew Dominic had been the subject of press attention. He'd had an affair with a high-profile, married politician, and the newspapers had made a meal over it. Dad had ranted about the effect it had on Storm Enterprise's shareholders, so I knew Dominic was losing money fast.

Getting married would fix his reputation and save his bank balance.

None of this was my problem.

Scarlet's emotional health, on the other hand, was. Her chance at having a good future.

As if sensing my reticence, the man leaned in. Even though I was in my flats, my six-foot height meant I was looking down on him. "Your sister is off the rails. You can help her. Why wouldn't you do that? Your father will let you take her in if you're married, am I correct?"

How on Earth did he know that? I gave a slow nod. From

behind me came the clamour of raised voices. Dominic's attention shifted to the source of the commotion, and his eyes widened as if in recognition. He gave me a short bow. "I have to leave. Call my assistant to set up that meeting, and we can finalise the arrangements. Just don't take a time over it. It serves us both to arrange this as soon as possible."

Then he was gone.

Rotating, I spied a vacant table in a dark corner. On the way, I grabbed a glass of water from a waiter then found a chair and laid my head back. My sister, Scarlet, nearly arrested again last week, worried me to death, and clearly Dominic knew enough about the situation to determine which buttons to push. It was the solitary reason I'd have to say yes, saving her skin and, separately, his, and why I hadn't yet laughed him out of town.

Not that I would do anything quite so unladylike.

A surge of frustration filled me from even entertaining the idea. I didn't want Dominic. He'd called me practical, and I was, but what about chemistry and heat and passion? I wanted more than the lacklustre relationships I'd so far suffered in my twenty-five years on the planet. Beth, my best friend, made a robot-Mathilda voice when I was being ultra-efficient, but inside I was like everyone else: desiring that overwhelming romance. The breathless appetite-quenching satisfaction that came from sex with someone I loved.

The love stories I devoured couldn't all be wrong.

If I took the marriage deal, on whatever terms, I wouldn't have the chance to find out. Then again, who's to say I'd ever find this relationship utopia. My last boyfriend had cheated, after all. Maybe a sham marriage and one-night stands could work. Passion based on the purely physical was better than nothing.

At the entranceway, a distance across the open hall, two

men emerged through the crush. Both tall, the men carried a watchful air as the event's patrons left a moat around them, and my interested gaze skipped over each as they shook off the security staff.

The dark-haired younger man had the kind of looks you could stare at for an hour and praise God for pretty people. But it was the man beside him who caught my attention. And held it. Because *holy hell.*

Not only because of his size—he was one of the tallest men I'd ever seen—but for the way people orbited around him, and how he held his powerful, large body with ease as he reached out a long arm to take a glass of what appeared to be water. He gave the waiter a polite nod, and I warmed inside.

Lifting my drink, I tried not to stare. *"Good luck with that."* I imagined my friend's stage-whisper. If only Beth could be here to ogle alongside me. She'd nab a cocktail, rest her chin on her hands, and goggle freely.

The room lights flickered over the doorway, as if showing off for the big man, and a lick of interest curled in my belly.

Power impressed me. I couldn't help the fact.

Then, like I'd switched on a neon light that said "Look over here, big guy!" the man's gaze swept over the busy space and locked onto mine. I started, but he didn't move on as would be proper. Instead, he angled his head and ran an attentive glance over me. A fair eyebrow raised, appreciation lightening his serious expression.

The babbling noise of the room ramped up, and I dragged in a breath. Heat snaked under my high-necked dress, maybe from the intensity or maybe from the humidity, and I tore my gaze away, fidgeting on the chair. *Wow.*

If I was to ever try a one-night stand, he'd be top of my list.

Then my head panged again, and I winced. My cue to leave. From my bag, I extracted my phone to book an Uber, and on the screen, a message already waited. Beth.

Testing testing, are you still alive? Did your dad make you do a speech?

I tapped out a reply.

Luckily, no. But he did tell a bunch of his colleagues that I'd be working for him soon. I should've just come home after lunch.

I'd journeyed to London this morning to see my family, and I could've been on the first train home to the house I shared with Beth. Instead, I'd gritted my teeth through an awful lunch, politely kissed my mother goodbye, booked into a hotel, then attended Dad's product launch. They thought I was getting the late train, though I hated travelling at night, otherwise I'd be forced to stay at my family's home. The mere thought had me shuddering.

Beth shot back an answer as Uber gave me a twelve-minute wait time.

Ugh, I'm sorry, honey. Want me to come get you tonight?

It was a generous offer, and a long drive, but I was too rattled by Dominic's offer and by no means ready to talk about it. Beth would expect me to be miserable as each visit to see my family took me a week to get over. But this... I needed to sleep on it.

Readying to leave, I let my gaze seek out the big man one last time. From first appearance, he wasn't the type of guy I'd usually find interesting. Rougher, less refined than a standard city-dweller. At a black-tie event, he was wearing jeans, so I guessed he was in the wrong room at the conference centre. He was a tourist, maybe. Though the way he and his friend had entered the place felt more purposeful than happy holidaymakers.

A mountain man, I mused, sliding my phone into its pocket in my bag. Used to harder living and working with his hands. Maybe he had a shack somewhere he emerged from each morning to cut wood and fetch water from a stream. He'd go swimming in a river some days.

Naked, obviously.

I grinned at my own fantasy, the levity of it the most exciting part of my evening. But my search of the event space was fruitless. The shy-looking model-type stood with his back to the wall. The interesting one had vanished.

More disappointed than I reasonably should be, I took a final sip from my water then eased myself up from the table. But as I stood, the strap of my sandal snapped, and I stumbled. My purse swung in a wide arc, knocking straight into my glass.

Down the glass fell, cracking on the seat. It shattered and rained razor-edged pieces over my feet. "Shit!" I squawked. And there was me, proud of how little I swore.

I danced away, but in the process, wedged my ankle against the chair leg, trapping a piece of glass. It stung. With a wince, I fell back onto the seat and clutched at my foot, losing my shoe. A sliver of glass stuck out from my skin. I touched the edge and nearly fainted.

Blood welled, and my head swam.

"What's happened here?" a deep voice sounded beside me.

I peeked up. And up.

It was the man. A *wall* of man, looking down at me. Sweet Jesus, he had to be close to seven feet tall. The top of my head wouldn't even reach his chin.

I opened my mouth and managed, "Be careful, there's glass. My drink fell."

Then, with the worst timing, a flood of emotion came over me. My evening had turned absurd. My tiny, stinging injury was nothing compared to the impossible offer my father's colleague had made me. Worse, I couldn't think of another way to help my sister than to accept him.

Marry someone I didn't care for.

Add to that the embarrassment of being a klutz in front of the most impressive man I'd ever seen, my horrible headache, and nausea from my lack of food, I wanted to curl up in a ball.

That was it. My head reeled double-time, my foot panged, and my brain checked out.

Like in an old-style romance novel, I swooned, and everything went black.

Read on...

ABOUT THE AUTHOR

JOLIE VINES is a romance novelist who lives in the South West of England with her husband and toddler son.

From an early age, Jolie lived in a fantasy world and is never happier than when plot dreaming. Jolie loves her heroes to be one-woman guys. Whether they are a huge Highlander, a touch starved earl, or a brooding pilot, they will adore their loved one until the end of time.

Her favourite pastime is wrecking emotions then making up for it by giving her characters deep and meaningful happy ever afters.

Want to contact Jolie? She loves hearing from her readers. Find her on Instagram and join her Fall Hard Facebook group

Printed by Amazon Italia Logistica S.r.l.
Torrazza Piemonte (TO), Italy

16852635R00180